TEACHING HOPE

A Whitebridge Novel

Sienna Waters

Copyright © 2023 Sienna Waters

All rights reserved

The characters and events portrayed in this book are fictitious. Any similarity to real persons, living or dead, is coincidental and not intended by the author.

No part of this book may be reproduced, or stored in a retrieval system, or transmitted in any form or by any means, electronic, mechanical, photocopying, recording, or otherwise, without express written permission of the publisher.

Find out more at www.siennawaters.com. And stay up to date with the latest news from Sienna Waters by signing up for my newsletter!

SIENNA WATERS

To N.–

My rock
xxx

CHAPTER ONE

Life wasn't supposed to be this way.

Ava Stanford blew a lock of red-blonde hair out of her face and wiped her forearm across her sweaty forehead, narrowly avoiding knocking off her glasses.

It wasn't as though packing was such hard work. But then, maybe she was just getting old. Maybe this was the price she paid for eating at her desk and skipping runs to grab ice cream and occasionally drinking more wine than was good for her.

"Forty three isn't old," Quinn said, putting a cup of coffee on top of a pile of books. "And you don't have to go."

"Forty three isn't exactly young," Ava said with a sniff. "I mean, statistically speaking, even if I live until my late eighties then I'm already half way done, right?"

"Ever the optimist."

"As for going, as much as I'd love to sleep on your couch for the rest of my life, it'd be a rough commute, don't you think?"

Quinn's nose wrinkled in thought. "I'm not sure Uber does trans-atlantic crossings," she said finally. She cupped her mug in her hands and perched on the edge of the sofa. "You know what I mean though, don't you?"

Ava sighed, got her own coffee and joined her best friend on the couch. "I do. And you're a darling. And I love and adore you. But truthfully, I do need to go. I need to do this. I need to… challenge myself."

Not to mention the fact that she needed to get away from the shattered remains of what her life *was* supposed to be like.

"You think teaching English kids is going to be more challenging than teaching American ones?" Quinn said with a snort. "They're all ties and tea, rather less of the guns and cursing, I'd have thought."

"It'll still be a challenge," Ava said. "It's a different way of doing things, a whole new bureaucracy to learn."

Quinn rolled her eyes and grunted in a non-committal way that made Ava laugh.

"It's for a year, Quinn. Not even a full year, a school year. I'll be gone all of, what, ten months? It'll be over in the blink of an eye."

"You're leaving me all alone to fend for myself," pouted Quinn.

Ava laughed again because in the whole time she'd known Quinn, going on a steady twenty five years now, the woman had never technically been alone. Quinn lived by the rule that an empty bed is a waste of space, and with her blonde hair and big blue eyes had no trouble filling the other side of her sleeping quarters when necessary.

"You mean that I'm leaving the male population to fend for themselves against your charms," Ava said. "You'll be fine. It's the twenty first century. We can Skype or Zoom or, hell, you could even come over for a visit."

"I might do that." Quinn lay her head back on the couch and looked at Ava.

"What?"

"Nothing."

"No, come on, what?" Ava said. "You can't give me that look and then not follow it up."

"What look?"

"You know, the one that makes me feel like I'm wearing a huge 'Handle With Care' sign draped around my neck."

Quinn blew out a breath. "Well excuse me for being worried about you."

"You don't need to worry about me."

"You could have fooled me," Quinn said. "Your entire life

turned upside down, three months of sleeping on my couch having nightmares, weeks of crying that you tried to hide from everyone, and now this."

"This?" Ava said.

"Yes, this. You going to England. You running away. You thinking that all your problems will disappear if you leave the country. Like you're some kind of Mafia Don avoiding the cops or something."

"Well, first, I haven't committed a crime," Ava said, patiently. "And second, I'm not running away. I have to come back at some point." Though what she'd be coming back to was another question. It wasn't like there was anything here for her other than Quinn and some horrifically painful memories.

"You're sure about this?"

Ava reached over and patted Quinn's knee. "I'm sure. I need to do this. I'm not running away, but I do need to get away. I need to clear my head and be away from things for a little while. You can understand that, can't you?"

"I suppose," Quinn sighed. "Though I'm not sure I can understand you wanting to be that far away from my signature Mango Martini."

"I can," said Ava, wincing at the memory of the hangover she'd had just last weekend. "And I'm going to adopt some healthier habits. Less drinking, more running. I'll come back a whole new me."

"Right," Quinn said. "In the meantime, is it too early to open a bottle of wine?"

"It's half past one."

"So... is that a yes or a no?" asked Quinn innocently.

"It's a 'get your ass in gear and help me pack up these books before the storage guys come to get them' and then maybe we can open a bottle."

Quinn groaned but got up and started packing anyway and Ava loved her for it. She couldn't help but wonder though just what she'd done to deserve losing her whole life and to be left sleeping on someone's couch at the grand old age of forty three.

THE AIRPORT SMELLED of cinnamon rolls and expensive perfume and Ava's hand was sweating around the handle of her suitcase.

"You're sure?" Quinn said for about the millionth time.

"It's a little late to back out now," Ava said, eyes scanning the departures board.

"It's not. We can grab a Cinnabon and hop on out of here. There's a revival of Cary Grant movies playing at the Westfield Theater, we could hit that up and then scout for Cary Grant lookalikes at the bar after."

"I'd prefer a Katherine Hepburn," Ava said, locating her flight number on the board.

"Since when have you turned down female Cary Grant lookalikes in suits?" Quinn said, sticking her tongue out. "You shouldn't be so limited in your thinking. As you keep reminding me, it's the twenty first century. You don't have to be male to impersonate Cary Grant."

"All things of which I'm very much aware," Ava said, gently steering them both toward the correct check-in line. "However, I paid a fortune for this ticket and I'm getting on this plane. And even if I weren't, I wouldn't be picking up Cary Grant impersonators in a bar. Male or female."

"Still too soon?" Quinn said, looking vaguely sympathetic.

"Too soon," Ava said, not at all sure when it wouldn't be too soon. In her heart she thought it would probably always be too soon. She was forty three already, maybe she should just give up, devote herself to her students.

"Maybe when you get back?" Quinn said, stepping forward to join the line just as a young man in a baseball cap swooped past her, almost tripping the both of them.

"Excuse me," Ava boomed. "Just what do you think you're doing?"

The man turned back, a look of anger on his face, but saw Ava, heard the tone in her voice, and promptly swallowed back whatever he'd really intended to say. "Sorry, ma'am," he said, stepping aside to let Quinn go first.

"I wish I could do that," Quinn whispered.

"It's all in the voice," confided Ava, though after twenty years of teaching high school it was second nature to her.

"Teach me your tricks, oh wise one."

"Hush," Ava said as she stepped up to the desk to take her turn.

The check in process was fast and efficient and a couple of minutes later Ava was pulling Quinn to one side.

"Smuggle me in your suitcase?" Quinn said plaintively.

"Too late, my case is checked already."

Quinn took a breath and looked toward the sliding door. "I suppose I'd better go then before the car gets towed."

"I suppose you'd better," said Ava, trying to sound a lot lighter than she felt.

Quinn turned back to her and took both her hands. "Divorce isn't the end of the world, Ava. I know it feels like it, but it's really not."

Ava felt herself grimace at the D word, which was ridiculous. It wasn't even the divorce so much that bothered her, though signing the papers would break her heart when the day came, if it was possible to break something that had already been trampled over and thrown down the garbage disposal.

No, it was everything that had gone before that truly bothered her.

That and the fact that her lovely, wonderful, perfect life had been destroyed.

"Don't let her ruin everything," said Quinn.

"Serena. You can say her name. Don't let Serena ruin everything." Saying the name stung but she kept on doing it, hoping that the word would hurt less over time, though so far her strategy didn't seem to be working.

Quinn squeezed her hands gently. "I know you need to leave for a while, I know you need to find yourself again, I do understand, Ava, I really do. Just... just don't forget that I'm here for you."

Quinn's eyes were brimming with tears and Ava felt a lump in her throat. "I'd never forget about you."

"Right, just you wait until you pick up some Keira Knightly lookalike over there, or maybe a royal princess or two. You'll have forgotten my name by the time the new season of The Bachelorette starts."

Ava shook her head and pulled Quinn into a hug. "I'm lucky to have you."

"You absolutely are." Quinn squeezed her and then let go. "Now off you go on your adventure."

"You're the one with the car that's about to get towed," Ava pointed out.

"Oh shit, I'd forgotten." Quinn leaned in, kissed Ava soundly on both cheeks and then ran off toward the doors. "Call me when you get there," she yelled over her shoulder.

Ava watched her disappear out into the sunshine and wondered for just a second if she was doing the right thing.

But then, what else was there to do?

She couldn't handle going back to school, couldn't deal with having to see Serena every day. So she'd lost not only her wife and her home, but her job as well. Then this opportunity had landed in her lap and it had seemed like the perfect solution, even if it was short term.

With a deep breath, she hiked her carry-on up onto her shoulder and strode toward the security line.

Ava Stanford was officially moving on. Both literally and figuratively.

CHAPTER TWO

"How do you know my name?"

Hope frowned and shrugged. "I mean, I gave it to you, so…"

"Yeah, but how do you know?"

Hope looked down at Alice's serious brown eyes and considered the idea of bringing up ice cream as a distraction. But she'd committed to answering her daughter's questions, whatever they may be, or, in this case, however challenging they may be. "Um, I'm not sure I know what you mean."

"Well, my name could be Bob," Alice said helpfully. "Or it could be Hope like yours. Or teddy, or cat or climbing frame or anything really."

This all sounded like a brewing existential crisis and Hope tried desperately not to look over at her own mother who was browsing souvenirs and doing a pathetic job of trying to hide her growing amusement.

"I suppose I just thought Alice suited you," Hope said.

"You? Or you and daddy?" Alice prodded.

"Well, both of us, of course," said Hope, feeling her guard go up at the mention of Noah as it always did these days.

"Huh," Alice said. "Gran? Did you choose my name too?"

"Oh no, love," said Caz from across the zoo shop. "That's a mummy and daddy job, not a gran job."

"So you could change it then?" Alice said, turning her

attention back to her mother. "If you wanted to."

"I suppose," said Hope carefully. "But I don't think I really want to. Do you?"

Alice pursed her lips in thought, then shook her head. "No, not really. I quite like Alice. And I've just learned to spell it properly even though it sounds like an S sound and there's no S."

"Well, that's a relief."

"But you won't just change it without telling me?" Alice asked.

"No," said Hope. "Absolutely not. No changing names without informing the other person first."

"Good," Alice said, picking up a stuffed meerkat. "Do you want to know how *I* know what my name is?"

"Um, yes, I suppose," said Hope, eyeing the price of the meerkat and hoping that Alice wasn't getting too attached to it.

"It's on the label in the back of my jumper," Alice said easily, putting the toy down and skipping off to the other side of the shop where a video of a baby elephant was playing.

"She's too smart for her own good, that one," said Caz.

"Mmm, I wonder who she gets that from," said Hope.

Her mother laughed. "You. You were exactly the same at her age. All knowing and all seeing."

Hope looked over at her daughter, all of six years old and thoroughly entranced by the video she was watching. Sometimes she didn't seem real, like she was a figment of Hope's imagination and one day she'd wake up and find that she didn't have a child at all.

"Hope?"

"Mmm?"

"You did it again."

Hope turned back to her mother. "Did what again?"

"Sort of... grimaced I suppose. Pulled a face anyway. When she mentioned her dad."

Hope sighed. "So?"

"So, all knowing and all seeing, remember?" Caz said gently. "However you might feel about Noah, he is her dad, and she's small still. You can't let your feelings infect hers. You know that."

Another sigh as Hope turned back to her daughter. "Yeah, I know. I do know. It's hard sometimes is all."

"Of course it is, I of all people understand that. Just be careful, that's all." Caz raised her voice a little. "Anyone want to go and see the penguins?"

Alice immediately tore her eyes away from the video. "I do, gran," she shouted in glee, running up to take her grandmother's hand. Hope trailed the two of them out of the shop.

It wasn't like she'd intended to end up like her mother. Not that Caz was a terrible role model. In fact, Caz was the strongest and best woman that Hope knew. But life had somehow conspired to turn Hope into a mini-Caz and sometimes she wasn't entirely sure how she'd gotten here.

Her own father had been out of the picture for as long as Hope could remember. It had always just been her and her mum. And she'd always sworn that if she had kids of her own they'd have a whole family, one like everyone else at school had.

Then Noah had come along, with his chocolatey-dark eyes and his easy smile and she'd fallen for him so fast she hadn't known what was happening. When she looked back on those days it seemed like it was always summer, like the sun was always shining. Mind you, she suspected that the sun always shone for Noah no matter what time of year it was, that was just the kind of guy he was.

Alice hadn't exactly been planned. But Noah's eyes had shone so brightly when she'd told him, and her mum's lip had trembled and she'd turned away before Hope could see the tears of happiness, and then she'd heard that little heartbeat on that stupid machine and she'd fallen in love all over again.

Not that she regretted Alice one bit. Quite the opposite. Alice was by far the best thing she'd ever accomplished.

No, the part that she regretted was the part where she'd assumed that Noah was around for the long haul.

That part she really could have done without.

A year ago everything had tumbled down.

A year ago, almost to the day, she'd been living in a little semi close to the school where she worked, the school that Alice was about to start at, with a child and a cat and a husband and a laundry pile higher than Ben Nevis.

A year ago, Noah had come home from work with his face uncharacteristically pale and had sat her down at the kitchen table and said his piece and now here she was, not just becoming her mother but a single parent *living* with her mother.

Because that's how she'd always planned things. Right.

"Can we have ice cream and can I have a Cornetto?" Alice said, tugging at her hand.

"Bit grown up that, don't you think?" said Hope, raising an eyebrow at her daughter.

Caz laughed. "Go on, let her have one, I'm buying."

Hope sighed but nodded and Caz and Alice went off to buy ice creams from the stand next to the polar bear enclosure and she watched the way Alice's dark curls bounced as she walked and it made her heart hurt.

No matter what anyone said Hope couldn't help but think that she'd fucked all this up.

It didn't matter in the end that she was turning into her mother, after all, Caz was brilliant. No, what really mattered was that Alice was turning into a little Hope, and that just didn't seem right. Not when Hope herself knew what it was like to grow up in a broken family, not when she'd always sworn that her kids would have the perfect parents.

"Strawberry or chocolate, mum?" Alice shouted.

Hope felt herself grin. "Strawberry."

"Told you," Alice said to her grandmother.

"Come on then," Caz said. "Better eat them before they melt."

THE CAR WAS standing in a shaded area of the car park and Hope was glad for the cool. It was hot, the kind of summer August heat she remembered from when she was a child.

"Do we really have to go?" Alice said.

Hope paused, wondering if a tantrum was in the offing, but

Alice looked like she was honestly asking. To be fair, she rarely acted up, especially now that Noah was gone. Sometimes Hope worried about that, like maybe Alice was being too grown up. "We do," she said. "Rosie needs feeding."

"Can I feed her?" Alice asked. She was adorably attached to Rosie, who was a grumpy, fat cat that Hope had found in the garden one day and who had promptly moved herself in. When they'd moved back into Caz's, Rosie had come with them, probably because she'd eaten everything even vaguely edible in their old neighborhood.

"You can," Hope said, unlocking the car doors.

"Then I suppose the zoo animals need feeding too, don't they?" Alice said as Caz helped buckle her into her booster seat. "Polar bears eat fishes and lions eat meat. But what about elephants, mum? What do elephants eat?"

Hope climbed into the driver's seat and frowned. "Um, I don't think I know."

"Mu-um, come on, what do elephants eat?"

"Christmas trees," Caz said.

"Mum, you're not helping," said Hope.

"No, I'm serious," said Caz, getting into the passenger seat. "They do. I saw it on the news last Christmas, people donated their trees and the elephants ate them."

"All of them?" Alice asked from the back seat. "Like every Christmas tree in the whole world?"

"Maybe every Christmas tree in Whitebridge," Caz said. "Maybe not the whole world."

"But what about when it's not Christmas," said Alice. "What do they eat then? Cos there's only Christmas trees at Christmas."

Hope carefully backed out of her parking space. "I know, why don't you save that question up for when school starts again? Then you can ask your teacher."

"You're a teacher," said Alice.

"No, I'm a school receptionist," Hope said.

"But it's ages until school starts again."

"It's no more than a week and a bit," said Caz. "So you can wait that long. How about a bit of a sing along?"

"Give me a minute," said Hope. "Let me find the way out of here. Once we're on the motorway then we can sing." She checked her rear-view mirror and pulled out onto the road.

"So when we get home I'm going to feed Rosie and then we're going to watch telly, right mum?"

Hope felt rather than saw Caz give her a look, so she was careful to keep her face and voice neutral. "Actually, your dad's coming to pick you up, did you forget?"

"Didn't forget," Alice said, face darkening. "But what about watching telly, you said I could."

Hope took a breath. "How about I tell daddy that you can watch telly?"

Alice brightened again. "Yeah, that sounds good. Or maybe daddy can stay at our house and watch telly with us."

Caz reached out and patted Hope on her knee. "Your dad's got his own house now, love," she said.

Not to mention his own girlfriend, added Hope mentally. She cleared her throat. "Oh look, there's a sign for the motorway. Shall we get that sing-song started? Who wants to go first?"

"Me, me," Alice cried, and began a noisy rendition of Nelly the Elephant.

Hope pulled the car into the slow lane of the motorway and found herself smiling. Okay, so she might not have planned life this way, but was it so bad? Her daughter and her mother were both making elephant noises and maybe things weren't perfect, but they could certainly be worse.

CHAPTER THREE

The house was better than Ava had expected. Not that she'd expected much of anything, to be honest. This whole teacher exchange program had been a blessing sent from heaven, but it hadn't exactly been well-planned, just well-timed.

But she was now the proud temporary owner of a charming little cottage at the end of a row of charming little cottages in a charming little town called Whitebridge. Ask her to point the place out on a map and the closest she'd probably get was London, but she'd work on the geography later.

She was just rinsing out a coffee cup at the kitchen sink when she saw movement in the garden. She pushed her glasses up on top of her head and squinted, seeing a very large, fat cat jump surprisingly nimbly up onto the garden fence.

Ava growled. The thing had better stay out of her yard. See? She was feeling proprietorial already.

So what if she'd been jet-lagged as all get out for the last three days? So what if climbing out of bed in the morning seemed like a chore? So what if suddenly the loss of Quinn was seeming like a gaping hole in her life that might be harder to fill than she'd expected?

It had taken leaving to realize that Quinn just might have been the one holding her together.

But she wasn't to be beaten.

The sun was shining, she'd dragged herself out of bed, and she was going to explore Whitebridge. She'd be damned if she was going to spend the next week in bed until school started. Apart from anything else, she needed food in the house. And toilet paper.

She stepped out of the front door and took a deep, clean breath, and found that actually, she was feeling slightly better.

Her mood continued to improve as she followed the leasing agent's hastily scrawled directions into town.

Whitebridge was a small place, but cute and seemingly well provided for. As she reached the main street she could see a small cafe, a library, a police station and pub. Ah, her heart jumped just a little, and a book store.

She grinned and decided to treat herself before getting any real shopping done.

As she got closer she could read the sign, The Queens of Crime, and her smile got even wider. If there was one genre that was going to keep her busy and cheer her up, it was a good, bloody murder. The shop bell dinged as she walked inside.

"Morning, help you?" said a voice.

"Sorry, I..." Ava looked around trying to locate whoever was speaking.

"Right here," said a woman with bright blue hair, popping up from behind a cash desk. "Help you with something?"

"Uh... I'm not sure?" Ava said, wrong-footed not so much by the question as by the person asking it.

"Woah, American, huh?"

Ava nodded.

"Ad will be pleased."

"Who's Ad?"

The blue haired woman grinned. "The owner's wife. Or the half-owner's wife. She's American. Ant, that's the half-owner isn't though. And there's me, I'm not American either, though I am the other half-owner and I'm Mila."

Ava more or less followed this. "I see."

"New in town or just visiting?" asked Mila, leaning on the

desk.

"New, I guess," said Ava, really not sure what to make of this, but spotting a Tana French book she hadn't read on the shelf in front of the cash desk. "Here until the beginning of next July. I'll be teaching at the local school."

"Ooo," Mila said, sounding thrilled. "That's exciting. You'll have to come to our book club. And just you let me know if you want some help. My husband's the local policeman, so we'll both look after you. Actually..." She peered carefully at Ava. "Actually, you'll probably meet him sooner rather than later. He usually comes up to the school at the beginning of term."

Ava was trying to read the back of the book when something gray and sleek swept past her legs, she squealed and jumped back.

"Oh, that's just Maigret," Mila said airily. "Shop cat."

"I see."

"Not a cat person?"

"No," Ava said firmly. "Very definitely a dog person."

Just as she spoke, there was an odd gurgling sound from behind the counter.

"One sec," Mila said. She ducked down and re-appeared with a small child who was grasping an Agatha Christie novel. "This'll be Ag."

Ava frowned. Small children were very much not her thing and it was hard to judge what gender this one was, let alone how old it was. And yet... "Is it old enough to read?" she asked.

Mila laughed. "Not yet, but she's working on it, she'll be there soon enough, I'd say. You looking to buy that book?"

"This and some groceries," said Ava, watching the child suspiciously in case it exploded with bodily fluids or something else equally unexpected or unpleasant. "Oh, and if you could point me in the direction of the local school, I'd like to check it out before I start work."

"Easy peasy," Mila said, she grabbed a pen as Ava handed over her book. "Hold her for a sec."

Before Ava knew what was happening she was grasping on to

a wriggling bundle of something that smelled faintly of cheese. The child looked up at her and said nothing. Ava said nothing right on back. Carefully holding the girl at arm's length she watched as Mila drew a small map and then hastily gave the woman her daughter back.

"Jesus," said Mila. "Good you're not teaching reception, eh?"

"Reception?" asked Ava, confused.

"Reception, like the first class of school, the one the little ones are in," Mila explained. "Just that you don't look like you're that comfortable around the real smalls."

"No," Ava said slowly. "Not really. Not been exposed much, I suppose."

Mila grinned. "Well come back and babysit any time you feel like it. I could do with a night down the pub. That'll be ten pounds for the book then."

Ava handed over the money in funny colored large bank notes, then made her escape before Mila could find another excuse for her to carry her child.

SERENA HAD ALWAYS done the grocery shopping. It was just the way things worked out. Ava handled the vacuuming and laundry, Serena did the shopping. For well over a decade Ava hadn't set foot in a grocery store, and she couldn't say that she missed it.

Whatever the local shop was though, it was nothing at all like how she remembered American stores. It was small, and the woman behind the counter was almost as wide as she was tall. But the place seemed stocked well enough, though Ava didn't exactly recognize most of the products.

She walked out of the shop to a cheery goodbye and got two 'good mornings' and one confused 'afternoon' from passersby as she walked the length of the high street.

A friendly place then. Not at all like her suburban home in the States. Jesus, she'd barely be out of her subdivision walking at this rate at home. It was pleasant, she decided. Different, but nice, not to have to drive, to have everything within walking distance. Nice even to have strangers greet her on the street.

Maybe Quinn had been right about teaching English kids. Maybe the teenagers here would be calmer, more polite, less antisocial.

Following the map Mila had given her, she took a short detour to walk past the town school.

In fact, she almost walked right on past it before realizing what it was.

The building was short and squat and red brick, older than she'd expected, enclosed in a large playground that had games etched onto the tarmac in yellow and white paint.

She paused to take a good, long look.

It certainly didn't look like anyplace she'd ever taught before. But then, that was the point of all this, wasn't it? Change, moving on, trying to piece her life back together.

Maybe she should join that book club. It was something different. Maybe she needed to change more than just her country.

Ava gripped hold of the metal railings that surrounded the small school, feeling them cool despite the summer warmth. She could change, she wanted to change, but she couldn't shake the feeling that she could change all she wanted but that horrible afternoon would still be there, would still over-shadow everything else, casting itself over every second of the rest of her life.

That afternoon when Serena had finally told her, not just that she was leaving, not just that she'd been cheating, but who she'd been cheating with.

Ava squeezed the railings so hard that rusty flecks of paint came off on her palms. She let go, brushing her hands off onto the sidewalk.

It was better not to think about things, better to move on, to keep moving, to stay in motion like some kind of shark. That way maybe the pain wouldn't catch up with her.

Keep moving. She'd told Quinn she was coming back. The

truth was though, that there was nothing to go back to except Quinn herself and Quinn had her own life to lead.

Just don't think about it, Ava told herself. Don't think, just move, let the future bring what it may.

She pushed herself away from the railings and started to walk toward home. As she passed the school gate she saw a proud blue and white painted sign. Whitebridge Primary School. She smiled. The sign looked hand painted and just as old as the building. Obviously, small as it was, the school was an important one. If it was a primary school then it was probably the best in the area, probably a central hub, maybe even a school that was difficult to get into, one that held gifted students.

She was still smiling as she turned the corner toward her new home. Yes, things were changing, but one thing wasn't. She still loved her job and she couldn't wait to get started.

As far as Ava Stanford was concerned, the new term couldn't start soon enough.

CHAPTER FOUR

Hope put the oven on to preheat and started running warm water in the kitchen sink. "It's not like I never leave the house."

"That's not what I'm saying," said Caz, seated comfortably at the kitchen table. "I'm saying that you should get out more as in, you know, get out."

"You're saying I should try and meet someone."

"Would that be such a bad thing?"

Hope sighed and pulled out a kitchen chair to sit on. "Mum, I've got bigger things to worry about."

"I'll look after Alice, you know I will."

"Not really the problem."

"Then what is?" Caz asked.

Hope pulled a face. She didn't really know how to answer that question. Maybe because there were too many answers. She wasn't ready to date again. She wasn't ready to risk herself, her heart, her trust. And she needed to protect Alice.

Besides, she was busy. What, with a job to do and a child to raise and her mother to look after.

"You're getting old before your time," Caz said, leaning forward. "Unnecessarily so in my opinion. There's nothing stopping you getting out there and finding a new partner, male or female, and building something new."

Hope had to smile just a little. She'd told her mother she

was bisexual when she was seventeen and Caz not only hadn't batted an eyelash, but had always been careful thereafter to be gender neutral in her assumptions. Which was endearing and supportive and somehow didn't make this conversation any easier.

"You worry too much about Alice. She'll be happy if you're happy. If there's one thing I've learned, it's that. Would you have minded if I'd brought someone home when you were her age?"

"I'm not sure I remember being her age," Hope said. "In any case, no, I wouldn't have minded."

"See?" said Caz, leaning back again.

"Ah, yes, but you never did bring anyone home, did you, mum?"

"Yes, well." Caz shifted in her chair looking uncomfortable.

"See? Not so much fun when we're dissecting your life, is it?" Hope laughed. "Fancy another cup of tea?"

"I wouldn't say no," Caz grinned.

Hope got up and put the kettle on. "If you want us to move out then all you've got to do is say so."

"That wasn't what I said now, was it?" said Caz. "Though if you want to talk yourself out of a place to stay, feel free. On my part, I love having Alice here and you're part of the deal, so I suppose I can put up with you being here too."

"Ta very much," said Hope, getting new mugs from the cupboard.

Caz got to her feet and got the milk from the fridge, putting it down on the counter before giving her daughter's shoulder a squeeze. "You know I love having you here too, little one. The two of you can stay for the rest of my natural life and I wouldn't be bothered. I'd prefer it, in fact. But the truth of the matter is that you should have your own life."

"Mum," Hope began.

"Yes, I know, I know, pot calling the kettle black and all that. But part of the pleasure of being a parent is you get to be a hypocrite sometimes. Or maybe you get to try and teach your kid lessons that you had to learn the hard way. Consider this me teaching you something that maybe I could have learned a wee bit earlier."

"It must have been lonely," Hope said, putting teabags in the mugs and not turning around because she didn't want Caz to see the look on her face. She knew that Caz put her own feelings and wants aside to look after her and bring her up, and she knew what a sacrifice that must have been.

"Sometimes," admitted Caz, sitting down again. "But then, there was always you. Little chatterbox that you were. Never a moment's peace with you around."

Hope snorted. "Yeah, I didn't inherit that from you, did I?"

"What's that supposed to mean?"

"It means that one of us spent half an hour bending the poor postman's ear this morning and it wasn't me," Hope said, pouring out the hot water.

Caz grunted in reply to this.

"How about we both stay out of each other's dating lives?" Hope offered, bringing mugs, a plate for the teabags, and the milk carton to the table.

"What dating lives?" Caz said.

"Mum."

"Fine, yes, whatever." Caz sniffed. "You know, you'll be back to work any day now. If you fancy a night out before school starts again then you've only to ask."

"Mum," said Hope, her tone more threatening.

"Fine, fine. Stay here watching Coronation Street with me and Alice and going to bed at nine every night," said Caz. "See if I care. Just as long as you're happy."

"I'm happy," Hope said, with more force than was really necessary. Or really true, for that matter.

Happy wasn't exactly the word she'd have chosen. Satisfied maybe. Content perhaps. Living in the little cottage she'd grown up in, surrounded by the two people she loved most in the world, wasn't a bad life. She was no fool though, she knew things could be better.

Making things better would involve risks though. Risks she

wasn't prepared to take. At least until Alice was a lot older than she was at the minute.

"Rosie!" shrieked Caz.

The big cat jumped up onto the kitchen table, knocking over the milk carton and then hastily lapping up the spilled milk.

"What's that about crying over spilled milk?" Hope said as she snatched a cloth from the sink.

"Very funny," said Caz. "You know there's no more milk in the fridge, don't you?"

Hope lifted Rosie off the table and wiped up the milk. "I'll go into town and get some more just as soon as Alice is back."

She'd no sooner said the words than the doorbell rang. Rosie fled back out of the cat-flap and Hope felt a small chill go down her spine.

"Be nice," Caz said.

"Aren't I always?" said Hope, even though the thought of having to see Noah made her feel slightly sick.

The second the door opened a ball of energy flew right at her and smacked her in the stomach so hard that it almost knocked the breath out of her.

"Mum!"

"Anyone would think you'd been gone a year instead of a night," Hope said, ruffling Alice's curls with one hand and holding the door open with the other.

"Er, hi." Noah shuffled from one foot to the other, his dark hair as curly as Alice's, his cheeks pink, and the tip of his nose white so that Hope knew he was as uncomfortable as she was.

"Hi," she said, plastering a big smile on her face for Alice's benefit. "Everything alright?"

"Uh, yeah, yeah," said Noah, running his hand through his hair. "Yeah, all good." He cleared his throat. "Just, um, we were... I was wondering if it'd be alright to have Alice over one more time. You know, before school starts again. We wanted to go to the cinema, if that's alright with you?"

Hope swallowed down her irritation at the change of plans. "Of course," she said, smile still wide. She'd never stop Alice seeing Noah. Even if she did want to get Alice back on early nights so she was ready for school.

"Great," beamed Noah.

"Hurray!" squealed Alice, her face screwed up with joy.

"Alice! Alice!" came a voice from the direction of the car.

Hope looked over to see a tall, thin woman climbing out of the passenger seat, Alice's red and white striped cardigan in her hand. She glanced over at Noah to see his eyes cloud over a little bit.

"That's Amelia," Alice said helpfully. "She's got my cardigan. I was too hot so she put it in her bag when we were at the park."

"I see," said Hope.

Of course she knew who Amelia was. Noah had told her everything she needed to know. To be fair, he hadn't tried to hide the fact that he had a new girlfriend, not when Alice stayed with him at least once a week.

It was just that she wasn't exactly prepared to meet her face to face.

Not when she was wearing yoga pants and a t-shirt that hadn't been white for at least the last ten washes. Not when she hadn't done her hair or even looked in a mirror so far this morning. Not when she wasn't prepared.

Maybe not ever.

"Here we go," said Amelia, slightly breathless from jogging over from the car, handing the cardigan to Hope who took it automatically.

"Thanks." The word came out shorter and sharper than she'd intended.

Amelia blushed and Hope took in her blonde hair and her blue eyes and her even features and wasn't sure whether she was relieved or offended that the woman looked nothing like her. Did that mean that Noah needed something different, or did it mean that he'd always wanted something different and hadn't liked her at all?

"I'm Amelia," said Amelia, holding out a delicate hand.

"Hope," said Hope, taking the hand for all of a second, then dropping it again.

"Well, we'd better be off," said Noah with false cheeriness. "Bye Alice."

"Bye dad," Alice said, already on her way to see her grandmother.

"I'll text you about the cinema," Noah said to Hope, taking Amelia's arm and steering her away from the doorstep.

"Yes," said Hope. "You do that."

She stood and watched as Noah opened the car door for Amelia and wondered if he'd ever done that for her. She watched until they drove away. Then she leaned against the doorframe and watched the empty street.

They made an attractive couple, Noah and Amelia. She wondered if people had ever thought that about her and Noah. Then she wondered how Noah could have moved on so fast. How he could have healed so quickly that he was ready to start seeing someone new. Except maybe he hadn't had to heal. Maybe Amelia wasn't all that new.

Hope wasn't an idiot. She knew she'd been left for someone. Whether or not Amelia was that someone, she wasn't sure. And she didn't know if she wanted to know.

In the end, did it matter?

"Mum, mum, gran says you're making biscuits, can I decorate them?"

With a sigh, Hope turned away from the street and closed the front door. "Of course you can, why do you think I made them?"

"Brilliant," Alice said, and she smiled Noah's smile and Hope's heart crumbled just a little more.

CHAPTER FIVE

"No, it's sweet," Ava said.

"It sounds terrifically boring," said Quinn. Her face on the tablet screen screwed up in thought. "Unless there are murders, like on PBS. Are there murders?"

"I hope not," Ava laughed. "And it's a lovely little town. You should see the school, it looks like something out of Charles Dickens."

"Yeah, not a great comparison," said Quinn, laughing now too. "But I'm glad you like it." She paused and clicked her tongue against her teeth. "So, uh, met anyone yet?"

"Jesus, give me a chance, Q. I've literally just got here."

"You've been there almost two weeks and school is about to start soon. I'd have thought that you were making the most of your free time and settling in." Quinn leaned forward so that her face zoomed large on the screen. "Are they not friendly, these English people?"

"I'm sure they're lovely," Ava said, shaking off the last dish that she'd been washing. The tablet was propped up on the kitchen windowsill. "I've met a shopkeeper and an odd bookstore lady. People say hello to me all the time, it's just…"

"It's just that you don't respond. You need to join in, Av. You need to, I don't know, join a club or something. Meet some new people."

"Aren't you the one that wants me back in the States?"

Ava asked, putting her dishcloth down. "And now you're encouraging me to build a new life here?"

"I want you to be happy."

"Fine. I am." Okay, a little lie never hurt anyone, right? But she felt immediately guilty. "Or I will be. Wait until school starts, I'll meet tons of people then." Out of the corner of her eye she saw a blur of fur. "Oh no, you don't."

"Oh, no I don't what?" asked Quinn.

"Not you, got to go, talk to you later," Ava said, flipping the tablet shut and opening the back door at the same time.

She ran out into the garden just in time to see the cat finish up its business and jump back onto the fence, disappearing over to the other side. Standing on tip-toes, Ava leaned over and saw a tail snaking through a cat-flap. She pursed her lips. "Got you."

❊ ❊ ❊

Alice stood over the little easel, her tongue poking out of one corner of her mouth in concentration as she dabbed paint onto the paper. The second Hope saw her, she couldn't help but laugh.

"Did you get any paint on the paper?" she asked.

"Of course," said Alice. Her hair was wrapped up in a shower cap, her face, hands, and an old shirt of Hope's were all plastered with paint. "I'm making a unicorn."

"On yourself?" Hope asked.

"Oh, leave her be," said Caz. "She's having fun, that's what counts."

"It'll be your kitchen cabinets that she gets paint all over," Hope said, depositing the shopping bags on the kitchen table as Rosie shot through the cat-flap and ran into the hallway and up the stairs. "What's wrong with her?"

"Probably messed with the wrong bird," said Caz, pulling paper towels off a roll and handing them to Alice. "Wipe your hands, love, you're getting paint everywhere. You'll spoil your picture if you touch it with those grubby fingers."

Alice did as she was told.

"What do we say?" asked Hope.

"Thank you, gran," said Alice as the doorbell rang. "I'll get it."

She ran off before Hope could stop her. Not that Hope was particularly worried. Whitebridge was a small town, if someone was ringing their doorbell chances were it was someone they knew.

"I got some nice ham for tea," she was saying to her mother as Alice ran at top speed back into the kitchen.

"There's a lady and she says that Rosie pooed in her garden," Alice stated matter-of-factly.

Hope looked at Caz who shrugged back. "I suppose next door's probably rented again," said Caz. "Can't say that I've noticed whoever it was though."

Hope sighed. "Alright, I'll deal with this." Alice skipped after her. "No, not you, young lady. You've got painting to do. And get gran to wash your face, I can barely recognize you. I might mistake you for a traveling fairy and throw you out."

"Mu-um," said Alice, but she was smiling under the paint. "It's me, Alice."

"That's what you say."

"Okay, okay," Alice muttered and went off to get her face washed.

Hope re-opened the front door to find an angry looking woman holding up a plastic bag of what she presumed was Rosie's business.

For a brief second her brain registered that the woman was attractive. More than attractive. She had black-rimmed glasses pushed up on top of red-gold hair that brushed her shoulders. She had green eyes, sharp cheekbones, and a firm chin. She had curves in the right places. Quite large curves, Hope couldn't help but notice with a faint blush of warmth in places she hadn't thought about for quite some time.

Her eyes traveled back up to the bag of poo that the woman was holding in her hand. It rather spoiled the whole effect.

"Can I help you?" she asked, trying to sound as neutral as she could.

*　*　*

The child that had originally opened the door was so covered in paint that Ava honestly didn't know whether it was a girl or a boy. It had said hello, then promptly slammed the door in Ava's face when she'd explained why she'd come.

The second time the door was opened, a woman was standing framed by light streaming in through a window on the staircase. She had long dark hair pulled back into a ponytail, and she was wearing yoga pants and a t-shirt. She looked like she'd just come in from a run and Ava immediately felt a pang of guilt.

She'd promised herself that she'd be healthier, that she'd run more, drink less, eat better.

"Can I help you?" asked the woman, lifting one eyebrow.

She had nice eyes, Ava thought, warm and kind, dark and framed by long lashes. Then she remembered that she was supposed to be angry. That she was angry. She held up the little baggie accusingly. "I think this belongs to you."

The woman's lips twitched into a slight smile. "Um, not personally, no," she said.

Ava refused to weaken, even when the woman's cheeks pinked a little which made her eyes shine. "Your cat is using my lawn as a toilet," she said.

"How do you know it's my cat?" The woman leaned on the doorpost, folding her arms.

"Because I saw it disappearing over the fence and then through the cat-flap in your door," said Ava.

"So you're spying on me and my family?" Another eyebrow raise.

"No, of course not," said Ava, taking a step back. "I was simply seeing where the cat went."

"You can't just go peering over fences. It's not right. It's not polite." The woman looked her up and down. "You're obviously not from around here, but you can't go around looking over fences."

"And you can't go around letting your pet defecate wherever they please," Ava said, not to be outdone.

The woman sighed, then shrugged. "Fine, I'll have a word with her about it."

"A word with who?" asked Ava.

"The cat, of course," said the woman, before closing the door firmly in Ava's face.

Well, really. Ava looked at the plastic bag in her hand and seriously considered pushing it through the letterbox, but thought better of it. Thought better of herself.

Honestly, if this was what neighbors were like in this country, she could count herself lucky that she wasn't staying long.

She marched back to her own house, determined to keep an eye open for the damn cat.

❃ ❃ ❃

"You're not worried, are you?" Hope said, putting the bedtime book down and looking at Alice's face serious on her pillow.

"No," said Alice. "Not exactly."

"Because you went to school last year and everything was fine," said Hope. "And you know that I'm always right there. I'm just in the office if you need me. All the other boys and girls don't have their mum there." She paused as a thought struck her. "Um, that isn't what's bothering you, is it? That your mum's there?"

"No!" Alice giggled.

"Then what's the problem?" Alice had been uncharacteristically quiet all evening, and Hope knew something was wrong.

"Well, you know how it was supposed to be Mrs. Bowen that was my teacher for upper infants?" Alice said.

"Yes," said Hope, stroking hair off her daughter's forehead. "And you know how Mrs. Bowen is having a baby so she won't be the upper infants teacher this year?"

"That's the problem," sighed Alice. "I already knew my teacher before I had school last year because she came to visit when I was in reception class. But now I don't know."

"And you're worried it'll be someone you don't like?" asked Hope.

Alice nodded, wrinkling the pillowcase under her head.

Hope smiled. "You've got nothing to worry about," she said.

"You don't know that. You don't know who my teacher's going to be either."

Alice really was too smart for her own good sometimes. She had a fair point though. The vacancy hadn't been filled when school ended, and all Hope knew now is that Jake Lowell, the headteacher, had found a candidate through a school exchange program that Hope couldn't pretend she understood.

"I do know that," she said to Alice now. "Because I know a secret."

"What's that?" asked Alice, suspicious.

"That all upper infant teachers have to be nice," Hope said airily. "It's a requirement. A qualification for the position. It's the first thing Mr. Lowell looks for. And you trust Mr. Lowell, don't you?"

Alice squinted in thought, then nodded.

"There, see, it'll all be fine," said Hope. "And you need to go to sleep, or else you'll be in no fit state to meet that new teacher tomorrow."

Alice screwed her eyes tight shut and Hope laughed before dropping a kiss on her head. "Night, kiddo."

"Night, mum."

Hope switched off the big light and closed the door until only a crack of nightlight shone out onto the landing. As she walked down the stairs she had a sudden memory of opening the front door that afternoon and she shook her head.

She really hoped that the new neighbor wasn't going to be a problem. It wasn't like she could keep Rosie inside. Maybe she should try to make friends. Or maybe not. She had enough to do as it was.

"Cocoa, mum?" she shouted through to the lounge.

"Please," answered Caz.

Alice wasn't the only one that needed an early night, she wasn't the only one expecting a busy day tomorrow. Hope yawned. She'd be off to bed soon herself.

CHAPTER SIX

"Good morning, good morning!" A tall man with thinning gray hair was holding out his hand and Ava took it.

"Good morning," she said. "Mr. Lowell?"

"Jake, please," he said with a pleasant smile. "I'm only Mr. Lowell in front of the children, come, come, there's coffee waiting in my office. I'm so pleased to see you."

"I'm pleased to be here," Ava said, it was a nice surprise to be welcomed so warmly.

"I know this is all rather last-minute," said Jake, leading her into an office that had a view over the fields behind the school and was lined in filing cabinets. "But that doesn't mean that we don't want you, far from it. You're a god-send."

"Not to worry," Ava said, taking a seat and accepting a cup of coffee. "It was pretty last minute on my end too."

"We had coverage all worked out, but then the supply teacher broke her leg, and, well, here we are. I should have been here earlier to welcome you and give you all the info you needed, of course, but I'm afraid my mother's been sick, and, well, things are far from ideal."

"It's really not a problem," Ava said. The coffee was strong and good, far better than she'd had at her previous school. "I've twenty years experience, I don't think there's much that I can't handle at this point."

"One of the many reasons you'll fit in perfectly, I'm sure," Jake said with a grin. "And I've had one of our other teachers go over the lesson plans that Mrs. Bowen left to ensure they're up to scratch, so for the first week everything's already planned out for you. All you'll need to be is a warm body, so to speak."

"Excellent," said Ava. This job was getting better and better. Maybe she should consider staying.

"After that you'll be somewhat on your own, though we do have the national curriculum that we need to follow," the headteacher was explaining. "It's not too complicated, but I'll have someone sit and go over it with you after school, just to ensure that you're up to date with the latest information."

"Perfect." Honestly, she expected him to offer to teach her classes for her any minute now. She sipped some more of the excellent coffee.

"You'll find Whitebridge Primary to be a nice school," Jake said, sitting back and crossing one ankle over the opposite knee. "We're a friendly bunch, the teaching staff are all quite close. The children are well-behaved for the most part, though there's the odd trouble maker like anywhere, I suppose. On the whole, our ethos is to support our pupils in becoming the best that they can be, whilst understanding that what's best for one child might not be the best for another, of course."

Ava cleared her throat. There was one thing bothering her. "Child?" she said. "Perhaps student or pupil is a better term?"

Lowell frowned but then shrugged and grinned. "Whatever you prefer," he said. "Now, everyone will start arriving around eight thirty or so. The children, sorry, students, will be in by ten to nine, and then the school day finishes at half past three. I'll get you the grand tour later, but for now we do have a fair amount of paperwork to take care of, so if you don't mind…"

He pulled out a fat folder and Ava sat forward, a pen already in her hand, ready to make everything official.

SHE'D COME INTO the school through a side door that had

been unlocked and had been shown straight to Lowell's office. But now that she was walking through the actual school corridors, Ava could tell that something was patently wrong here.

"The staff room is that door through there," Lowell was saying with a gesture.

The walls were painted white and blue and Ava was busy trying to figure out what wasn't right, so she simply nodded as the headmaster went on.

"There are pupil toilets here, the staff toilet is right next to the staff room, absolutely don't give a student the key to that, please."

"Right," said Ava, and she suddenly got it.

The coat hooks that were lining the corridor came up no higher than her waist. That was what was wrong.

"If you need help, or if there's illness or injury, just come right up to the front desk that you saw by my office. Hope, our receptionist, will be happy to help out wherever necessary."

"Right," said Ava. "Um, actually—"

"You'll be glad to know that we're a small school," Lowell went on. "You'll have only twelve in your class just at the moment, though of course, enrollment is open all year."

"Yes, lovely. Um, if I could ask a question?"

"Not enough time, I'm afraid," Jake said with a jolly smile. "Your classroom will be this one right here and you should find everything you need in there."

"No, I, uh, wait," Ava said, starting to feel quite desperate. A dawning realization was making her hands sweat and making her mouth dry.

"Now, we're running quite late. I really didn't expect all that paperwork to take so long," said Jake. "But it's all fine. Hope, our receptionist, did the parental meet and greet, and Amy from the classroom next door has kept an eye on yours for you, they've already got reading books out and they'll be ready for you."

"But—" Ava said.

But it was all too late. The headmaster was opening the door and stepping aside and Ava was standing in the doorway as twelve pairs of eyes swiveled in her direction.

She looked on in horror at twelve miniature desks and twelve miniature chairs, at a tiny classroom sink that reached only as far up as her thigh, at bookshelves that reached her knee, at the brightly colored alphabet border that stretched around the room, at the soft beanbags and cushions, at the dollhouse and the stack of toys in the corner.

And for a long moment she thought she might pass out, as in actually faint, like some damsel in a Victorian novel.

"Children," Lowell said, his voice modulated but authoritative. "This is your new teacher, Ms. Stanford. What do we say?"

"Good morning Ms. Stanford," said twelve reedy little voices.

"I don't understand," Ava hissed, turning back to the headmaster. "There must—"

"We ask for good manners at Whitebridge Primary," Lowell said, frowning slightly at her. "Good manners and politeness help us all get along nicely together."

"Right," said Ava, losing track of things again.

"So?" said Lowell, nodding back toward the children.

"Ah, right." Ava turned back, took a deep breath, and smiled. "Good morning, children."

"Where are you from?" asked one little boy.

"You sound like you're on the telly," said another.

"There must have been some kind of mistake," Ava said, forgetting to lower her voice.

"Why? Are you not from the telly?" asked the second boy again.

"Or maybe she is," said a little girl. "And then it's a mistake her being here and being our teacher and all."

"There's no mistake," Lowell said firmly. "Now, I'll let you be getting on with things, Ms. Stanford. Good morning, children."

"Good morning, Mr. Lowell," chorused the children.

The headmaster closed the door firmly, leaving Ava standing in front of it looking at twelve eager little faces and wondering just what she was supposed to do.

"We're doing reading time," said one of the girls helpfully.

"Oh," said Ava. "Okay, that sounds nice." She spied a red book sitting on a large desk at the front of the room.

"You'll need to do the register," added the same girl, who had dark curly hair.

"The register?" asked Ava.

"Yes, you know, to make sure that everyone's here. It's in that red book," said the child. "But we're all here, aren't we?"

"Yes," chorused a set of voices.

Ava took a deep breath. She had no choice here. It was all a mistake, but it wasn't like she could fix it right this second. Someone had to run this classroom and just at the moment that someone had to be her.

She walked to the desk, picked up the red book and opened it to find a list of twelve names. Well, that was a start.

"Alright then," she said with far more confidence than she felt. "Clara Buxton?"

"Here," said a girl with fair pigtails.

"Carter Edwards?"

"Miss?" said a voice.

Ava looked up. "Please just answer with 'here' or 'present,'" she said.

"Yes, but miss?"

She took a breath, control. That was key. Control was the key in any classroom, no matter how old the students. "We're doing the register right now," she said, proud of herself for remembering the right word. "We'll have questions after. Carter Edwards?"

"Here," said a voice. "But miss?"

"I said we're taking attendance," Ava snapped.

"We know," said the little girl in the front row with dark curly hair. "But we're all here and the problem is Daniel."

Ava frowned. "Who's Daniel?" She looked down her list and found his name.

"Me," said a boy at the back with a hang-dog look on his face.

"Well, he's here, so I don't see the problem," said Ava.

"There is a problem," said the curly-haired girl looking quite serious. "Because Daniel's done a wee."

"Daniel's what?" squawked Ava, looking around in alarm.

She tilted her head and sure enough, a puddle was growing around the small boy's small chair. She swallowed, thoroughly out of her element and unsure of what to do.

"You need to send him to the office," said the curly-haired girl.

Ava nodded. "Right. Um, Daniel, off to the office please." The boy stood up and squelched toward the door and even Ava felt a pang of pity. "Do you, uh, need some help?"

Daniel shook his head.

"It happens all the time, miss," said Miss Curly-Hair. "He knows what to do, don't you Daniel?"

Daniel nodded grimly and opened the door.

Ava turned back to the register and marked him as present. She had no idea what had gone wrong here, and she was going to sort it out at the earliest opportunity, but just at the moment she had a classroom to run, and her professional pride was enough to overcome her discomfort around small children.

She'd take attendance, check the lesson plan on her desk, and keep them occupied until recess. After that, well, she and Jake Lowell needed to have a serious discussion.

CHAPTER SEVEN

Hope's day hadn't exactly started off well. She and Alice had both woken up late and it had been a rush to get into school. Then, just when she was sitting down to get on top of the normal start of term paperwork, Amy Littleton, the lower infants teacher who had been Alice's class teacher the year before, stopped by the office.

"Slight emergency," she'd said.

Hope, who'd always had a bit of a soft spot for Amy, smiled sympathetically. "What can I do to help?"

"Um, actually you're under orders from Jake to come handle the parents for upper infants and get the kids settled."

"But… I thought we had a new teacher?" Hope said, standing up and switching her screen off.

"We do," said Amy. "She's in his office now getting everything formalized. But he's running behind, you know that his mum was ill, don't you?"

"How is she?" asked Hope as the two women walked down the corridor.

"Mending, I think. But he's still a bit disoriented. I'm sure he's on top of things now, but this summer hasn't been a great one. And now we've got this new teacher. Ava Stanford, by the way. I only caught a glimpse, but she seems nice enough."

"I hope so, Alice was worried."

"I'm right next door," Amy reassured her. "If anything goes

wrong, I'll jump in. But she's really experienced apparently."

Down the corridor, Hope could see small faces already lining up outside the classroom, and a host of parents were holding hands and making assurances and she sighed. "Alright, I'll get this lot settled. Reading books?"

"You got it," Amy said, hurrying off to her own classroom. "Quiet reading time, and Jake said Ms. Stanford will be in in ten minutes or so. I can keep an ear open for them until then."

After allaying parental worries, giving Alice a secret hair ruffle so as not to embarrass her in front of her friends, and settling the upper infants, Hope had gone back to her desk and she was just starting to count dinner money contributions when Jake Lowell strode up.

"Thanks for helping out, Hope," he said with a grin.

"Not a problem." Hope couldn't contain her curiosity. "What's she like?"

"Ms. Stanford? Seems pleasant enough. A good member of the team, I'd say. Highly qualified, very experienced." Jake ran a hand through his thinning hair.

"But?" Hope asked.

"Nothing. Just, well, she seemed a little... nervous perhaps?"

"Well, first day of a new term and all. First day in a new school even. She's got the right to a little stage fright."

He grinned again. "Maybe that's it. Have a chat with her at break time, will you Hope? Make sure she's getting off on the right foot, making friends, getting support, that sort of thing."

"Of course I will," said Hope.

"Brilliant," said Jake.

Just then there was the sound of small feet shuffling down the hallway. Both adults turned to see a small, damp figure heading their way.

"Oh dear," said Hope. "That'll be Daniel Monroe. And on the first day of school already."

"Poor Dan," said Lowell with a sigh.

"He'll grow into himself," said Hope. "Or grow into his bladder, I suppose. They all do eventually." She smiled as Daniel got closer. "Morning Dan, need a bit of help there?"

The child nodded solemnly. "Sorry, Ms. Perkins. Sorry, Mr. Lowell."

"Nothing to apologize for, Dan," Jake said cheerfully. "Accidents happen to the best of us. Just this morning I spilled an entire cup of coffee all over my kitchen table."

"Did you?" Daniel said, looking faintly mollified. "What did your mum say?"

Hope laughed. "Mr. Lowell doesn't live with his mum any more, he's a grown up."

Daniel frowned. "Who does your washing then?" he asked. "And how come you still wake up to go to school? My mum says that without her waking me up, I'd sleep all day."

"Grown ups do all those things for themselves," Hope said, standing up.

Daniel pulled a face. "Doesn't sound good that," he said. "Being a grown up sounds horrible."

Jake laughed. "It's not all bad. Now, why don't you let Ms. Perkins take you to the nurse's room for a clean up and some spare trousers?"

"Yes, please," Dan said.

Hope took his hand and they began the slow walk to the nurse's room.

"Don't forget about break time and Ms. Stanford," Jake called after them.

"I won't," Hope said.

But when the break bell rang she was still busy helping Daniel into a new set of clothes and finding clean socks for him. She didn't worry too much. She was sure that Amy Littleton would pick up the slack.

AND SO THE day went. At lunchtime she had to run out and pick up the stationery supplies that had been delivered at the post office and didn't get back until long after the bell rang, having stopped for a sandwich in town.

At afternoon break she was embroiled in a fight with the aging photocopier in the back office and had hands covered in toner.

And by the time the end of school bell rang she was exhausted and ready to do nothing more than pick up Alice and go home.

She packed her desk up, switched her computer off, and turned just in time to see Alice bounding down the corridor toward the office.

"No running in the corridors," she reminded her daughter.

"But school's finished," protested Alice.

"Rules are rules for a reason. You don't run in the corridor because you might get hurt, or because you might hurt someone else." She took Alice's hand and they started to walk together toward the side door. "Now, how was your first day back at school?"

"Daniel wet himself again," said Alice.

"I know," said Hope, with damp memories.

"And there was a spider in the window but then we were all scared but then Ms. Stanford said we should give him a name and then now we have a class pet." Alice stopped in the doorway. "Except Ms. Stanford said he'll have to go to see his family so maybe he won't be there tomorrow. That's a bit sad, isn't it? Except seeing his family will be nice, I suppose."

Hope ushered Alice toward the playground and the school gate. "Speaking of Ms. Stanford, what's she like?"

She felt guilty that she hadn't even greeted the woman. But to be fair, it seemed like today the universe was conspiring against her. Every single time the bell rang she was away from the office. It was only the first day, she reminded herself. She'd make up for it tomorrow. It wasn't a good idea to get on the bad side of Alice's class teacher.

She turned back in just in time to hear Alice saying "poo lady."

"Alice Perkins," said Hope in a strangled voice. "I don't want to hear you say that phrase again, is that clear?"

Alice stopped and looked up at her mother. "Yes, but—"

"But nothing," Hope said. "Never again."

Clara Buxton was making a bee-line for them. The Buxtons lived just around the corner from Hope and Alice and the two girls often walked home together. Alice glanced at Clara, then at her mother, then nodded. "'kay."

"Good. Come on then, let's go girls."

The two girls trotted off in front of her and Hope followed along. She sighed. From the nickname, it sounded like Alice didn't like her new class teacher, which was a shame. But then, Hope supposed that all children had to have at least one teacher they didn't like. It was a learning experience.

And perhaps Ms. Stanford wasn't that bad. Maybe she was just a little stricter than Alice was used to. Hope resolved to make far more of an effort to meet the woman tomorrow.

As it turned out, she didn't have to wait that long.

CAZ WAS PULLING a baking tray out of the oven when the doorbell rang.

"I'll get it, mum," said Hope. "Alice, dinner's almost ready," she called up the stairs as she went to the front door.

She opened the door and stopped still.

On the front doorstep was the same blonde woman holding what Hope assumed was a different plastic bag. Or at least she hoped it was.

"Another gift from your feline," said the woman.

"And you're presenting it to me," said Hope sourly. "How lovely."

"I really don't want this to become an issue between us. We do have to live next door to each other," the woman went on. "But this is unconscionable. You can't just allow your cat to use everyone's gardens as toilets."

"It's not exactly easy to stop her," protested Hope. "What would you actually like me to do about it? I could sit down and discuss it with her, maybe have her sign some sort of contract, would that work?"

"Well, now you're being silly, aren't you?"

The woman swept off her glasses and pushed them on top of her head in a movement that gave Hope a memory of feelings she'd rather ignore. She filed that away for later. Note to self: women with glasses on their heads are sexy. By the time she returned to the conversation the woman was halfway through some kind of diatribe about cats in general.

"Hold on," Hope said. "Just stop for a minute there. Rosie is an outside cat and always has been, I can't keep her inside all the time, it'd be cruel."

"Oh, can we keep Rosie inside, mum?" came Alice's voice. "She can sleep in my room, in my bed even."

Hope opened the door a little wider as she turned to see her daughter coming downstairs, a doll under one arm. "No," she began. But something about Alice's face stopped her.

"Alice?"

Now Hope turned to look at the woman on her doorstep. "You know her name?" she said. She remembered that the woman had stalked Rosie over the back fence and was suddenly furious. "You spied on us long enough to learn my daughter's name? That's... that's terrifying and creepy and I'm in a good mind to call the police."

"No, mum, please don't," Alice said, coming closer. "You can't call the police on Ms. Stanford 'cos then I wouldn't have a teacher again."

Hope looked down at Alice, mouth half-open, then back up at the woman on the doorstep, then shook her head in disbelief.

The woman cleared her throat. "Um, Ava Stanford," she said, holding out the hand that wasn't clutching a plastic bag of animal droppings.

"Hope Perkins," said Hope, taking it.

"School secretary?" the woman said in a slightly less stern voice.

Hope nodded.

For a long moment the two of them regarded each other. Then Alice spoke. "You said it's tea time," she reminded her mother.

"Right," said Hope. "Yes, it is."

"I'll let you go then," said Ava Stanford, snatching her hand away from Hope's. "I'll see you tomorrow, Alice." And she turned and stalked away.

Hope closed the door and then closed her eyes, leaning her forehead against the cool of the wood.

"I did try to tell you, mum," Alice said. "I tried to tell you that she was the… the you-know-what-lady, but then you just told me not to say that anymore, so I stopped."

"Right," said Hope, wondering just how bad of a first impression she'd made and whether the relationship could be at all salvageable at this point.

"I won't call her the P-O-O lady anymore," Alice said. "Because now she's Ms. Stanford."

"Right," Hope said again.

For God's sake. What were the chances?

She sighed and followed Alice into the kitchen for dinner. Ms. Stanford was a bitch, not that she'd tell Alice that. The problem was that now she was going to have to pretend that she wasn't. And Hope really wasn't that good at pretending.

CHAPTER EIGHT

The headmaster crossed his very long legs and sat back in his desk chair. "I'm not sure I completely understand."

Ava stopped herself rolling her eyes. "What's to understand? There was some kind of mistake, that's all. I don't teach elementary school, I teach high school."

"You're not qualified to teach primary school children?" he asked, a worried look passing over his face.

"Well, yes, I suppose," Ava said. "I mean, I have a general teaching degree and I did a rotation of heavily supervised elementary teaching. Heavily supervised," she said again to underline the words.

"Well then, I'm sure it will all be just fine," smiled Jake.

"No, no it won't," Ava practically screeched. She'd wanted to deal with this yesterday afternoon when school ended. But unlike in her US schools, when she'd gone back to the admin offices after the bell rang, they'd been empty and locked. So instead, she'd been forced to come in early.

"It's just a case of the nerves," Jake said soothingly.

"No," said Ava. She got up out of her chair and paced around the small office. "I'm not experienced doing this, I have no idea what's going on, I can't teach these children." She sighed in exasperation. "For God's sake, I'm used to teaching teenagers about the symbolism of color in The Great Gatsby, or the use of metaphor in T.S. Eliot. I'm not used to singing the alphabet song ten times a day."

And even that she'd got wrong nearly every time, with the kids correcting her pronunciation of 'zee' to 'zed.'

Jake leaned forward now and put his hands on his desk. "I see," he said, sounding sad and slightly irritated. "Alright, I suppose I can take this up with the program administrators. I'll give them a buzz and see what they have to say. That's the best I can do for the moment."

Outside, Ava could hear the high sound of children's voices in the corridors. The bell was about to go any minute. "And what about right now?" she demanded.

Lowell shrugged. "I can't work miracles. You'll have to go in there and do your job. You have lesson plans written out for you, you got along fine yesterday, you'll just have to hold on for the next couple of days until we can sort something out."

"But you are sorting something out?" Ava said, pushing for a promise.

With a weary sigh, the headmaster nodded. And then the bell rang.

Out in the corridor, Ava felt like she was walking through fog. She was tired and had only herself to blame. She'd spent half the night on Zoom with Quinn, talking through what had happened, trying to figure out a way to solve the problem.

In the end, they'd each opened a bottle of wine and had ended up no closer to a solution, though Ava had come close to tears at the thought of missing her old life.

And now, well, she supposed that Jake Lowell was right, there wasn't much that could be done at the moment. She'd have to buckle down and hope that the exchange program would correct their mistake.

In the meantime, she had children to deal with.

Small ones.

Including the precocious daughter of the irritating woman next door.

She shook her head as she stepped to the side, narrowly avoiding a running boy.

Who would have thought? She supposed that Whitebridge was a small town and it was somewhat inevitable that her neighbors would end up being her students. Still though, right next door? And with a badly-behaved cat to boot?

Plus, of course, the woman was the school secretary or receptionist or something. Just to add insult to injury. The one person that Ava would have thought she could rely on to get a little help and it turned out to be the one person in town that she'd already pissed off. Perfect.

A small girl yelped and Ava practically had to dance to get out of her way.

This was not turning out quite as she'd imagined. Though if she'd wanted a change she supposed she couldn't change much more than this.

The fact remained though, she was completely unsuited and under-qualified to deal with small children. And that was the end of it.

Another boy bumped into her and Ava took a step back and years of training took over. "Stop!"

She didn't shout exactly, but her voice carried and the busy corridor ground to a halt as dozens of pairs of eyes turned to her. Ava put her hands on her hips.

"No running inside. No shouting inside. No bumping inside. Now please calm down and get to your classrooms."

There was a second of silence, then the crowd of children began to move again, more calmly this time, with a buzz of light chatter as they made their way to their classes.

"Nicely done," said Amy Littleton, who was standing outside her own classroom. Her face wrinkled into a smile. "I see they teach the 'teacher's voice' in the States as well."

Ava grinned. "How would we survive without it?"

Amy was laughing as she went into her classroom and Ava wondered if maybe she could hit the woman up for some tips. After all, Amy's kids were even younger than her own, so she must have some idea of how to deal with them.

She took a deep breath before she opened the door and walked into her classroom. There seemed to be children everywhere she looked. One was on top of a bookshelf. Teacher voice, she reminded herself.

"Good morning, children."

"Good morning, Ms. Stanford," mumbled a chorus of voices as twelve children fought to get back to their seats.

Ava suppressed a smile as she watched them all clamber back into their chairs. Maybe she could do this after all. At least for a few days.

THE WHITE BOARD marker felt heavy in her hand and Ava was beginning to question her sanity.

"No, listen carefully," she said. "I give you four cats on Monday. On Tuesday, I take two cats back again. How many cats do you have?"

Nathan Jackson rubbed his nose with his hand and then said: "Three."

Ava bit her tongue to stop herself shouting.

When she'd seen math on the curriculum she'd had a quiver of fear. But then she'd figured that even she could teach six-year-olds math. Indeed, the exercises had seemed quite easy and the class had been doing well up until right now. Three times she'd asked Nathan the question, and three times he'd given the same, wrong answer.

"Four cats minus two cats is how many cats?" she tried.

"Two," Nathan said with confidence.

Ava frowned. "Alright, so if I give you four cats and then take away two cats, how many cats do you have?"

"Three," said Nathan with equal confidence.

Ava was about to snap when she had a sudden thought. "Nathan, do you already have a cat at home?"

The small boy nodded with a grin. "So when you give me four cats then I have five cats and when you take two cats away then I have three cats," he said.

"Right," Ava said. She put down the white board marker. She

was exhausted and really couldn't handle any more of this. She glanced down at the lesson plan that was on her desk. Whatever was next was going to start early, her math teaching career was at an end. "Let's put our books away and…" She peered at the lesson plan. "And get ready for art."

"Hurray!"

There was a bustle of busy noise as everyone put away their math books. Ava read the lesson plan a little more carefully. The children were supposed to paint insects, since insects were the over-arching theme for the next couple of weeks. Later there'd be a story called James and the Giant Peach, which was somehow insect related. But first, painting.

"The art cupboard is over there, miss," piped up Alice, pointing to a cupboard to one side of Ava's desk.

"Thank you, Alice," said Ava.

She breathed a sigh of relief. Art. That was easy. Even she couldn't screw this up. She might even get to sit down for a few minutes. What could possibly go wrong?

SHE LOOKED AROUND the classroom and couldn't see a surface that didn't have at least some paint on it.

The normal collection of various skin-colored faces that looked up at her were now purple and green and blue and, in the case of Carter Edwards, a rather startling yellow.

Not only that. The neat outfits that the children had worn into school this morning, with their white polo shirts that had the school logo and their blue pants and skirts, were now equally kaleidoscopic.

Ava let out a small moan that she hoped no one heard.

It hadn't started badly. The children had taken paints and brushes and paper and had settled down to work with quiet industriousness. It had taken a good ten minutes before Ava noticed that Clara Buxton had painted the top of her desk as well as her paper. And another minute before she'd seen that Adesh Khatri's centipede had extended down onto the floor.

Things had gotten rather worse since then, and asking the children to wash their hands had resulted only in paint all over the sink as well as the wall.

Ava moaned again. What was she supposed to do? She had no idea how to clean all this up, not to mention what to do about the children and their uniforms.

"Ms. Stanford?" said a small voice.

She looked down and saw Alice's solemn dark eyes. "Yes, Alice?"

"I think we'd better ask my mum for help, don't you?"

Ava closed her eyes and sighed. What other choice was there? "Yes, Alice," she said. "I think we'd better."

CHAPTER NINE

Hope looked up to see a host of literally multi-colored children walking down the hallway. As they got closer, Alice waved, and Hope could see that the pupils were absolutely covered in paint.

She stood up and came to meet them all in the corridor in order to prevent them touching anything with paint-covered hands.

The small group stopped when they got to her, twelve bright faces smiling up at her, their teeth white against the colored paint. Only Alice looked vaguely uncomfortable. Well, Alice and Ava Stanford, who was standing at the back of the group with an embarrassed look on her face.

Hope examined them all, one by one. Paint not only on their faces, but in their hair, on their clothes, everywhere.

"Ms. Perkins," Ava Stanford began.

Hope held up a hand. "Before Ms. Stanford says anything, would any of you like to tell me what the problem is here?" She glared at the line of children.

"We've got paint on us," Nathan Jackson said.

"Even on our clothes," added Daniel Monroe.

Alice sighed. "We didn't wear our painting aprons," she said.

Hope nodded. "Ms. Stanford is new here and doesn't know the way we do things. But you aren't new, are you?"

Twelve heads shook simultaneously.

"So next time, perhaps one of you could help our new person learn the rules. Like that we wear our painting aprons when we paint."

"Yes, miss," said a bunch of sad voices.

Ms. Stanford coughed. "Do you perhaps have a solution for us, Ms. Perkins?" she asked, quite politely Hope thought.

Hope held up a finger to indicate they should all wait and then went quickly to her computer to check the class schedules. She gave a satisfied nod and went back to the corridor.

"It's just as well that you all have PE this afternoon. Does everyone have their PE kit?"

"Yes, miss," said twelve voices.

"Good," said Hope. "First, we're all going to go into the nurse's office and I'm going to give each of you a plastic bag to put your dirty clothes in. You will get undressed, you will put your clothes in your bag, and you will wash your hands and faces in the big sink there. Ms. Stanford and I will be in to help you momentarily. First, she and I will go and get your gym kits so that you have something to change into."

"Yes, miss," chorused the class.

"Any questions?"

"No, miss," they all said.

"Alright, I'm going to get Mr. Lowell and he'll supervise until Ms. Stanford and I get back."

Once Jake was escorting the children to the nurse's office and they were all well out of ear-shot, Hope finally turned to Ms. Stanford.

"What on earth were you thinking?" she said. "Letting them at the paints without aprons on?"

"I… I didn't know." The woman at least had the grace to blush.

"You didn't know?" screeched Hope. "What kind of teacher are you? You don't let a bunch of six-year-olds paint without protecting their clothes. It doesn't take a genius to work that out."

Ava drew herself up tall. "Then I shall know for next time," she said coolly. "In the meantime, what do you suggest I do about the mess?"

Hope shook her head. "I don't know where you're from, but it's obviously some kind of clown town. And then someone else has to clean up after you."

"I've been cleaning up after your cat for the last week," Ava pointed out.

"And this is payback?" asked Hope. "Come on, we need to get the kids' PE stuff otherwise they'll be running riot half-naked back there."

She marched off down the corridor, letting Ava Stanford follow behind, still shaking her head at the idiocy of the woman. Seriously, what kind of teacher lets their kids loose with paints?

But she was nowhere near as angry as she got when she opened the classroom door and saw the state of the room.

"Do you have any control at all of these children?" she said, turning to Ava in disbelief.

"Of course."

"Well, it doesn't look like it," Hope said. "This is unbelievable."

"There's been a misunderstanding," said Ava. "I don't teach young children."

"You *shouldn't* teach young children by the looks of this." Hope stared around and then came to a decision. "Alright, there's no point crying over spilled milk. You get the PE kits back to the kids, get them dressed up and then take them outside and do PE out there. You're lucky the sun's shining. While you're doing that, I'll get in here cleaned up so you have a classroom to come back to."

There was a slight pause. "Thank you," Ava said eventually. She said it as though it hurt.

Hope rolled her eyes. "It's not like I've got much choice," she said. "And after that, I'll prepare a note for the kids to take home explaining about their clothes. At least it's all washable paint, it should all come out."

"Right," Ava said.

Hope turned to her. She didn't look so high and mighty now, did she? Not now that she was the one in the wrong. How a teacher could let a class get so out of control was beyond Hope. But then, maybe Ava Stanford wasn't the brilliant teacher she'd been made out to be.

Maybe she was a fraud.

And Hope wasn't planning to pick up the slack for her. The woman was arrogant and irritating, and if she was going to put herself in a position to get fired, well, Hope wasn't going to stop her. The sooner Ava Stanford was gone from the school and from next door, the happier and quieter life would be.

They could always get a supply teacher to cover the class. She was sure they'd find someone.

"Er, thank you," Ava said again. Her green eyes were sparkling and Hope wasn't sure if she was angry or about to cry.

"Just get those gym clothes to the kids," she said. "And then get out of my way so I can deal with the mess you've created."

ALICE HAD GONE home with Clara Buxton with promises that she'd be well-behaved and she wouldn't complain when Hope came to pick her up for tea at home. Which left Hope slowly cleaning up her desk and getting ready to go home for a nice quiet coffee with her mum before resuming parenting duties.

To be honest, she thought she deserved a nice slice of cake to go with the coffee after the day she'd had. It had taken an hour and a half to get Ava Stanford's classroom into a presentable state again, even with Amy Littleton helping out at break-time.

She was exhausted and not at all in the mood for staying on after school when Jake Lowell cornered her in her office.

"Hope."

"Jake."

He scratched his head. "We've got a problem."

"Is that problem called Ava Stanford?"

"Yes," he said, honestly. "There's been a bit of a misunderstanding, you see."

"I know, she's a secondary school teacher, not a primary

school one. You called this teaching exchange program place, I suppose?"

He nodded. "That's just it though. They don't have anyone else to send us. Oh, they apologized profusely, though they pointed out that Stanford's completely qualified to be here, just inexperienced. But in the end, their positions are all happily filled and there's nothing they can do for us until the next influx of teachers, which won't be until next school year."

Hope sat down on the edge of her desk. "So, we'll get a supply in."

"It's not that easy," Jake said, leaning up against the wall. "I can't find anyone who's willing to do the whole year, or even the whole term. Which would mean having different teachers in at least every week, and that's not good for the kids."

"You're not making me feel good about this, Jake."

The headmaster ran his fingers through his hair. "I've got a solution, but it might not be completely ideal."

"What's that then?"

He sighed. "Listen, I talked with her and she's willing to stay on. I mean, she's not happy about it, but when I pointed out that the alternative was to go back to the States, she said that she'd spent the money to come here and couldn't go home yet."

"Fair enough, I suppose," said Hope. She sighed. "I suppose this isn't really her fault either, is it?"

"It's not," Jake agreed. "It's not anyone's fault. Let alone the kids'. And that's what's important here, you know that. I'm sure you agree, especially with Alice in Ava's class."

Hope lifted an eyebrow. "Why do I get the feeling that you're winding up to ask me something I'm not going to like?"

"Ava can stay, but she's obviously unable to control that classroom by herself. At least right now until she gets a bit more experience. We can agree on that, can't we?"

"I suppose," Hope said.

"And yet, having her stay is the best option that we've got at the moment."

"I suppose," Hope said again.

Jake pinched the bridge of his nose between his forefinger and thumb. "And the only way I could persuade her to stay on was if I got her some help."

"Like a classroom assistant," Hope said, nodding. It was a fair idea. Ava could do the teaching, the assistant could help out with the extras, like ensuring the kids wore painting aprons and making sure Ava was doing age-appropriate lessons.

"Well, Amy's agreed to help Ava with her lesson planning and making sure she's sticking to the curriculum," said Jake. "But she can't be in the classroom, obviously, she's got a class of her own. Which is why I thought of you."

"Me?" Hope said, jumping up. "Are you kidding? I've got a job, in case you hadn't noticed."

"I know, I know," said Jake. "But it's the best solution I can come up with. You're great with the kids, Hope, you know you are. You've been here forever and you know how things work here. You're sensible and anyone here would trust you with their kids. You're in the perfect position to help."

"And what about my actual job?"

"Getting a temporary secretary is a lot easier than getting a temporary teacher."

"Well, thanks a lot," Hope said, stung.

Jake straightened up. "Look, I know it's not the greatest thing in the world, but I can't come up with anything better. I need your help. We need your help. The school needs your help. Please, Hope. I'm begging you."

Hope sighed. She didn't want to do this. She didn't want to have to go around fixing Ava Stanford's problems and cleaning up her messes, which was exactly what Jake was asking her to do.

On the other hand, she wanted her daughter to have a decent education, and at least if she was in the classroom she could make sure that that was happening.

"You'll just have to be in the classroom during teaching hours," Jake said. "And, well, I'm sure I can squeeze something out of the budget to make the salary a little more attractive."

"A raise?" Hope said.

Jake nodded.

She narrowed her eyes at him. "A pay raise that I get to keep after the year is over when I return to my normal receptionist slash secretary duties?"

He sighed but nodded.

"Fine," she said. "It's a deal."

CHAPTER TEN

The garden needed weeding and the lawn could do with a mow, but Caz kept the flowers looking nice and at the end of the day it was nice to be able to sit in the late summer warmth. Or it was when Hope wasn't sitting opposite her ex-husband.

"Well," she said. "You're the one that wanted to talk. So go ahead and talk."

Noah shuffled in his chair then gripped the armrests with his hands, a sure sign that he was trying to stop himself fidgeting. Whatever this was, it must be big. He knew how much fidgeting irritated Hope, so if he was consciously stopping himself then he was trying to make a good impression.

"It's about Alice," he said slowly.

"No shit," Hope said, folding her arms and sitting back in her own deck-chair. "I wasn't thinking it was about the cat."

Noah gave a weak smile. "Right."

If Hope looked closely, she could see Alice's head bent over a coloring book at the kitchen table. Caz was keeping her busy, keeping her out of the way for this impromptu set of negotiations. "Go on then. What about Alice exactly?"

Noah scratched his nose. "It's just, uh, you know, we really like having her around."

"We?" Hope said. "We? As in you and your girlfriend?"

"Okay, I told Amelia this was a bad idea."

"Did you? How strangely perceptive of you," Hope said. She felt brittle, like her skin could break at any second and then all the anger would come pouring out.

"We just wanted to help."

"Right."

Noah held up his hands. "Listen, I'm Alice's father."

"And when have I ever tried to stop you seeing her?" Hope demanded.

"You haven't," said Noah. "And I'm just saying that maybe I'd like to see her more."

"Maybe?"

"No, I would. We would. We'd like Alice to feel just as welcome and at home at our house as she does here."

Hope blew out a breath. Jesus. "Listen, the agreement was every other weekend and half the holidays, plus one weekday evening as long as she's back by seven. There's a reason that we agreed to that. Alice needs stability."

Noah rubbed at his eyes. "Are you sure that the reason isn't that you want stability, Hope? Maybe it's just you being controlling."

"It's me looking after Alice's best interests."

"And what do you think I'm doing?" asked Noah.

"If you're suddenly so concerned about Alice's best interests then..." Hope cut herself off. 'Then you should have thought about that before you dumped me and our family for someone so skinny she might break in half at the next gust of wind,' had been what she was planning on saying.

"It's important that Alice feels comfortable at my place," Noah said.

"It's important that Alice has a regular schedule and knows what's happening and when. Not to mention that she gets a good night's sleep before school," said Hope. She stood up, hoping that Noah would take the hint.

"Hey, there are rules at my place too, you know?" he said. "I don't just let her run wild. I'm as good a parent as you are, Hope. Something that you seem to forget often enough."

"Do I? What about that time you left her sitting in a petrol station as collateral against the wallet that you forgot?"

Noah rolled his eyes. "That again. How many times do I have to tell you, the Buxtons were there and keeping an eye on her. I popped home to get some money, I was gone all of ten minutes."

Hope gritted her teeth.

"Fine," Noah said, getting up. "This is obviously pointless. But we're not done. We're going to talk about this again when you've calmed down and had time to think about it."

Hope showed him out of the house thinking that there wasn't enough time in the world for her to consider his proposal and agree to it. Alice stood next to her and waved goodbye to her father, a sight that always left a little chip in Hope's heart.

"How about we make some fairy cakes?" she said.

Alice's face lit up. "Really? Can I decorate them?"

"Obviously. There's no one else around here to do it, is there?"

Alice grinned and skipped off to the kitchen and Hope followed, her steps slower than usual.

THE CLASSROOM WAS barer than she'd expect. But then, she supposed that Ava's kids had spent so long painting their desks and the floor that they hadn't had time to make something to put on the walls yet.

Ava's back was to Hope, but she turned as the door clicked shut.

"Ah."

The black-rimmed glasses were on top of her head again, pushing back her hair and making her cheekbones look even sharper. "Ah?" Hope said. "That's all I get? Not exactly a warm welcome."

Ava put down the folder of lesson plans she was carrying and took a visibly deep breath. "We haven't got off on the best foot," she said.

"Funny that," said Hope. "I don't generally take to strange women knocking on my door holding bags of cat poo, but then, maybe that's just me."

"Listen," Ava said. She was getting pale, a spot of color high on each cheek. But she took another deep breath and Hope could see that she was trying. "Listen, I'm sorry about that. But perhaps we could try and separate our work and home lives?"

Hope pressed her lips together into a tight line, but nodded. It was a fair enough request. Besides, they were about to be spending five days a week together for the foreseeable future, so some kind of compromise had to be made.

"Fine," said Hope. "Home and school. Two different people. Got it."

"Good." Ava held out a hand.

Hope looked at it. "What am I supposed to do with that?"

"Well, traditionally, I think you shake it," Ava said, a twitch of a smile on her lips.

Reluctantly, Hope took the hand. It was warm and softer than she'd thought and as she took it the idea crossed her mind that she might find Ava Stanford attractive.

It was an idea that she immediately dismissed as ridiculous. There were a thousand reasons why Ava Stanford was not attractive. She hated Rosie, for one. And the fact that she looked somewhat sexy with her glasses pushed up on her head did not in any way over-ride any of the nine hundred and ninety nine other reasons why she was a pain in the backside.

"I am very grateful that you're here," Ava said, letting go of Hope's hand.

Hope took a breath to answer then had to remind herself to play nicely. "Thank you," she said as politely as she could.

"You've heard the problem from Mr. Lowell?"

"Jake explained everything."

Ava nodded and for a second Hope could see a flicker of doubt in her eyes. She couldn't possibly be nervous, could she? Not this woman who carried herself with the confidence of someone far more important, who knocked on strangers' doors, who flew halfway across the world for a temporary job?

What was there to be nervous about? Okay, she wasn't

supposed to be a primary school teacher, but these were only little children. It wasn't like they were going to be an equal match in a fight. Not that Ava should fight her students, but still.

"So how do you want this to work then?" Hope asked, interrupting Ava who'd been making some kind of excuse for the exchange program she was on.

"Oh," said Ava, looking surprised. "Well, I'll teach, obviously, and, um, I think your role is to stop me doing anything stupid."

"Like letting six-year-olds paint their desks."

"Yes," Ava said a little more coolly. "That's about the sum of it."

"Alright," said Hope. "What's on the agenda for today then?"

"Reading, science time and math this morning."

"Maths."

"What?" Ava said.

"Maths, we call it maths here. You can't confuse the children by using the American word."

"Right," Ava said looking like she might want to punch Hope. "I'll remember that."

"I'll get the graded readers out then," said Hope, turning away before Ava gave in to the impulse to punch her.

For a few minutes they worked in silence, the only sound that of books hitting desks.

"Are you alright?"

Hope paused, then turned. "Why do you ask?"

Ava looked faintly guilty. "You just looked kind of tired."

She'd been so angry with Noah, with the idea that he just wanted to waltz in and take Alice whenever he felt like it for as long as he felt like it, that she'd tossed and turned last night thinking of all the things she should have said to him.

"I'm fine."

"Fine," Ava said so that Hope wasn't sure if she was agreeing or if it was a question.

"Not that it's any of your business."

"Not that it is," said Ava. Her eyes were sparkling a little and she was almost smiling.

"What about you? Are you alright?" said Hope, deliberately

poking.

"I'm fine."

"Fine," mimicked Hope.

"Not that it's any of your business."

"Not that it is," said Hope.

Ava took a step closer, then another. "Would you tell me if you weren't fine?"

"Probably not," said Hope honestly.

"And yet it could be my business. You do work in my classroom, after all." Ava's lips were kind of hypnotic as she spoke.

"Our classroom," Hope said. And Ava was stepping even closer.

For a long second there were only centimeters separating them and Hope smelled Ava's perfume. Something mild and masculine, something with sandalwood and spices. Her heart began to beat a little faster and Ava's eyes narrowed.

Then the school bell rang and Ava stepped back and the moment was broken.

CHAPTER ELEVEN

Ava felt like she'd been beaten in the boxing ring for a full twelve rounds. Her back hurt from bending over desks that were too small, her feet hurt from standing so much, and her brain hurt from trying to follow the derailing trains of thoughts of six-year-olds.

"I'm just taking these to the photocopier," Hope said, holding up a stack of forms for the forthcoming parents' evening.

"Right," said Ava. "Uh, thanks."

"I'm your classroom assistant, it's my job," Hope said brusquely, before walking out of the classroom.

Ava sighed and collapsed into a chair the second Hope had left. Somehow it had seemed important not to show weakness in front of the woman. Hell, she was weak enough already without having the younger woman think that she was too old for the job.

Maybe she was too old for the job.

She stretched out her aching legs with a moan of pleasure.

Not that Hope didn't make things easier, she absolutely did. The burden of just what she was supposed to do if one of the tiny beings in her charge wet themselves, or worse, was very much lightened.

On the other hand, the tension in the room had sky-rocketed.

It was painfully obvious that Hope didn't like her, and Ava didn't really blame her.

After all, they hadn't gotten off to the best start. And now Hope was being roped into doing a different job just so that she could clean up Ava's messes. Which Ava could very much appreciate was not something Hope particularly wanted to do.

On the other hand, Hope was no superstar herself. Okay, so she was great with the kids. But she was otherwise snappy, and she nearly never took her eyes off her own daughter. Ava wondered just how smothered little Alice must get at home.

But Ava herself wasn't supposed to be here. That was the only thought that kept echoing around her head. She wasn't supposed to be here.

Yet what choice had she had?

When Lowell had told her that the program couldn't help reassign her, she'd had to make a decision. A decision that had come down to staying here to tough things out or going back to the States to nothing. A few substitute teaching hours and a wild hope that she didn't run into Serena somewhere on the teaching circuit.

A futile hope since there were only so many schools in the district and Serena worked at the largest. The school that Ava had once called home.

So sticking it out had been the only option. Now here she was daily placed in a room with twelve small children that seemed to have some sort of inherent death-wish, or at least mess-wish, and a woman who looked fabulous in yoga pants but who hated her.

Wonderful.

She did look good in yoga pants though, Ava conceded. Not only that, but she looked good in the tight jeans that she wore to work, complete with Converse and open-necked shirt. That was the kind of uniform Ava could get behind.

Eugh.

Thinking of behind and Hope in the same sentence was not a good idea. It awakened feelings that Ava had almost forgotten existed. Feelings she wanted to forget existed.

What the hell was she thinking? It wasn't as though she didn't notice attractive women. She was divorced, not dead. But Hope? Seriously?

She blew a raspberry at herself and the classroom door opened pretty much simultaneously.

"Ah," said the headmaster. "Interrupting something?"

Ava laughed. "No, just me lost in my thoughts is all. Is there something you need?"

"Oh, nothing too important," Jake said with an absent-minded grin that Ava was beginning to recognize meant that he was going to tell her something immensely important.

"Oh?"

"Just that the inspectors will be in in a couple of days. Nothing to worry about. Just do your best and teach to the curriculum and you'll be fine. No worries."

The door was already starting to close. "Wait!" Ava cried. "What?"

The door opened again and Jake stuck his head back in. "Inspectors."

"What inspectors?" asked Ava, starting to panic. "What are they inspecting for? Will they come in here? What happens if the inspection goes wrong?"

She had visions of Nathan Jackson painting an inspector's pants. Or worse, Daniel Monroe peeing on them.

"It's fine, it's fine," Jake said. "OFSTED, school inspectors, they just make sure everything's up to scratch. But like I said, teach to the lesson plan you have and you'll do just fine." He paused for a second. "Hope is here, isn't she?"

"In the copy room."

His face cleared. "Well then, it'll all be alright. I'll talk a bit about it in the staff meeting tomorrow. But really, I'm sure they'll give you the benefit of the doubt, being new and a foreigner and all."

Ava wasn't at all sure she wanted the benefit of the doubt, or that she wanted to be inspected, or that she really understood what was being inspected and why. But before she could ask any more questions, the headmaster had gone and she could hear his shoes clopping down the corridor outside.

She was still worrying about what had just happened, and was busy googling OFSTED, when Hope returned holding her photocopies.

"You look like the world's about to end," said Hope.

"What's OFSTED?"

Hope put the pile of papers down on the desk. "It's the government department that oversees standards in education, you know, makes sure we're teaching the kids to read and write and not to, I don't know, hold their breaths and dive for pearls or something."

"They're inspecting me."

Okay, so she hadn't wanted to show any further weakness in front of Hope, but she didn't have much of a choice just at the moment. It occurred to her that the inspection involved Hope just as much as herself. Maybe Hope was just as shit-scared.

Hope shrugged. "They do it every now and again. It's not a big deal. Well, I mean it is if you're a failing school, but we're not." She stopped. "You've got a lesson plan, right?"

Ava nodded.

"Then don't worry."

"That's easy for you to say," Ava snapped, irritated that no one seemed to be taking her concerns particularly seriously.

"Well, I'm not the one being inspected, am I?"

"Very helpful. And totally unnecessary," Ava said.

"Sorry, I've been too busy lecturing my cat about using the toilet outside to keep up with my etiquette lessons," Hope said, one hand on her hip.

Ava rolled her eyes. "Are you ever going to let that go?"

"Are you?"

"That rather depends on whether or not your cat appears in my garden again."

"See, I thought we were going to separate our home and work lives."

"You were the one that brought this up," Ava pointed out.

"I did," agreed Hope. Then she cocked an eyebrow. "Are you

still dwelling on that inspection?"

Ava frowned. "Well, no, but—"

"Then distraction achieved," said Hope, picking up the purse that was hanging on the back of the closet door. "Besides, you have nothing to worry about. I'll be here."

And with that, she walked out.

Ava shook her head and wondered if she'd ever met anyone quite as irritating as Hope Perkins.

THE EVENING WAS warm and Ava enjoyed the feeling of being outside. She enjoyed the feeling of being in Whitebridge, if she was being honest. Not that she'd made herself part of the community yet. But it was nice to be somewhere small for a change.

And nice to be somewhere where she could walk home past a nice bookstore, she thought as she saw that The Queens of Crime was still open. She needed something new to read, something to distract her and take her mind off the disaster that was her personal life and the potential disaster that her professional life was becoming.

She clinged through the door and a blue head immediately popped up from behind the counter.

"Oh, it's you," Mila the policeman's wife said.

"What are you doing down there behind the counter?" asked Ava curiously.

"Hiding," Mila said confidently. Then she put her head on one side examining Ava. "You worried that I've got Ag down here again?"

"Ag?"

"You know, the baby that you so inexpertly held?"

"Oh, yes," said Ava. "Um, I mean no. It's your workplace, you can do what you like in it."

"Is that Ad?" came a voice from the back of the store. A young woman appeared, her hair messy, a flannel shirt and ripped jeans on, but wearing a friendly smile.

"Not Ad," said Mila, turning to her. "Honestly, Ant, do all Americans sound the same to you?"

The woman laughed and looked at Ava. "Which means you must be the other American in town, making you the new teacher."

"That's me," Ava said.

"We've heard you're terrible," said Mila.

"Mila!" The other woman pulled a face at Ava. "Sorry. I'm Anthea, by the way, most people call me Ant. And don't mind Mil, she doesn't have a filter."

"I'm only being honest. I don't put much stock in rumor, but you should have seen the way she held Ag, like she was going to explode or something. The little ones aren't really your thing, are they?" She turned to Ava for confirmation.

"I, uh, well, not really," Ava allowed. "But I'm here for experience, so…"

"Not worried about the OFSTED inspection, are you?" Ant asked.

Ava looked from one to the other and then Ant started to laugh.

"Yeah, keeping secrets in small towns isn't really the done thing," she said. "Jake Lowell dropped in on his way home and told us about the inspection. But I'm sure you'll be fine."

"And Hope Perkins is there to help, isn't she?" put in Mila. "So it'll be alright."

Really. They knew everything. Ava wondered if there was a point in having curtains on her windows, or whether there were already cameras in her cottage.

"Hope's a good woman," said Ant.

"Mmm," said Ava, not wanting to commit to that one.

"She is," said Mila. "She's had a tough time of it, what with the divorce and everything. But she's got a heart of gold."

"Not unattractive either," Ant said.

"You know, I just came in for a book," Ava said needing to put a stop to this conversation before it got any further out of control.

Ant narrowed her eyes and then grinned. "Hope's a touchy

subject, eh?"

"Hope Perkins is not a subject at all as far as I'm concerned," said Ava. "Now, can I choose a book in peace or not?"

She stalked off into the shelves but was sure she heard a faint giggle behind her as she left.

CHAPTER TWELVE

"Why aren't you wearing your school cardigan?" Hope asked as Alice walked into the kitchen.

"Ms. Stanford says we don't have to if it's warm," Alice informed her. "And she says in America children don't wear school uniforms at all. They wear anything they like."

The kettle boiled and Hope was glad of an excuse to turn around so that she could roll her eyes without Alice seeing. "Go and get your cardigan please," she said as patiently as possible.

"But why?"

"Because I said so. Because it's part of your uniform. And because you don't know what the weather will be like later. It might get colder."

Alice trotted off back up the stairs to get her cardigan and Hope shook her head.

"Why do you hate her so much?" Caz said, putting down her cereal spoon.

"Hate who?"

"Ava Stanford," said Caz, picking her spoon up again. "You know, you get the same look on your face when Alice talks about her as you do when Noah's name gets mentioned."

"I do not," protested Hope.

"Looking at your own face now, are we?"

Hope took her coffee to the kitchen table. "I don't hate her. I just... She's annoying. She was annoying the first time I met her complaining about Rosie and she's annoying now. It's annoying that she can't do her job properly, it's annoying that someone else, namely me, has to clear up after her, and it's annoying that she's here at all."

"That's a lot of annoyances," agreed Caz. "In fact, some might say it's protesting just a little too much. That maybe you're not as annoyed as you're making out. Maybe Ava Stanford is getting under your skin for other reasons."

"Like what, mum?" Hope asked, daring her mother to say what she feared she was going to.

"Look, like it or not you have to work with the woman," said Caz, ignoring Hope's provocation. "And to be fair, this new job is only temporary and it got you a nice raise. So maybe you should try to play a little more nicely with your new friend."

"Mum's got a new friend?" asked Alice coming back into the kitchen with her cardigan on inside out.

"No," said Hope.

"But she will have," Caz said.

"Mum, stop interfering."

"You know I'm right," said Caz. "Spend a little time being less annoyed and trying a bit harder. It can't be easy on her. She's all alone here, after all, isn't she? What's the story there?"

"I've got no idea," said Hope suddenly realizing that actually she knew nothing about Ava at all. She didn't even know where she came from in the States.

"What's the story where?" Alice asked, tucking into her cereal.

"Little pitchers have big ears," Hope said to Caz.

"I do not have big ears," said Alice, which made them both laugh.

THE SCHOOL WAS uncharacteristically quiet. Mostly because the inspectors liked to see children playing outside at lunchtime, rather than finishing projects or running in and out as was more usual.

Hope had rushed her sandwich in the staff room and come

back to the classroom in order to get the art materials ready for the first part of the afternoon. When she walked in, Ava was standing at the window, watching the kids playing.

"It's going alright," Hope said, remembering that she was supposed to be playing nice.

"Only because the inspectors haven't been in here yet," said Ava, obviously stressed. Her hands shook a little as she tucked a lock of hair behind her ear.

"Oh, please," Hope said. "We've all told you it's going to be fine."

"I wish I had your confidence."

For once, Hope found that she couldn't be irritated. The blunt admission on Ava's behalf made her understand that the woman truly was worried.

"I'd have thought you were brimming with confidence," Hope said, pulling pots of paints out of the art cupboard.

"What's that supposed to mean?" Ava leaned against her desk, crossing her arms.

"Just that, well, I suppose it's quite brave, isn't it? Coming to a new country all alone, striking out for independence and all." Hope put the paints down. "I suppose you could have run away when things didn't turn out as you expected, but you didn't. You're sticking around. That's brave too." And it was. Her mother was right. She should try to be more charitable. God, she hated it when Caz was right.

"It's not that brave," Ava said.

"Right."

"No," said Ava. "I mean it, it's not. I mean, maybe if I were leaving something to come here it would be. But I didn't. So it's not as brave as you might think."

Hope sensed an undercurrent of something. "Not leaving anything? You mean you don't know anyone back home? You don't have a job?"

Ava startled her by laughing. "No, that's not what I meant." She got serious again. "I'm just being self-pitying is all."

"Self-pitying?"

Ava looked as though she might not respond, then her shoulders lowered a little and she said: "Recently divorced."

"Ah." Hope felt a pang of sympathy. "I could have entered the self-pity Olympics after I got my divorce," she said lightly. "Mind you, some days I still could."

"It doesn't get any better then?"

Hope shrugged. "I suppose it depends. On the circumstances. On whether kids are involved. I mean, there are a lot of factors. Was your ex-husband an asshole? Did he hurt you physically? Was there someone else involved? You know how it goes."

Ava looked at Hope for a long minute until Hope started to realize she might have said something wrong. Then Ava obviously came to a decision.

"My ex-wife wasn't an asshole," Ava said. "Mostly."

"Jesus." Hope felt blood rush to her cheeks. "I'm an idiot, I assumed and that's wrong. I'm sorry."

Ava waved a hand. "It's not important. It happens. Being straight is the norm, I get it. And Serena mostly wasn't an asshole. Luckily, there's no kids involved."

Hope pulled a face. "Not messy then? Well, given your ability to get kids messy whilst doing something as clean as maths, that might be a good thing."

"It might," Ava said, a smile tugging at the corner of her mouth.

"So she wasn't an asshole mostly..." Hope said, aware that she was prying but also aware that Ava wouldn't hesitate to stop her if she went too far. Besides, she was supposed to be playing nice, getting to know the woman better, right?

"She left me for someone else," Ava said.

"Ouch."

"A man."

Hope raised an eyebrow and whistled. "Double ouch." She sniffed. "Mind you, is that better or worse? I mean, being left for another woman is being left for competition. Being left for a man, isn't that more like being left for something that you couldn't provide, something you don't have?"

"Oh, I have," said Ava.

Her voice was loaded with meaning but it took a second for Hope to realize what she was saying, and then she was so shocked that she burst out laughing. "Uh, I'm not sure that was quite what I was talking about," she said, when she'd recovered. "Also, what you keep in boxes under your bed is definitely none of my business."

"No, I know what you meant," said Ava.

Hope found that she was trying very, very hard not to think about Ava and sex toys, which proved very, very distracting. Distracting enough that she missed the first half of what Ava was saying.

"... in the end I suppose it was the sense of betrayal. Him being such a close colleague and all," Ava said as Hope tuned back in. "What about you and Alice's dad?"

Hope sighed. "Noah? I wish it was so simple. I mean, I suspect that there was someone else, but I don't really know. He just came home one day and sat me down and told me he was leaving."

"And you didn't try to find out?" Ava asked, uncrossing her arms and putting her hands on the desk behind her.

Hope shook her head.

"Didn't you need to know for the divorce?" pushed Ava. "Hell, didn't you need to know for your own sanity?"

Hope took a breath and let it out slowly. "Maybe," she said. "But Alice didn't need to know. And in the end, that was more important."

Ava looked at her for a moment, then gave a short nod. "Alice is important to you, isn't she?"

"She's my daughter, of course she is."

The bell rang and Ava suddenly stood up straight, the nerves back. Hope smiled at her. "It's going to be fine."

THE CLASSROOM FELT larger when it was quiet, with all the kids gone home. Hope pulled out her purse and considered what she was going to do.

The inspection had gone fine, just like everyone had said it would. The kids had been happily painting insect parts when the inspectors arrived and all had been chatty and communicative. Ava had shown full control of the classroom and the inspectors had been smiling as they left.

And Hope thought that maybe she and Ava had made some kind of connection. Maybe this was a cause for celebration. Maybe Caz had been right and she should try harder. So she smiled as she closed the closet door.

"It went pretty well," she said.

Ava nodded. She was sorting through her lesson plans for the following week. Amy Littleton had been helping her square away some ideas.

"So, um…" Hope started. Her mouth got dry. Maybe this was a mistake. No, come on, it was nothing. It wasn't like she was asking the woman on a date or anything. "Er, do you fancy a drink?"

"What?" Ava said, eyes snapping straight up to look Hope in the face.

Hope felt color rise to her cheeks. "I just meant as a celebration, that's all. Just a quick one. My mum's taken Alice home. We could stop in at the pub. I, uh…" She trailed off.

Ava looked back down at her papers. "I don't think so," she said.

Fuck.

There went that connection she'd thought they were building. "Oh," said Hope. "Alright then."

She hitched her bag over her shoulder and walked to the classroom door. She should have known better. She'd had Ava pegged as a bitch and one moment of weakness in a conversation didn't change that, did it?

"Hope?"

She turned back.

"Thank you," Ava said. "For today. Thanks."

And suddenly Hope wasn't quite as angry as she had been.

Alright, she wasn't *not* angry. But she wasn't thinking of pushing her hosepipe through Ava's letterbox either, so that was an improvement. Maybe.

CHAPTER THIRTEEN

Alice was dancing around the kitchen wearing angel wings from last year's nativity play and her football shorts. Hope pulled a piece of spaghetti out of the pot and examined it closely.

"Do you think that angels might wear, oh, I don't know, white dresses and the like?" she asked Alice, deciding the pasta was about ready. "Rather than a football strip, I mean."

"Mu-um," Alice said, and Hope could almost hear her eyes rolling. "It's the twenty-first century. Angels can wear anything they like and even boys are angels so some of them wear football shorts."

"Right," said Hope, in solid agreement, suddenly realizing that Alice wasn't going to be small forever. One day she'd be a teenager and the eye-rolling would start for real and Hope wasn't entirely sure she was prepared for that.

"I'm not sure that dancing in the kitchen is a good idea," said Caz, coming in from the garden. "But I like the look. Good to know that even Man U supporters get to go to heaven."

"Everyone gets to go to heaven," Alice said definitively. "As long as they want to. They have to have, um, consent?" She said the word uncertainly.

"They have to give consent," said Hope, hearing Ava's voice in the word. "Did Ms. Stanford tell you that?"

"Not the heaven bit," said Alice. "But the consent bit. It's important to have, wait, give consent for things and to ask for it as well so you don't make other people feel bad or make them do things they don't want to do. Like if I want to play legos and you don't want to play legos if I make you play legos then that's against your consent and it's wrong."

"I see," Hope said. Alice had the essentials at least. "Well, would you consent to eating some spaghetti?"

"Yes," said Alice seriously.

"Then go take those wings off," said Caz. "Otherwise you'll get sauce all over them."

Hope picked up the pan of boiling pasta and water and turned just as Alice was scooting past her. She squealed, fumbled, and managed to practically throw the pot at the sink, narrowly avoiding splashing her daughter. "Al! No running in the kitchen!"

Alice froze, looking at the puddle of water on the floor.

"Accidents happen," Caz said. "And that's all it was. No one's hurt, right Alice?"

Alice nodded and looked up at Hope. "Sorry."

Hope sighed. "Go and change those wings, go on, let's see if I can rescue this spaghetti out of the sink."

"I'll get the mop," said Caz as Alice walked ever-so-carefully toward the stairs.

Hope went to the sink, gratified to see that most of the spaghetti had made it into the strainer sitting there anyway.

"I was meaning to talk to you," Caz said, as Alice's footsteps disappeared upstairs.

"Mmm?" said Hope.

"About going out one night early next week. Monday maybe."

Hope spun around and lifted an eyebrow. "You don't need to ask me for permission to go out," she said.

"Good," said Caz, coming back with the mop. "Because I wasn't asking permission exactly, I was—"

She never finished her sentence. Her foot slipped out from under her as it hit the edge of the puddle of water and Hope watched in horror as her mother came down hard onto the floor, smacking her head against the edge of the kitchen cabinet as she fell.

"Mum!"

There was a millisecond that felt like an eternity before Caz moved. "It's fine, I'm fine."

Hope rushed to her, bending over. "You're not fine."

"Well, I've not broken a hip," said Caz, a look of relief on her face.

"But you cracked your head going down." Hope pressed her fingers into her mother's scalp, watching her wince as she did so. "And that means a trip to casualty."

"No, no, don't fuss," Caz said, struggling to stand up.

Hope helped her up and stationed her on a kitchen chair. "I'm not fussing, mum. You gave your head a good bang, we're getting it checked on, no complaining. Let me just call Noah."

She gave her mother a glass of water and grabbed her phone from the kitchen counter, keying in Noah's name and then pacing into the front hallway as the phone rang.

The phone rang and rang and Hope peered anxiously out of the window next to the front door. Voicemail picked up and she hung up, immediately dialing Noah again. Rosie hopped over the hedge and Hope opened the front door to call her in, phone still in her hand.

The cat slinked past her and the phone went to voicemail again.

"Damn it," Hope said, already dreading the thought of taking a wiggling six year old to the hospital. She had no choice but to go. Caz wasn't getting any younger and Hope wasn't going to let her take chances.

But taking Alice as well wasn't ideal. She could kill Noah. She knew that he'd be home from work by now. Why wasn't he picking up his phone?

"Everything alright?"

Hope turned to see Ava, bag over her shoulder, walking up the short path to her front door. "Fine," she said, still salty from Ava's refusal to have a celebratory drink.

"Yet it's obviously not," said Ava, stopping.

Hope growled. "If you must know, my ex isn't picking up and I need to take my mother to the hospital. Which means I now need to wrangle Alice into something that isn't fairy wings and football shorts and drag her with me too."

"I see." Ava bit her lip and Hope saw a look of something cross her face. Regret perhaps? She really wasn't sure. "That doesn't sound like a healthy place for Alice to be."

"It's probably not," said Hope, irritated even more now because of course it wasn't and she didn't need Ava to point that out. "And we'll be there for hours, well past her bed time."

Ava closed her eyes for the briefest moment and Hope knew what she was going to say and prayed for her to say it even as she hated depending on Ava to say it. "I suppose I could…" Ava began.

"Could you?" said Hope far too quickly. "It'd be such a help and I'll be as fast as I can. Dinner's already made. You just have to sit with her while she eats and then she can watch TV for an hour. She can shower herself and get into bed, then read her a story. That's all." She had another thought. "And feel free to eat too, there's plenty of spaghetti."

Ava blew out a breath looking quite exhausted, but nodded. "Let me just put my bag inside and get my book and I'll come over."

"Thank you, thank you, thank you," Hope said, knowing full well that this wasn't something that Ava wanted to do and feeling like she was taking advantage but not sure what other choice she had.

"I TOLD YOU I was fine," grumbled Caz as they walked up the garden path.

"And I told you that it was better safe than sorry," said Hope. Her bag rattled with the painkillers they'd been given for Caz's headache.

"Well, now it's close to midnight and I'm exhausted, so forgive me if I go and take my shower and get into bed when we get in."

"Of course," said Hope, feeling slightly guilty. She'd forgotten the time and now it was so late. Ava must be fuming.

She unlocked the door quietly and let her mother go inside first. The light was on in the living room. "Go on upstairs," she told Caz. "I'll deal with Ava."

"Make sure you thank her," Caz said.

Hope rolled her eyes because no matter how old she got, her mother was still her mother. Like she'd forget to say thank you.

She pushed open the living room door and then stopped.

Alice and Ava were on the couch, a red-blonde head against a curly-dark head, both breathing deeply, a book between them. Ava's glasses were askew and Alice had biscuit crumbs around her mouth. And both looked very relaxed and very, very asleep.

Hope leaned against the doorway. Wouldn't it be nice, said a little voice in the back of her head, to have this all the time? Wouldn't it be nice for Alice to have more than just a divorced, split-up family?

Ava's face was softer in sleep, her features less sharp and Hope had the feeling that she was seeing the woman without her shell. How hard must it have been to have been left like that. To have built a life based on one thing only to have it snatched out from under her. Ava must be hurting, she must ache with it every day. Yet she still showed up, still did a job she was so obviously uncomfortable doing.

Hope couldn't help but feel sympathy. Sympathy and... and something else. Something warm and growing inside that she really didn't want to think about. Especially right now when Ava had one arm around her daughter.

Perhaps something could happen though. Maybe she was ready for that now. Maybe she could be a little nicer, a little more forward and who knew? Ava was around until the end of the school year, after all. Perhaps something could develop.

For a second, Hope had an image of Ava's hair splayed out on her pillow like a fairy crown and she had to shake her head to clear the picture.

Ava wasn't so bad.

"Oh, you decided to come home then?"

Hope turned her eyes back to the couch to see Ava awake. "Sorry?"

"You could have called," said Ava, obviously irritated. "We tried calling you."

"I had my phone switched off, it's a hospital," said Hope.

"Well, little miss over here didn't want to sleep without saying goodnight to you."

Hope sighed. "You should have put her in bed. She was pulling one over on you, getting you to let her stay up later than her bedtime."

"Well I'd have known that if you'd have picked up your phone," said Ava, carefully extracting her arm from behind Alice's head.

"She's got school tomorrow," said Hope, thinking of the tantrums that were likely to erupt from a tired Alice in the morning.

"She's not the only one," sniffed Ava, standing up and picking up her book off the coffee table.

"Looks like you won't be lacking for sleep though," Hope said pointedly.

Ava huffed. "Is your mother alright?"

"Fine," Hope said as Ava approached, book under her arm. "Just fine."

"I'll be going then."

Ava got to the door and Hope didn't move, too taken aback by just how fast she'd gone from 'Ava's a misunderstood and actually nice person' to 'I might just have to poison her milkbottles on the doorstep in the morning.'

Ava frowned and then turned to squeeze past Hope in the doorway and Hope held her breath. For the shortest of instants Ava was brushing past her and Hope felt that warmth again and then the front door was opening and Ava was leaving and Hope was sighing and wondering just why Ava had to be so incredibly annoying.

CHAPTER FOURTEEN

There was, Ava thought, no point trying to avoid a relationship with Hope altogether. She was walking to school, the fall air still warm but with a hint of the burning smell of falling leaves. After all, she had to work with the woman.

However, she could certainly do a better job of not getting involved.

Truthfully, when Hope had asked her out for a drink her heart had skipped a beat and she'd suddenly remembered what it was like to be nineteen and falling in love for the very first time.

Some sort of biological short-circuit, no doubt.

And it had scared her. Scared her enough that she'd, very sensibly in retrospect, turned Hope down flat.

It was sensible. Sensible because Ava wasn't interested in dating again. And even if she were interested then she wouldn't be interested in someone as obviously irritating as Hope Perkins.

But then she went and invited herself into Hope's life by offering to babysit her daughter. As though she didn't get enough of small children at work.

Alright, so Alice had actually been rather entertaining to be around. But that really wasn't the point, was it?

So what was the point, Ava wondered as she walked through the school gate. She was early enough that there was only a scattering of children in the playground.

Maybe the point was that she was changing, just as she'd promised herself. Change was always uncomfortable. But it was happening. She was drinking less. She'd been running twice this week already and it was only Wednesday. And, apparently, she was looking at women.

Looking, not touching.

Hope Perkins was, indisputably, attractive. Not that that meant a thing. It really didn't. Okay, maybe it meant that Ava's heart could still function, as battered and broken as it was. But it definitely didn't mean that she was willing to risk said heart on anyone else.

And if she were willing to take that risk, it absolutely, completely and definitely wouldn't be on Hope Perkins.

She pushed open the door to her classroom and screeched. "What on earth are you doing?"

"Fixing the planets display," Hope said, tongue sticking out of one corner of her mouth and tottering on the very top of a ladder that was blatantly not tall enough.

"You're going to kill yourself," said Ava, dropping her bags.

Without thinking, she rushed to the ladder and reached up, clutching Hope's calves, one in each hand, to steady her.

"I've got it," said Hope, wobbling as she straightened out Mercury on its string.

"No, I've got you," Ava said.

Only then did she realize what she was doing. Only then did she realize that she was holding on for dear life to Hope's very warm, very shapely legs. Only then did she realize that perhaps she shouldn't be quite so close. She cleared her throat, unsure of what to do, wanting to let go and not wanting to let go at the same time and all the while her heart was throbbing to let her know that it was very much alive, very much not down and out no matter how broken down it might have seemed.

"It's fine, I'm fine," Hope said, letting the display swing back into place. "Watch out, I'm coming down."

Ava let go as though Hope were burning hot and took a step back just as Hope backed down the ladder. Hope turned and then they were nose to nose.

Ava cleared her throat again.

Fantastic. She was developing a nervous tic. Just what she needed.

"I told you I got it," said Hope, but her voice was a little quieter and her eyes were flickering, shining in the morning sun.

"You did," Ava said, entranced by those eyes, wondering what it would be like to see the world through them.

"It's, um, it's all fixed now."

"Uh-huh." Hope's cheeks were flushing a pale pink and Ava thought that she might be blushing too and then they'd match and…

"So, um," said Hope.

"Uh-huh," Ava said again.

"If you could, uh…"

"Ah, yes, of course." Ava blushed even deeper red and took a large step back, freeing Hope who had been trapped between her and the ladder. She cleared her throat one last time. "Don't use the ladder alone," she said brusquely, moving away and picking up her bags.

"Why not?" Hope asked, folding the ladder up.

"It's dangerous."

Hope snorted. "As if. It's a tiny step ladder. It's fine."

"Everything's fine with you, isn't it?" Ava said, depositing her bags on her desk. "Always fine. Right up until there's an accident and you have to go to the ER."

Hope leaned the ladder up against a wall and pulled a face. "Speaking of, I didn't thank you for last night. I'm sorry, I was tired and out of sorts when I got home and that's no excuse, but seriously, you were a life saver."

Ava sniffed. Alright, so maybe she didn't regret helping out. It was the neighborly thing to do, wasn't it? Nothing more than that. She hadn't been at all interested in seeing inside Hope's house. And she'd definitely not looked in the bathroom cabinet.

One peek. She'd had one peek. Then slammed it closed and gone back to read a story to Alice.

"It was nothing."

"No, it was something. A big something, and I really appreciated it," said Hope. "I, uh, well, I'd meant to grab some flowers for you on the way back, but it was so late…"

"Just as well you didn't," Ava said, opening up her bag. "Can't stand the things."

"Flowers?" Hope asked, coming closer to the desk. "Who doesn't like flowers?"

"Me." Ava looked at her over the top of her glasses. "Leave them in the ground where they belong. Don't kill them to present to someone you're indebted to."

Hope raised an eyebrow. "Right. Okay. I'll remember that."

"I doubt you'll have future cause to present me with anything, let alone flowers," Ava said sharply.

Hope lowered her eyebrow, cheeks flushed, and backed off. "Yeah. Doubt it," she said, as she walked back over to take her ladder back to the appropriate closet.

QUINN'S FACE GLOWED weirdly orange on the tablet, but her eyes were bugging out and she was practically yelling. "You did it, I knew you would! How hot is she? Tell me every detail."

Ava frowned. "What are you talking about?"

"What are you talking about?" Quinn asked, looking confused now. "I thought you went to this woman's house. Hope. What's she like? Is she hot?"

"I went to her house to babysit her kid while she took her mother to the hospital," Ava explained.

"Oh," said Quinn. Then she brightened up. "But is she hot?"

"It's not like that," Ava started.

Quinn laughed. "It starts that way though. And I'm so happy for you, happy that you're finally taking an interest again, that you're starting to live again."

"Q, calm down. She's my classroom assistant, I simply did a favor for a neighbor, nothing more, nothing less."

Quinn peered at Ava through the screen. "Right. So, is she

then? Hot, I mean."

Obviously, Quinn wasn't going to let this go. Ava sighed. "I suppose," she said, grudgingly, because she couldn't deny the fact that Hope was attractive, that would be lying.

"Hmmm. So you noticed?"

"And?"

Quinn shrugged. "And nothing. It's obviously a touchy subject, I'll leave it alone." She paused for a second. "She's single though?"

It was Ava's turn to shrug. "I think so, I don't really know. I know she's got an ex-husband and she lives with her mom. She doesn't seem to get out much."

"Neither do you," pointed out Quinn.

"What's that supposed to mean?"

"That it's seven thirty on a Wednesday evening and you should be, I don't know, bowling or on a date or doing anything other than talking to your gorgeous best friend."

"I'm about to be doing anything other than talking to you in a minute," Ava said. "Quit pressuring me. I'm not dating again. End of story. Can you not let me be heart-broken in peace?"

"That's the thing though, isn't it?" said Quinn. "You can't be heart-broken forever. You need a heart to live. If you let it languish away in that dark pit of despair, well, eventually you'll keel over and die."

"Cheerful, thank you."

"You're forever welcome." Quinn smiled and her eyes danced and Ava couldn't help but smile back. "Listen, I'm encouraging you, that's all. You've had a tough time, Ave. But you're not dead yet. You're all of thirty eight."

"I'm forty three."

"Shit? Really?" Quinn said, pretending to look surprised. "Well then, strike everything I just said. You're an old maid, spend your time alone at home. Have you looked into getting a cat?"

"Don't talk to me about cats," said Ava. "And you're not funny."

"Oh, I am," grinned Quinn. "I'm also about out of time. Lunch break's over and it's back to work for me. I'll talk to you soon, okay?"

"Soonest."

"And Ave? Never say never, eh?"

Ava sighed. "Fine. I won't say never."

"And if this one's hot, don't let her escape," said Quinn, leaning in and switching off the call so that Ava couldn't respond.

Ava shook her head and folded the cover back over the tablet. Quinn just never gave up. Maybe because Quinn had never actually been heart-broken. She'd never taken anything or anyone seriously enough to hurt herself. Not like Ava. Not like how things had been with Serena.

She got up and went into the kitchen to pour herself a glass of wine.

Just one, she promised herself.

One glass and an early night, she had school in the morning.

And Hope would be there as always. Ava had a sudden image of herself clinging on to Hope's legs as she shuddered on a ladder and took a large gulp out of her glass. Okay, a glass and a half then, she thought, topping her drink up.

CHAPTER FIFTEEN

Caz was shelling peas at the kitchen table and Hope watched her hands with their long fingers and knobbly knuckles.

"You know they make frozen peas nowadays," she said. "No shelling involved."

"I'm not a fool. These ones taste nicer," Caz said comfortably.

"I feel like I'm in a Victorian novel."

"Cheeky," said Caz. She sniffed. "So, the other day, we were talking about something and then I fell and hit my head on that water you so cleverly spilled."

"I apologized," Hope said, pulling a face. "It wasn't like it was intentional. And you said something about going out."

"That's right." Caz threw a pod into the bag and a handful of peas into the pan. "I'm going out. Tuesday night, as it happens now."

"Fine by me," said Hope. "Not that you need my permission, as we've already established."

"Neither do you."

Hope pulled a pea pod out and chewed on the end of it. "What's that supposed to mean?"

"Just what I said. If, say, you wanted to go out, you wouldn't need my permission."

"Right," said Hope. She didn't quite know what her mother was saying. That or she didn't want to think too carefully about what she might be saying. "So who're you going out with then?" she asked, trying to steer the conversation away from herself. "Bingo?"

"Not bingo," said her mother.

"Girls' night out then," grinned Hope. "We'll leave an aspirin and bottle of water by your bed."

"Nope," said Caz calmly shelling peas. "Not girls."

"Well, who then if it's not— oh."

Caz looked straight at her daughter. "Oh indeed."

Hope took a breath and tried again. "I mean, that's nice, mum. It's good. You're, um, you're getting out and, uh…"

"And dating," filled in Caz. "At least that's what I heard you youngsters call it nowadays."

"Dating." Hope felt a little faint. Not that she wasn't happy for her mother, but she'd never considered Caz actually dating before. She'd always seemed happy alone, which now that Hope thought about it, was sad.

"He's a nice man. I met him at the shop the other week. We've run into each other a few times now, actually. He's just moved into a place over by the church."

"Right, okay, sounds… good."

"Not that I need your permission," Caz said with a smile. "But my point still stands. If you wanted to go out at all, if you wanted to *date*, then you should go ahead and do it."

Hope snorted a laugh. "And who exactly would I date then?"

Caz shrugged. "That Ava Stanford seems alright now that she's calmed down about our Rosie."

Hope inhaled so fast she almost choked on her pea pod. "Ava? Are you serious?"

"Why not?" Caz said, dumping another handful of peas in the pan. "She's attractive. Single. She must like children if she's a teacher. You could do worse."

"She's…" Hope struggled with the many reasons that she shouldn't be going anywhere with Ava Stanford. "She's annoying," she said finally, unable to put anything else into words.

"Annoying," echoed her mother, looking faintly amused.

"Annoying," Hope said with a finality that suddenly she didn't quite feel.

She was saved from further questioning by the ringing of her phone. She saw Noah's name on the screen and picked it up immediately. Alice was with him this afternoon and she just prayed that nothing had gone wrong.

"Is she okay?" she barked into the phone.

"What? Who?" asked Noah.

"Your daughter," spat Hope.

Noah laughed. "Alice is fine. We're at the park. She's racing Amelia on her new bike."

"You got her a new bike?" Hope felt anger boiling up in her stomach. "I thought that was going to be a Christmas present."

"It's ages until Christmas," Noah said. "And besides, she won't be able to go out on it in the winter, will she? It's better now so that she can get some use out of it."

Hope bit her lip. Alice was an only child. It was important to her that her daughter didn't grow up spoiled. And it was important that Noah didn't try to buy his daughter's affection with pricey gifts.

"And that's not why I called," Noah went on.

"It's not?" Hope asked, wanting to bring up the bike again but really not wanting to fight over the phone. She'd talk about it with him when he brought Alice home, she promised herself.

"It's not," Noah confirmed.

"What is it then?" Hope got up and left her mother to shell peas in peace. She went into the living room and sat down, propping her feet up on the coffee table.

"It's about what we were talking about the other day in the garden."

Hope felt the anger again, bubbling up inside her. "I said all I had to say."

"I didn't," Noah said firmly. "I meant what I said, Hope. I want to be involved in Alice's life. She's my daughter as well as yours."

"What exactly is it that you want, Noah? An extra weekend a

month? An extra week during the summer holidays?" Hope was tired of this. She didn't want to argue. She didn't want to bargain and negotiate with Noah.

"I want half custody," said Noah, loudly and clearly. "Fifty-fifty."

Hope laughed, unable to help herself. "You're kidding."

"I'm not. I'd prefer to settle this amicably, Hope. I really would. I don't want to involve lawyers and the like. I think you and I can work this out. But I'm serious about wanting Alice with me half the time."

Hope opened her mouth, but no words came out.

"I'll give you a bit of time to think about it," Noah's voice crackled over the phone. "But I'm not letting this one go."

Then he was gone and Hope was left, tears welling up in her eyes, wondering just what she was supposed to do now. Living without Alice half the time was unthinkable. She couldn't imagine Alice not being there every morning when she woke up.

THE CHILDREN WERE sitting cross-legged on the carpet, faces rapt as Ava finished the day's chapter of James and the Giant Peach. Hope sat quietly at the back, watching Ava's face as she read.

Contrary to every expectation that Hope had had, Ava had proven herself to be a more than fitting teacher for the upper infants class.

Sure, she might be trained better for older kids. But now that she'd got her feet, Hope could see that Ava was truly gifted at this. Gifted in a way that only the best teachers were. She had empathy and control, she was firm but fair, she reveled in teaching new skills and information. And it didn't matter how old her students were, they saw her true interest, her passion for what she did, and responded to it.

All of which was to say that whilst Ava certainly had hiccups every now and again, such as when she sent Sara Gonzalez alone to the toilet and didn't check on her before the kid had blocked the sink and flooded the bathroom, she was far from a terrible teacher.

In fact, Hope was starting to think that Alice might actually be lucky to have Ms. Stanford as her class teacher.

The children groaned.

"No, no, there's more tomorrow," Ava said, grinning. "But for now, it's home time. Go on, off you go. Goodbye, class."

"Goodbye, Ms. Stanford," they chorused, before rushing off to get coats and bags.

Hope started picking up chairs and putting them on desks so that the floor could be cleaned as the children filtered out of the classroom.

"Bye, mum," Alice called.

"I'll be home in half an hour, be a good girl for gran."

Only when the class was empty did she finally breathe a sigh of relief that the day was over. She was exhausted, she'd barely slept last night thinking of Noah and Alice.

"Not a bad day," said Ava. "Not a bad day at all."

Hope nodded. "Yeah."

Ava frowned at her. "You alright?"

Hope turned away, attending to the chairs at the next table. "Of course." But even as she spoke, her voice thickened and she could feel the tears starting again. She really thought she'd already cried them out.

"Slightly less than alright then," said Ava, coming around so that she could see Hope's face. "Obviously none of my business, but would you like to tell me what's going on?"

Hope gulped, tried to control herself but couldn't, then gave up. "It's Noah, he wants half custody of Alice," she said, getting the words out in a hurry in case she broke down. She felt a tear run down her cheek.

"Oh," said Ava. She pushed her glasses up on top of her head. "Oh dear."

Hope gave a hiccuping sob and sniffed, blinking furiously to try and stop herself losing control.

"Oh dear," Ava said again, coming a little closer. Close enough that Hope felt warmth emanating from her, close enough that she could see each eyelash, that she could see soft peach down on Ava's cheek. Close enough that suddenly her heart was beating awfully fast and her mouth was drying up.

Ava raised a hand, bringing it up so that it was close to Hope's face but not quite touching, obviously intending to wipe a tear away and Hope held her breath, waiting for the inevitable touch.

But it didn't come.

The moment lasted too long and then Ava was moving her hand away again.

"I'm so sorry," Hope said. "I shouldn't lose it at work like this."

"No apology necessary," Ava said, shuffling back a little. "I can imagine that this must be pretty distressing for you."

Hope nodded. "It is."

Ava started stacking more chairs. "Obviously, you have to be thinking about Alice though."

"Obviously," said Hope, moving around to the other side of the table to get the chairs there.

"Well, would it be so bad for her to spend half her time with her father? She obviously loves him."

Hope stared at Ava through the chair legs and shook her head. Of course Ava didn't understand. How could she? She didn't have kids of her own, she just didn't get it. "This isn't a topic for discussion," said Hope, anger biting into her words.

"Okay," Ava said. She moved off toward her desk and Hope watched her.

Just how was it that every time she was starting to think that Ava Stanford was an actual decent human being the woman managed to make herself annoying enough that all Hope wanted to do was slap her soundly?

However she did it, it was clear that Ava Stanford was strongly in the running for the title of most irritating person in Whitebridge. Perhaps the country.

CHAPTER SIXTEEN

"Close the door please, Adesh, you weren't brought up in a barn."

The boy closed the door and put his bag on his desk just as Clara Buxton ran in, leaving the door gaping wide behind her. Ava sighed and went to the door, closing it herself.

"Anyone want to tell me why we keep the classroom door closed?"

Alice put her hand up straight away and Ava nodded at her.

"Because we're sometimes too noisy and the door helps make us sound quieter."

Ava smiled. "Good. That's one reason. But also because remember that it costs money to heat classrooms and when the weather is getting colder we need to keep our doors closed so that we're not heating the outside."

"But what about the birds, miss?" asked Carter.

"They have feathers," said Ava, not missing a beat.

"And what about the animals, like foxes and dogs and cats?" asked Daniel.

"They have fur," Ava said, again, not getting wrong-footed.

Could it be that finally she was getting the hang of this? She wondered sometimes if the children in her care shouldn't be lawyers they were so good at finding loopholes and applying logic. They kept her on her toes, and she was starting to find that she actually liked it. Better the unarguable logic of a six year old than the puffing sulkiness of a fifteen year old.

"We keep the classroom doors closed," she said with finality. "Now, let's talk about our spelling test, shall we?"

Ava managed through pure force of will not to look at Hope for most of the morning. She needed to distance herself, she'd decided. Because like it or not she did think that Hope was attractive, as well as vastly annoying. So keeping out of her way as much as possible seemed like the wisest of plans.

Whatever Quinn might think, there was no way that Ava was ready to be involved with anyone again. Especially not someone like Hope. Someone irritating.

Though there were points in her favor, of course. Like the way she looked wearing yoga pants. Or the fact that any kind of relationship would necessarily come with a time limit, since at some point, Ava would have to leave.

Then came the thoughts of the future, black and empty and terrifying and Ava had to bring herself back to the present. Just in time to see Daniel wiggling in his seat.

"Daniel, toilet please, now."

"Oh, but miss…"

"No buts, off you go, please."

He skipped off and Ava got down to testing the list of spelling words the children had taken home the night before.

KEEPING HER DISTANCE was a lot easier when Hope wasn't actually in the room. For that matter, it was a hell of a lot easier when they weren't both trying to put materials away in the same storage cupboard.

Even with the door wide open, Ava could smell Hope's scent, flowery and feminine, and found herself brushing up against Hope's arm as she put crayons away on the top shelf.

"I can do this," she said. "You go off to the staff room for a coffee."

"I'm the assistant, this is part of my job," Hope said, not turning around.

"Miss, miss, can I stay inside and read my reading book?" came a voice from outside.

Ava poked her head around the door and saw Nathan Jackson. "Absolutely not. It's good for you to run around in the fresh air. Off you go." The boy was never still, he needed to work off some energy before he had to sit down again.

She went back into the cupboard, reaching up to get some paper and heard Nathan's footsteps.

"You should let him read if he wants to," Hope said.

"You should try not disagreeing with me for once," Ava said, without really thinking.

"You think I deliberately disagree with you?"

Ava took a breath. "That was uncalled for. I'm sorry."

"But you think I deliberately disagree with you?"

"Sometimes," Ava said carefully.

There was an awkward silence that lasted a second too long and then there was a bang and sudden darkness as the cupboard door was slammed shut.

"What the hell...?"

Footsteps hurried away and there was another bang as the classroom door banged shut.

Ava turned from the shelf just as Hope did and suddenly they were standing face to face in the darkness, close enough that their bodies were touching, close enough that Ava could feel Hope taking a breath.

"What?" she asked, voice huskier than she'd intended.

"Nothing," said Hope.

"No, go ahead," Ava said, striving for politeness and achieving coldness instead, though the last thing she felt with Hope's breasts pressed against her chest was cold.

"Well, I don't want to disagree with you," said Hope.

"But..."

"But, well, perhaps you should have been clearer when you told the children to close the classroom doors."

"Ah." It was getting hard to find words. Maybe there wasn't enough oxygen in here. Ava's heart rate started to climb.

Definitely there wasn't enough oxygen in here.

"Just a thought," Hope said, her voice was getting deeper. She moved, her hand coming up to tuck a lock of hair behind her ear and her elbow brushing against Ava, forcing Ava to close her eyes at the contact.

"A thought," she echoed, her own voice getting deeper. "You seem to have a lot of those."

"Like you don't."

There was a vent at the top of the far wall and light was coming through from the corridor, just enough that Ava could see Hope tilting her head, enough that she could see the curve of Hope's lips. An air vent. So there was enough oxygen. Huh. And yet her heart was still tripping in her chest.

"I have ideas," Ava drawled, the words coming out sexier than she'd intended.

"Do you?" asked Hope, moving a tad closer, just close enough that the light caught on those lips again.

Ava could feel her own breath catching in her throat, could hear her brain yelling at her to stop, could hear other parts of her anatomy urging her on, pushing her forward. "Well, we are stuck in a cupboard until recess is over," she breathed.

"And whose fault is that?"

Ava let out a breath. "See? See what I mean about disagreeing? Every time I do something, say something, you have to go in the opposite direction. You have to blame me or argue with me. Do you know how absolutely infuriating that is?"

Hope snorted. "Like you're the only one. Every time I finally start to think that you might actually be a decent person, you ruin everything by opening your mouth."

"By opening my mouth?"

"You heard me," Hope said, pressing herself against the shelves. "And now we're stuck in here because you can't give children simple instructions."

"Oh, not for long," said Ava. "Don't think that I want to be in here with you." She raised her voice. "Help!"

"Help," Hope shouted, a little louder as though this was a

competition.

"Help!"

There was a rustling outside of the door, then the handle clicked open and Amy Littleton was standing there looking somewhat surprised.

"Nathan Jackson locked us in," Ava said by way of explanation.

"Don't ask," said Hope, marching out of the cupboard and then out of the classroom.

Ava watched her go. Honestly. The woman would strain the patience of a saint.

ALICE WAS SITTING at a desk, tongue sticking out of one corner of her mouth coloring in a picture. Ava thought how much she looked like her mother sometimes.

School was finished and Hope was taking care of some photocopying, leaving Alice sitting at her desk and waiting to be walked home.

"Is it weird?" Ava asked her.

Alice looked up from her coloring. "Is what weird?"

"Having your mom work at the school?"

Alice grinned. "I like having mum work here, it's nice."

Ava nodded and wondered how to get across what was really on her mind. "I can see how it's nice," she said carefully. "But I just meant, well, you see your mum all the time at home and then you see her all the time at school as well."

Alice sniffed and nodded, going back to her coloring. "That's good though," she said.

"Is it?" asked Ava. She could see how protective Hope was of Alice and had wondered how Alice felt about things. Apparently, she liked it. Or she didn't know different.

"It's good because then mum's not all by herself."

"What do you mean?" Ava asked curiously. She really shouldn't be grilling a child for information on her mother, but she couldn't help herself.

"Well, my gran does her volunteering so she's not at home and now my dad doesn't live with us anymore, so if my mum didn't come to school then she'd be on her own. Except for Rosie. But mostly Rosie likes to be outside." Alice looked up. "You can't be cross at Rosie for going to the toilet in your garden, you know, it's only natural."

Ava decided not to touch that subject, so she just nodded. She hadn't gotten the answers she'd expected. It seemed like perhaps Alice was just as protective of Hope as Hope was of her daughter. "That's a nice picture," she said to deflect the situation.

"It's a cat like Rosie except this cat is a doctor because that's what she wants to be and you said we could be anything we wanted to be if we worked hard."

"Huh," said Ava, looking at the scrawls on the paper and trying to discern which exactly was the cat. "Is she a doctor for people or for other cats?"

Alice looked up at her and Ava felt the weighty stare, as though Alice thought she was quite unbearably stupid. "Other cats, of course."

"Of course," agreed Ava.

"How could she reach all the way up to see people patients?" Alice asked. "She's only a cat."

"Right." Ava grinned as Alice went back to her picture.

Apparently she still had a lot to learn about children's imaginations. But then, with Alice to teach her, she didn't imagine it would take that long to learn.

"Do you like my mum?" Alice said, still coloring.

"What?" The word came out as a screech.

"My dad's got a new girlfriend, her name's Amelia and she's really nice," Alice said. "So I think it's about time that mum found somebody, don't you?"

Ava swallowed. "I, uh, don't really think that's any of our business."

"That's what grown ups say when they don't want to talk about things," said Alice airily. "I was just thinking that if you wanted you could find my mum a boyfriend or a girlfriend. It would be helpful and mum's helpful at school to you, so…"

"Ah."

Alice looked up again. "I think she doesn't have time to find a friend because she's looking after me all the time even though sometimes I stay with Gran or with my dad. But it'd be nice, wouldn't it? Cos having friends is nice."

Ava nodded weakly, aware that she was now very much out of her depth with this conversation. Alice bent her head over her paper again and Ava busied herself with some lesson planning. By the time Hope came back they were both silently working.

CHAPTER SEVENTEEN

Hope sat silently, legs crossed as best as she was able given the fact that she was sitting on a chair designed for a six year old. At least Fay and Allen Buxton weren't any more comfortable. Allen looked as though he was folded in half.

But both were sitting and listening eagerly to Ava tell them about Clara's progress and art with the look that parents always had on parents' evening, one of puzzled bemusement and pride that they'd created something with a life of its own.

Hope, however, had more important things to worry about than Clara's ability to paint fine detail (above average) or maths skills (dubious at best).

Because try as she might, she couldn't forget the fact that she was pretty sure that she and Ava Stanford had almost kissed in the stationery cupboard yesterday at morning break.

Pretty sure because even though it hadn't actually happened, she'd seen Ava's head tilt in a way that nearly always came before a kiss and because, perhaps, now that she was thinking about it, she sort of, might have, maybe, wanted it to happen.

Who was she to deny biology? That heart-pumping, knickers-twisting, belly-warming feeling could only be one thing, and she was a grown woman, she knew exactly what it was.

Then, obviously, Ava spoiled it all by, well, by being Ava.

Couple that with the fact that despite trying extremely hard to stay awake she'd fallen asleep by midnight last night, by which point her mother had still not come home.

Okay, so Caz was firmly in her bed this morning, but still.

Apparently the date had gone well.

She was trying hard not to be uncomfortable about the fact that her mother was dating for what felt like the first time. Caz deserved happiness, just like anyone else. Hope couldn't help but feel a little edgy about it though, mostly because try as she might she couldn't shake the feeling that Caz had put her entire love life on hold for her, Hope.

So she was responsible for her mother's abstinence.

Presumed abstinence.

It wasn't a nice feeling at all. She wanted her mother to be happy and as much as she'd enjoyed growing up with Caz's undivided attention she didn't think that she'd have minded a step-father. Or even an occasional male visitor.

Caz had taken that decision out of her hands, however, by turning herself into a nun for so many years, leaving Hope feeling now like she was somehow responsible.

A feeling that she didn't want Alice to have.

Which led her all the way back to the stationery cupboard and yesterday morning.

There was something there, Hope knew that. Some kind of magnetic something, that thing that drew together people who really shouldn't be together, that thing that drew a fine line between wanting to slap someone silly and wanting to screw their brains out.

Ava Stanford undoubtedly walked that line.

The only problem was, Hope didn't know which side of the line she was currently falling on, given that she changed her mind every millisecond and jumped back and forth over the line like it was some kind of demented skipping rope.

"Clara has fine reading skills," Ava was saying. "She's at least a grade above the class average, so there's something to be proud of."

"Oh, we've read to her since she was a wee one," Allen Buxton said proudly.

"Even before that," said Fay. "When she was in my belly we read her books."

"You... you read to a fetus?" Ava asked, disbelievingly.

Fay Buxton blushed. "The books said we should."

"I'm not sure I'd credit that with your daughter's current reading skills," said Ava. "However, she is certainly a good reader. Which is more than I can say for her math skills."

The problem with Ava, Hope had finally figured out, was that she was a closed book. Alright, she was also occasionally rude, far too forthright, and lacked diplomacy. But mostly it was the book thing.

It was like she was protecting herself, building a shell around herself so that nobody could see the squishiness inside.

Which was a shame because Hope rather liked squishy people. Or at least people that could hold down a conversation for more than two minutes without turning it into an argument. People who could show emotions other than irritation.

So if she truly was thinking about starting something, and she might not be, then she'd first have to wriggle underneath that shell and pry pieces off. A job she wasn't sure she wanted. Or that Ava wanted her to do really.

Hell, what did Ava want? There was a question.

For a few seconds in that cupboard Hope could have sworn that Ava wanted her. Now though, all Ava looked like she wanted was a glass of wine and a lie down. Which perhaps wasn't unusual given that Fay and Allen Buxton were the last in a long line of parents.

"All in all, Clara has made satisfactory progress," Ava was saying.

"What about the nativity play?" asked Fay.

Hope rolled her eyes and then saw Ava looking at her in confusion. "It's far too early to be casting that now, Fay," she said equably.

"It's something to keep in mind though, isn't it?" asked Fay anxiously. "Because Clara was so good as Mary last year in lower infants and, well, she has her heart set on doing it again. Just something to think about."

"I'm not at all sure we're having a... a nativity play," Ava stepped in.

"Oh, but you have to," said Allen. "It's part of our cultural heritage, you can't not have a nativity play."

"We have at least two non-Christian children in the class," Ava said. "Perhaps more, I don't investigate that sort of thing. I'm not sure a nativity is appropriate."

Allen sighed and rubbed his nose. "I suppose," he said.

"It's something for us all to think about," Hope said brightly. She stood up which prompted everyone else to stand up.

"Yes, well, thank you Ms. Stanford," Allen held out his hand and Ava took it.

"We're certainly glad that Clara has such an... unusual teacher," added Fay.

They waited until the parents were out of the room before Ava collapsed into her chair. "What do you think that meant? Unusual teacher?" she said.

"Probably exactly that," said Hope easily. "Not the norm. You know, you being American and everything."

"Is this nativity thing required?" asked Ava.

"No idea. We can run it past Lowell. It's tradition, but there's nothing wrong with subverting tradition if that's what you're into."

Ava grunted and stretched out her legs, lifting her arms and yawning and looking far more human than Hope had ever seen her look before. Her shirt lifted, baring a sliver of pale skin that caught Hope's eye and made her stomach contract.

She tore her eyes away. Maybe Ava did want something. Maybe Ava wanted the same something as she did.

Outside it was dark, the classroom lights streaming through the windows, and in the corridors was the soft hum of parents chatting to each other. The school was a different place at night.

A quieter, more relaxed place.

"So, um, that's us done," Hope said casually. Maybe now was the time for that drink. She could ask, couldn't she? If she decided to.

"Not quite."

Hope frowned. "No, I'm sure the Buxtons were the last."

"Not quite," Ava said again. She sat up straighter, crossing her legs again. "There's you."

"Me?" Hope laughed. "But I'm here all day, I know how Alice is doing, you don't need an appointment with me."

"Don't I?" asked Ava. She tapped her pen on her desk. "Alice is certainly a bright child. She's meeting every milestone and exceeding the averages in every classroom skill that we have. You should be proud of her."

"I am," Hope said, sitting down in her own small chair again.

"Yet being a fully developed child is so much more than just succeeding intellectually, isn't it?"

"What exactly is that supposed to mean?"

Ava sighed. "I've been debating whether or not to bring this up, but as Alice's class teacher I really feel like I have to."

"Bringing what up?" Hope could feel prickles rising on the back of her neck, could feel anger building in her stomach.

"You are... very protective of Alice."

"She's my daughter."

"I know that, and a certain amount of protection is necessary. But perhaps you're going a little too far."

Hope took a breath, trying to calm herself. "Meaning?"

Ava looked at her steadily. "I see the way you talk about her father, and how you feel about her father taking more responsibility with Alice. Something that could be good for a young child, but something you feel Alice shouldn't have. I sense that perhaps you have trouble... sharing Alice, in a way that might not necessarily benefit her."

"Sharing Alice? Sharing my daughter? She's a person, not a pizza," said Hope.

"A bad choice of words," said Ava. She held up both hands. "I've offended you and that wasn't my intention. I'm sorry."

"Sorry?" Hope was angry but knew that letting that anger out would be a mistake. "It's none of your business."

Ava inclined her head. "Right."

"So, is that it? We're done here?"

"Unless there's anything else you'd like to know about Alice's progress, which, again, is excellent."

"No, I think I know my daughter better than you do."

"Obviously."

Hope crossed her arms and Ava stood up. "Well then, I suppose we can leave."

"Fine." Hope went to get her jacket from the cupboard.

She waited as Ava collected her bag and then locked the classroom door and then they both went out into the playground.

Ava paused at the school gate.

"Arguing is a lot easier when you get to storm off," she said. "In this case, we're neighbors. Would you like me to wait for a few minutes and let you get ahead of me?"

Hope stared at her for a long moment and then started to laugh. She couldn't help it. The idea of Ava following her home like a lost dog was funny. "No," she said. "No, not necessary."

Ava smiled. "Good. I didn't want to walk home alone."

They began to walk side by side down the lane. Hope swallowed. "I do get a little over-protective at times," she admitted, not liking the way the words sounded but knowing they were true.

"You're a mother, you have every right to be," said Ava.

"Maybe." She thought about Caz dating again, thought about the way it made her feel to know that her mother had missed out on things because of her. "But maybe I could try to be a little better about that."

"It's none of my business," Ava said.

"Right," said Hope.

And they walked the rest of the way home in silence.

CHAPTER EIGHTEEN

All day, Ava watched Hope with the children. She was good with them, kind and patient, good in a way that Ava wasn't sure she could mimic.

Not to say that she was doing badly, she really wasn't. In fact, she'd surprised herself. Now that she'd taken on the challenge of teaching younger children she was enjoying it and learning more than she'd thought possible.

But Hope seemed so natural with them and Ava didn't think she could ever be that way.

She shouldn't have mentioned her feelings about Alice, she recognized that now. Or perhaps she should have been more careful, more diplomatic with her words. Clearly, Hope didn't want to hear the truth.

Which made Ava wonder if Hope wanted to hear the truth about other things.

Like about how Ava was relatively sure she'd come within about an eighth of an inch of kissing the woman.

So much for keeping her distance. Still though, she'd done well since then. She'd stayed out of physical touch and was slowly coming to the conclusion that this was probably part of her healing. Finding women attractive was natural, after all.

Hope was bent over, her backside in the air, zipping up Nathan Jackson's jacket against the cool autumn chill of the afternoon. Ava tried not to stare and ended up almost tripping over Daniel

Monroe who was looking solemn.

"What's the problem, Daniel?" she asked.

"I was thinking, miss," he said, face screwed up in concentration.

Ava thought she'd better tread carefully. "Ah, yes? About what?"

"You know, I don't think I've had an accident for two weeks," he said solemnly. Then he leaned in a little. "I think that's cos of you, you know."

"Me?" asked Ava, surprised. "I'm no magician, Daniel."

He scoffed. "I know that. It's just that, well, you get so upset when I have an accident and then it makes you cross so I think that maybe the wee just gets scared and runs back inside."

Ava opened her mouth before she realized that actually, she didn't know how to respond to that. In the end, she just said: "I see."

"Thanks, miss," Daniel said, jogging off toward the door. "It helps a lot now that I don't have accidents."

Ava bit back a smile as he went. Good to see that she was having some positive effect, unintended though it might be.

"Ready for this?" Hope said, appearing at her elbow.

Ava jumped. Hope was close enough to touch, closer than Ava had told herself she'd allow. Because she wasn't looking for anything, she'd decided. She took two steps toward her desk. "Ready for...?"

"Staff meeting," Hope filled in. "Remember?"

"Right," said Ava, who had completely forgotten. "Well then, we'd best be getting on with it. Let's go."

By the time they got to the staff room everyone else was already seated. Ava perched on a wooden chair, and Hope sat on the arm of Amy Littleton's armchair. Ava looked around. Five teachers, plus Lowell whenever he arrived. Hardly a huge educational establishment. Yet as far as she'd seen, every teacher was caring, patient, and kind, truly dedicated to what they did.

It was nice, she thought, to be part of such a small community. It was nice, she suddenly realized, to be part of something. To belong to something. She smiled to herself. This was what she was looking for, to belong.

"I'm here, I'm here," Lowell said, coming through the door. "And I won't keep you long. Is there anything anyone wants to bring up first?"

"We need more soap for the kids' toilets," Amy Littleton said.

"It's on order," Lowell replied. "Anything else?"

Everyone looked at each other and shrugged. There was nothing. They'd had a regular staff meeting just two days ago, it was Jake Lowell that had called this after school meeting.

"Right then," Lowell said. He stood tall, raking his fingers through his thinning hair. "I've uh, I've got some news. Not good news, I'm afraid."

"Uh, don't say OFSTEAD's coming again," said Frank Meyer who taught the upper juniors, the oldest children in the school. "We've done our bit and we did well from how I understand it."

"You did," agreed Lowell. "We all did. And no, this isn't to do with inspections. In fact, I think it's important to stress the fact that we did very well in our inspections and what I'm about to tell you has no relevance at all to teaching standards at the school."

Ava frowned. Something was coming, she could feel it. Something bad. She could tell from the way Lowell was standing, from the way he was struggling to put into words what he had to say. She started to feel a little sick.

"The thing is," started the headmaster. "Well, there's no easy way to put this really. The thing is that we've been put on the closure list."

"What?" It was Hope that reacted first. "The closure list? What on earth for? You can't be serious."

Ava looked at her, sensing this was very serious and not quite understanding. Surely the closure list didn't mean what she thought it meant?

Jake skimmed his hand through his hair again. "I'm afraid I am serious," he said. "And again, this has nothing to do with teaching standards or competence. The truth of the matter is that Whitebridge Primary is a small school and our numbers are dropping. It's beginning to be unfeasible economically to keep the school open."

"But—" began Hope.

Lowell held up his hand. "Nothing is decided yet. The way I understand it is that three of us small schools from the local area are on the list and at least one of us will be closed with the kids being diverted to one of the others. We'll know more in a few weeks, but the council won't be sitting on this one for long."

Ava felt a sharp pain go through her chest. She blinked hard, not letting herself lose control. And when, a few minutes later, Jake Lowell sent them all home, she hurried back to her classroom.

✽ ✽ ✽

Hope couldn't quite believe what she'd been told. There was no way that the school was being closed, not on her watch. There had to be something they could do and she was willing to sit with Jake for as long as it took to discuss options.

But Jake waved her away. "I know, Hope, and we're going to do everything we can. But there's a council meeting tonight and I need to get there, so I don't have time for a chat right now."

Slightly mollified, but still reeling, she looked around to see Ava hurrying off down the corridor. Slowly, she followed, thinking that perhaps the woman had forgotten something and that they could walk home together.

When she reached the classroom though, Ava was standing with both hands on her desk, her head bent.

"Ava?" Hope heard a slight sniffle but she could have been wrong.

"I have a few things to do here," Ava said, voice tight.

Hope stepped further into the room, closing the door behind her. Ava turned at the sound and for a second, Hope saw a glimmer of tears in her eyes. "Ava? Are you alright?"

"Fine."

"Yet you're not," said Hope, coming closer. "Is it about the closure?"

Ava sighed. "I just... I was just thinking that I was starting to belong here."

"You are," Hope said. "But even if you weren't, the closure shouldn't affect you too much. At most you'll have to go home a term early."

"Home."

The way she said it made Hope think it was a dirty word to Ava. "Surely it wouldn't be such a big deal to go home a little early," she said, trying to comfort Ava even though she didn't truly understand what was wrong.

"Home?" Ava said again. She shook her head. "There's nothing there, Hope. Nothing. You don't understand. My life imploded the second my wife left me. I have no house, no family, and next to no job, unless I feel like working with my ex and her new boyfriend every day."

"There have to be other schools," Hope began.

"Sure," said Ava miserably. "But it all means starting all over again. It all means finding a place where I fit in, where I can belong. I came here to change, to try and, I don't know, get over things, find a new me. And just when I thought that perhaps it was all starting to work, perhaps I was beginning to heal, it all gets snatched away again."

Hope put a hand on Ava's arm, half-expecting her to move away, but she didn't. "We're not closed yet," she said. Seeing Ava like this, so human, so near to tears, was somehow both touching and scary.

"But we might be soon."

It was the 'we' that did it. The sign that Ava truly was a part of the school, that she truly did care, that this wasn't just a temporary thing, that she wasn't just a high school teacher that had been flung into Whitebridge by mistake. She was more than that. She was a part of things now.

And she wanted to be a part of things.

Ava turned to Hope and her eyes were glistening again and Hope took a big breath and did the only thing she could.

She kissed her.

CHAPTER NINETEEN

It was only a kiss.

How many kisses had she had in her lifetime? Thousands at least. And this was just one of them. Barely significant in the grand scale of things. Weigh this one kiss up against the thousands of others, or against the millions of other minutes in her life and it barely made a dent.

So why did it feel like something was happening? Why did it feel like angels were supposed to be singing or the earth should be moving or something else equally trite and unrealistic?

Why were her eyes closing? Why was she suddenly finding that she was falling into Hope, that she was tasting her, feeling the softness of her, feeling the press of her hipbones, feeling the heart-bursting sensation of Hope's hands cupping her face?

For an instant, Ava responded. For an instant she had no control, she let her body take over, and her body was very, very definite about one thing: it wanted to be kissed by Hope Perkins.

Ava's hands were already moving to Hope's back, already ready to pull the woman closer, when her brain stepped into the equation and cleared its throat.

Ava practically jumped back.

Hope froze.

"I, uh, we, uh, you should really be leaving," Ava managed. "I'm sure Alice is wondering where you are."

"Alice knows where I am," said Hope.

She was standing her ground and Ava admired that. No running away from embarrassing moments for Hope. She was standing there tall and proud with no shame about what she'd just done. Which rather made Ava want it to happen again.

Until her brain once again cleared its throat, a little louder this time, like a librarian at an increasingly rowdy patron.

"Yes, well, she might be worried anyway," Ava said weakly.

Hope rolled her eyes. "Noah's picking her up for the weekend."

"So I'm an excuse to avoid your ex, am I?" asked Ava more sharply and much against her better judgment.

Hope was still calm, which given that momentous occurrence of just moments ago, was something of a miracle and Ava envied her her poise. "Not in the slightest."

Ava sniffed. "I see."

Hope's mouth twitched a little at the corner. "Feeling better now, are you?"

"Better?" asked Ava because just at the moment she was feeling both far better and far worse than she could remember feeling in recent memory. Her legs were still shaking, for one. But then there was the memory of Hope's delicate fingers touching her face.

"You were upset," said Hope. "About the school closure?"

"Ah, yes, right." Ava swallowed and made an attempt at pulling herself together. "But, as you said, we're not closed yet, are we?"

"An admirable change in attitude," said Hope. She stepped closer. Close enough that Ava could only imagine another kiss being the result. "Glad to see that I could help you."

"Help me?" Ava's voice was somewhat strangled and she wasn't sure whether it came from panic at the thought of being kissed again or because she really wanted to be kissed again and was saving up precious oxygen in the event that Hope came closer still.

Hope smiled and shook her head. "You're quite something, Ava Stanford."

"I am?" Still strangled. She really needed to work on that.

She couldn't go through romantic encounters sounding like a squawking chicken.

Her legs wobbled even more. Romantic encounters.

"You are," agreed Hope. "And I'm not going to say I'm sorry for what just happened, because that would be lying. I'm not sorry in the slightest, not one jot."

"You're not?"

Hope shook her head. "But if you'd rather ignore the fact that it happened, I suppose I can live with that."

"Ignore it?" said Ava. "That's your suggestion." She stepped away and her voice went back to normal. "Just pretend nothing happened? Seriously, you are absolutely the most irritating—"

She was cut off by Hope's hand on her arm.

"You don't need to do this," Hope said quietly, dark eyes calm and kind. "We don't need to make everything an argument. You know what I meant. I simply meant that I'm not going to push anything. I understand that you might not be in a place where kissing seems important or necessary to your life. No hard feelings, no regrets. No follow ups necessary. That's all."

Ava opened her mouth but no words came out so she shut it again. She simply nodded.

"Alrighty then," said Hope. "I'll leave you to your evening."

She picked up her purse from the closet and walked out of the classroom without looking back, leaving Ava to watch her go with a sharp feeling in her chest and an overly-warm sensation in her stomach. And possibly in other areas of her body.

IF SHE TRIED very hard, she could ignore the fact that anything had happened. It was actually easy at the beginning. She just paid more attention to the leaves changing color, or to the bite of chill at her nose.

But then she'd forget that she was supposed to be paying attention to those things and remember instead the press of Hope's lips against hers.

Which was ridiculous.

This couldn't happen.

She was too tired even to think of all the reasons that nothing could happen.

Yet her mind circled back again and again to the kiss and again and again she felt warm inside, she felt her body responding to it.

Which was exactly why she needed a distraction, she told herself, as she marched through the door of the bookstore.

"Back again?" Mila chirped, popping up from behind the counter.

"Behind the counter again?" responded Ava because honestly, what was the woman doing down there?

"You're out of luck this time," said Mila. "Ag's here. So if you're allergic to babies then you'd best skedaddle." She reached down and pulled up the wriggling infant.

"Is that really the best way to treat customers?" Ava asked. "I mean, telling them to skedaddle doesn't seem like a great way to make money."

"You're the one that treated my daughter like she was a uranium bomb."

"I did not."

"You did too," Mila said.

"I was... having a bad day."

Mila snorted.

"No," said Ava, suddenly determined that she was going to put this right. She was good with children. Okay, she was getting better with children. "I was. Hand her over. Come on."

Mila looked at her doubtfully, but Ag was gurgling and holding out her arms already, so finally she passed her daughter over and Ava took her in her arms.

"Hold her head a bit better," Mila said. "And put an arm under her bum, yes, like that."

Mila's arms were full and suddenly she was looking into deep blue eyes that regarded her with infinite curiosity. "See?" she said, voice lowering. "I can do this."

"Huh," said Mila. "I suppose you can. Which is a miracle

all things considered. Mind you, I've heard that the kids are well into you. They think the sun shines out of your... nether regions."

"Do they?" Ava asked, somewhat surprised. She really hadn't considered whether or not her students liked her, but now she was considering it, she found it gratifying that they did.

"They do," said Mila, stretching out her arms to take Ag back. "She's got a book and a teething ring down here. Hold her too long and she's likely to drown you in drool."

Ava hurriedly handed the child back. She might have changed but she hadn't changed that much. "I'm looking for a distraction."

"Well, our new releases are over there." Mila pointed to the table.

Ava started to look at them. "It must be odd," she said as she looked. "To have someone that dependent on you, I mean."

Mila laughed. "You're telling me. If you'd have asked me five years ago I'd never have thought that I'd have the life that I have now."

Ava looked over at her. "Any regrets?"

"You kidding?" Ava swept back her blue hair. "I've got a fine policeman for a husband and a beautiful daughter." She put her head to one side. "I suppose we don't always know best what we want, do we?"

"So how did you know?"

Mila shrugged. "I don't know. It all just seemed to come together. I think you have to be open to things, open to the idea of things. Open to the possibility that anything can happen."

Ava snorted at this. "You're telling me. My wife left me for another man, trust me, I'm open to the possibilities of anything happening."

"Not exactly what I meant," said Mila.

"Then what did you mean?" Ava was curious now.

"Just... Life is hard," Mila said. "It makes us hard, you know? Like we spend so much time getting hurt that we forget how to be vulnerable. We build up this protective wall and then, inexplicably, we expect other people to scale that wall in order to find us. Which is stupid really."

"Are you suggesting I... rent out climbing equipment?"

Mila laughed. "No, but that you remember how to be vulnerable. I think that's how we change, that's how we find out what we want. Protecting yourself from hurt is all very well, but sometimes it's the getting hurt that changes us, that makes us realize we need something. Or don't need it."

"Aren't you the little psychologist?"

"You asked," Mila said. "But in the end, there's always a million reasons not to do something, but you only need one to do it. Have you ever noticed that?"

Ava was about to say that she hadn't, but then the words sank in and she realized that Mila was right. She grunted in response instead and picked up the first book she'd seen that looked faintly interesting. "I'll take this."

Mila started to ring her up and Ava handed over her money and escaped out onto the street.

Something had changed. She'd changed. Which was the whole point of being over here, wasn't it? She'd changed and as much as she'd said she wasn't ready for anything to happen, maybe she was. Maybe she needed to put herself out there again.

Something had changed and that kiss had meant something. Of course it had. If it hadn't, if it had been unwelcome, she'd have pushed Hope away. But she hadn't done that. Because she'd wanted it.

Because as ornery and irritating and annoying as Hope could be, she was also gentle and loving and kind. Because as much as Ava might say she didn't want to date, she missed being with someone. Because change had to happen.

And perhaps the first step should be recognizing that something had indeed happened. Something scary and terrifying but not altogether terrible.

She needed to talk to Hope.

CHAPTER TWENTY

The knock came just as Hope was about to sit down with a cup of tea and an episode of something soapy that she'd never watch in front of her daughter. For once, she had the house to herself, so she wasn't exactly pleased at the knock on the door.

She changed her mind when she opened the door and saw Ava standing there.

"Hmm. I think this is the first time I've seen you on my doorstep without a bag of animal dung in your hand."

Ava, who had been looking pained and pale, actually cracked a smile at this. "No cat poop."

"Promise? Because I'm not sure I want to let you in if that's going to be involved." She paused. "That is, presuming you want to come in?"

The kiss had been a spur of the moment thing. For once, Ava had looked human, had acted human, had been a part of town life, part of Hope's life. And she'd been upset and, well, attractive.

Hope didn't regret what she'd done. After all, you couldn't hope to get without asking. For a moment there, she'd even thought that Ava was going to break out of her shell and actually let something happen.

Then Ava had stepped away and, clearly, the event had all been too much for her. Whether or not she was interested wasn't exactly the question. The kiss had been brief, the touch of their lips so short that Hope almost couldn't remember the sensation. But it had been long enough for Hope to feel Ava kiss her back.

The more important question was whether or not Ava could handle this. Hope knew a fragile soul when she saw one, and Ava was as fragile as fine china.

Not that Hope was as robust as all that. One wrong look and there was always the chance that she'd crumble into dust and live as a spinster the rest of her life. She wondered how Rosie would get along with more cats. Maybe once Alice left home she could fill the house with them.

She snapped back to attention. Ava was still standing on her doorstep.

"So, do you?" she asked. "Want to come in, that is."

Ava took a breath, then nodded. "I do."

Hope stood back and let Ava come in before she closed the door. "Coffee? Tea?"

"Um, I'd rather just... get on with things."

Hope felt a giggle coming on and bit her tongue firmly to stop it. She was pretty sure that Ava wasn't propositioning her for sex, but if she were, Hope wouldn't put it past her to do so in exactly those terms. "The living room?"

Ava nodded and went into the living room, perching uneasily on the edge of the couch. Hope sighed. Clearly she was going to need to take things in hand here. At least a little.

"Alright, we're both adults here," she began.

To her surprise, Ava held up her hand to stop her speaking. "Actually, if you don't mind, I'd rather..."

Hope nodded. "Go ahead."

Ava sat up straighter. "I'm broken," she said, and held up her hand again when Hope tried to interrupt. "No, let me, please. I'm broken. Losing my wife was the worst thing that has ever happened to me. It broke me in ways that will never be fixed. I understand that. I also understand that I came here to change, to try to move on, and, well, I'm trying to do that."

She paused and took a breath. Hope wondered if she was supposed to say something yet. But Ava wasn't finished.

"You kissed me." Ava's eyes flashed green. "And I'm not going to pretend that I didn't enjoy it. I'm not going to pretend that I don't find you attractive. I do."

Hope bit her lip. So this was Ava opening her shell. It was... strangely disconcerting and confusing. Much as she wanted Ava to be honest with her, she really wasn't entirely sure what was happening.

"I find you attractive but I'm broken."

Hope could hold her tongue no longer. "So what?" she said. "You don't want me to touch you again? I can understand that, though I think it's a shame."

Ava blinked, swallowed. "Not exactly," she said slowly.

"So what exactly?" Hope asked, remembering now how irritating Ava could be.

Ava let out a breath. "A lot of people wouldn't be interested in a broken woman."

"I'm not a lot of people," said Hope. "And you're forgetting, I'm not exactly un-broken myself."

"I'm not forgetting," said Ava.

Hope sighed. "We're adults, Ava. Adults come with baggage. But in the end, we have to take risks, it's the only way we change. You took a risk coming here. I took a risk kissing you."

"Why?"

Hope spluttered with surprise laughter. "Are you asking why I kissed you?"

"Yes," Ava said earnestly.

"Because you're attractive and infuriating. Because I wanted to. Because... hormones, I suppose."

"Right. It was... it was a nice kiss."

"It was," agreed Hope.

Ava pushed her glasses up onto her head and Hope almost fainted. "It's not that I don't want you to touch me again," she said. "It's that I want us both to know what's going on, and just at the moment I feel like we're groping around in the dark."

"Sounds fun," Hope couldn't help but say.

"I'm not the only one that can be infuriating." Ava crossed her legs. "Someone today told me that I needed to remember how to be vulnerable."

"Sounds like someone smart," Hope said, getting the sense that maybe this conversation wasn't going badly.

"She's got blue hair," said Ava, as though blue hair meant someone couldn't be smart.

"That would be Mila." Whitebridge was a small town. "And she is smart. You do need to be vulnerable. We all do. That's the only way we let other people in. You can build a big old garden wall or you can open up your front door. Guess which one gets you the most visitors? Assuming you want visitors, that is."

"I'm being open," Ava said. "I'm being honest with you. I like you. God knows why. But I do. I'm interested. There. I said it. I'm interested but I'm not at all sure where this is going or whether I can handle it."

"Fair," Hope said, picking up her mug from the table. "How about... no pressure?"

"No pressure."

"Look, I'm not asking you to marry me," Hope said. She put her cup down again and moved forward on her chair until she was closer to Ava. "But I do like you. And you like me. So maybe we could... see where things go?"

"See where things go."

"Are you going to repeat everything that I say?" Hope asked. But Ava had been open with her, so it was only fair that she was open back. "I'm not sure either," she said. "To tell you the truth, Noah is the only person I've ever... been with."

Ava's eyebrows about shot off her forehead. "Say what now?"

Hope shrugged. "I've had other boyfriends and girlfriends. But in terms of, um, being intimate, Noah was the only one. So starting everything all over again is just as confusing and frightening for me as for you. You're not the only one that needs to take things slowly."

Hesitantly, Ava reached out a hand and put it on Hope's knee. Hope felt her insides melt into jelly. She really hoped she could take things slowly. But Ava's touch was enough to make slow the last thing on her mind.

"Slowly," Ava said, her voice low and deep.

Hope nodded. "Slowly."

Ava's hand moved up her leg slightly and Hope felt a tickle of desire run over her skin. "This slowly?"

"Maybe a little faster," said Hope, eyes half-closing as Ava's fingers moved up her thigh.

"You can be demanding."

"So can you," Hope said.

"You have no idea," drawled Ava.

Hope flashed her eyes open. If they were being careful, being slow, then she needed to stop this. She took Ava's hand in her own. "We have time. Time to figure out what we want, what this is, if it's anything."

Ava's cheeks were flushed pink. "We do," she agreed.

"Then we're going to try this?"

Ava took a breath. "Yes."

Hope grinned, leaned in and cupped Ava's face in her hands, wanting to kiss her again, wanting to do more than that.

The front door opened. "I'm back," Caz called.

Ava jumped a foot in the air and then hurriedly stood up. "I'd better be going."

"You can stay," offered Hope.

But Ava was already leaving, already pushing past Caz in the hallway and going outside.

"What was all that about?" Caz asked, putting her shopping bags down. Then she looked up and saw the silly smile on Hope's face. "Aha."

"Mum…"

"Hope Perkins, did you kiss the girl next door?" Caz said, putting her hands on her hips.

"She's hardly a girl."

"And that's hardly a 'no'," said Caz. She grinned harder. "How about I put the kettle on and you tell your old mum all about it."

"Only if you're going to finally spill the details on your apparently booming love life," Hope said as she followed her mother into the kitchen.

"Like that is it?" said Caz. "Alright then, we can keep our little secrets for a while, happy?"

And Hope was happy. Happier than she'd been for a long time. Happy and very, very sexually frustrated...

CHAPTER TWENTY ONE

The call came at around four in the morning and Ava wouldn't have answered it except that she was already awake. Or still awake. One or the other.

As it turned out, taking things slowly was a euphemism for being all turned on with nowhere to expend the energy. Still, at least her libido was all present and correct. Ava couldn't remember feeling like this since she was a teenager in love with her poetry teacher.

"Ava Stanford." She assumed it was an American call, given the time difference and all, and was gratifyingly correct.

"Ava? This is Stan Gardener over at Milton High."

"Milton High?"

Six months ago she'd have immediately known what he was talking about. But with thousands of miles between them, she was suddenly disoriented.

"That is Ava Stanford, right?" Stan said. "English teacher supreme and poetry club sponsor?"

Ava laughed. "Yes, yes it is. Sorry, Stan, I'm just a bit all over the place. I'm out of the country right now."

"Really? Anywhere good?"

She knew that he meant somewhere sunny, somewhere hot with beaches, not Whitebridge at all. But she couldn't help smiling. "Yeah," she said. "Somewhere good."

"Good for you, we all deserve a break," he said. "God knows, I could do with one most days."

She might be awake, but it was still four in the morning and there was the slimmest chance that she might sleep at some point. "What can I help you with, Stan?"

"Right, yes, well, it's like this. The head of our English department is about to quit. It's about time, he's got enough years on him and he's been known to bark at his students when frustrated. Anyway, not the point. The point is that we're talking about interviewing candidates for the job and your name came up."

"My name?"

"I know, I know. I told the board that you wouldn't dream of leaving Alton High, but they twisted my arm and asked me to make the call anyway."

A job. A new job. A job away from Serena and her new love, a job that she could love and make her own. A week ago she'd have been on a plane. A week ago it would have seemed like all her dreams had come true.

So why was she now so reluctant to jump at the chance?

"Actually, I've left Alton," she said, not knowing until just that second that it was true. Technically she was on sabbatical, but she wasn't going back. Not to the school, anyway.

"Really?" said Stan in a way that signaled he was eager for more information.

"Really. I'm, uh, I'm spending a year on exchange, teaching in the UK."

"That's wonderful, just the kind of experience we're looking for. We're talking about a September start anyway, so that should fit in with your plans."

"I see," Ava said.

"So? Can I put your name in the hat?"

She blew out a breath. Whitebridge wasn't forever. It couldn't be forever. The only reason she was reluctant to say yes was because she'd kissed Hope Perkins, and that was a foolish reason to turn down an opportunity like this.

Yes, she was interested in Hope, but Hope herself had pointed out that they weren't getting engaged or anything.

Plus, it wasn't like she was signing a contract. It was a statement of interest, that was all.

"Sure," she said, as calmly as she could. "Why not? And thanks for the heads up, Stan. I appreciate it."

"Not a problem. We'd love to have you on board, Ava, you know we would. Say hi to the folks over there from me, and don't drink too much of that tea, I've heard it gives you gall stones."

"I'll remember that," Ava said with a grin. "Bye, Stan."

She hung up, put her phone back on the night stand, and snuggled back down into bed.

But she didn't go to sleep. Too many thoughts were running through her head for sleep to come.

AMY LITTLETON SAT on the very edge of the desk, her legs crossed. "I don't know if it's that easy," she said.

Hope rolled her eyes. "We can't just sit around and wait for the council to make a decision. That's giving up."

"But it is their decision to make," Ava put in.

"Still though," said Hope. "We have to do something. This is our school. It needs saving. We can't let it just slide through the cracks like this. What about all our kids? What, we're going to put them on buses and ship them off to a whole other town?"

"They wouldn't be going to Mars," Amy said. "Besides, whichever school or schools stay open, they're sure to hire on at least some of us. They'll have extra kids, so they'll need extra teachers."

"I wouldn't be so sure about that," said Ava. "If their numbers are as low as ours, they might not. There are twelve kids in my class but I'm allowed to have thirty. The key stage 2 kids have no class size limit at all."

"Look at you, knowing your key stages," said Amy. "But you're right, I suppose." She sighed.

"The first thing you should do is get the parents involved," Ava said. "Look at Hope, she's already upset at the idea of sending Alice off somewhere else. You can bet that the other parents will feel the same."

Amy nodded. "Makes sense. We could get some kind of petition going, send it to the council."

"The only thing that's going to change the council's mind is more kids," said Hope.

"For someone called Hope you seem to have little of it today," Ava said.

"Sorry, didn't get much sleep."

Ava felt her stomach twitch. She wondered if Hope hadn't been sleeping for the same reasons that she hadn't been sleeping.

Mila had said she should let the walls down, let herself be vulnerable, be open to things. What she hadn't mentioned was that in doing so, Ava would unleash some kind of lust monster. Now that she'd committed to seeing Hope as something other than an irritation, it seemed like she couldn't see her as anything other than a temptation.

"Alright, I'll get working on a letter to the parents," Amy said, hopping off the desk-edge. "I'll send it to you two tonight and you can let me know what you think."

She scampered off to her own classroom and Ava was alone with Hope for the first time all day. For the first time since they'd decided that they were going to… take things slow.

"Didn't sleep much myself," Ava admitted.

Hope raised an eyebrow. "Blame me all you like," she said. "I've been blaming you."

"Well, I'm only half blaming you," said Ava. She tapped the papers on her desk into a neat pile. "I'll blame Stan Gardener as well."

"Who's that?" Hope asked, pulling her light jacket out of the cupboard.

And Ava realized that not only had she not told Hope about the job offer, but that she'd forgotten about it herself until just this instant. So busy lusting after her classroom assistant that she couldn't remember she had a potential solution to all her problems.

"Um, he's a teacher. A head teacher," Ava said.

Hope raised her eyebrow again and Ava quickly filled her in. She spoke fast but saw the moment that Hope's face dropped anyway.

"That's great," Hope said, when she was done.

"You don't say that like you mean it," said Ava.

"I..." Hope breathed out through her nose. "No, it's great. It's good that you have something to go home to, a place that you could belong in. That's what you've been looking for, isn't it?"

"It is," Ava said. "But, just so you know, I didn't commit to anything. I mean, the possibility is open, but so are other possibilities."

It seemed important that Hope understood that, even though Ava didn't know what other possibilities there could possibly be. But things changed. She'd changed. Maybe something else would come up.

Hope's face lightened. "Other possibilities," she said, moving in so that she was standing within feet of Ava. "You know, I rather think that other possibilities were on my mind last night."

"You're not the only one," Ava admitted before she could stop herself.

"Am I not?"

Ava narrowed her eyes and looked at the plumpness of Hope's lips, the lips that she'd spent at least twenty minutes thinking about last night. In between thinking about other body parts.

"You're not," she said. This time she was the one that took the step forward, so that now only inches were between them.

"Would you care to elaborate on the possibilities that you were considering?" asked Hope, dark eyes wide and innocent.

"Well, I could," said Ava, voice deep. She leaned in even further. "But it might be easier to show you."

Before she could stop herself, she was putting one hand

behind Hope's head, tangling her fingers in long, dark hair and pulling Hope's face closer and closer until finally their lips met.

Then Ava felt her heart beat harder, felt the blood rushing through her veins, felt the warmth between her legs as Hope's tongue slipped into her mouth and she knew that she couldn't stop this. That she didn't want to stop this.

Whatever else was happening, whatever else they were building or not building, her body was definitively telling her one thing. It was ready. Ready for all those fantasies she'd had last night, ready to jump into something.

She crushed her mouth onto Hope's, pulling her in tighter and tighter so that she could feel the curves of Hope's body against her own. Then pushed her, pushed the both of them, until Hope was stumbling backward and Ava was holding her up against the wall by the blackboard.

"Here?" Hope asked, pulling away, eyes clouded with lust.

"There's always the supply closet," mumbled Ava, bending her head to kiss Hope's neck.

"What happened to taking things slow?" Hope said into Ava's hair.

"Fuck slow," Ava said into Hope's neck.

Hope groaned and Ava felt Hope's hips bucking up against hers, felt Hope's need and want coming to the surface.

Then a phone rang and Ava found herself being pushed away.

"Sorry, sorry," Hope said, rushing to her purse. "Sorry, but that's my mum's ringtone. She's looking after Alice."

Ava closed her eyes and nodded, getting her breath back. Perhaps it was for the best. This was hardly the appropriate location for anything to happen.

"Sorry," Hope said again, answering the phone.

Ava turned to collect her things. She'd walk Hope home in the autumn evening and behave herself. For now, at least.

CHAPTER TWENTY TWO

Hope checked her watch but it didn't make the queue move any faster. She sighed and hitched up the package under her arm and tried to be patient.

"Hope?"

She turned to see Mila grinning behind her, balancing baby Ag on her hip. "How are you doing?"

"Well, my life isn't as exciting as yours," Mila said. "But we're all doing just fine."

"What do you mean?" Hope shuffled one place further up the line.

"I'm not the one with exotic foreign admirers," Mila said with a sniff.

Hope sighed. "Is nothing secret around here?"

"Hardly anything," Mila said. "Have you heard that Ad and Ant are taking Lilian on a cruise?"

Hope laughed. "And the reason things aren't secret around here is you, isn't it?" She checked her watch again.

"It's not my fault people tell me things. And am I not right? Does our fancy American school teacher not have a crush on you?"

Hope felt herself blush and Mila laughed.

"Alright, alright, I'll stop prying. But just so you know, I think it'd be a great choice."

"If she sticks around long enough for anything to happen," said Hope, glancing again at her watch.

"In a hurry?" asked Mila.

"Kind of. I didn't expect the queue to be so bad at this time of day. I only popped out to mail this for the school, but Alice finished a half hour ago now and I really should get back for her. I'm sure she's fine with Ava, but still."

"It's Ava now, is it?" Mila said. "She seems like a jumpy one, was asking me how I knew what I wanted the other day. I told her to be more vulnerable, but she's like a wounded bird, that one."

"She's fragile," Hope agreed. "But then, I suppose most people are after a divorce, aren't they?"

"I hope I don't have to find out," said Mila, bouncing Ag. "But I suppose so. She just seems like she might be her own worst enemy."

Hope thought about how Ava could turn from entrancing to infuriating in the space of a second and nodded. It did sometimes seem like Ava was sabotaging things. But as long as Hope knew that, well, she could compensate for it, couldn't she?

Which was more than she could say about Ava's job offer. There was nothing she could do about that. Not that she was planning on anything long term. Or anything at all really. She'd meant what she said. What happened, happened, and she'd be grateful for it.

And it wasn't like she didn't know that Ava was leaving at some point. In a way, that made things easier. There couldn't be anything serious.

"Listen," Mila said. "Why don't I take that package for you? I've got to stand in line anyway, you can get back to Alice."

"Would you mind?" Hope said. "I wouldn't normally, but this is the problem with trying to do two jobs at once. Receptionist and classroom assistant."

"I thought Jake was getting a new receptionist in?" Mila said, taking the parcel from Hope.

"So did I," Hope said, checking her watch one last time. "Thanks Mil, I owe you one." And she rushed out of the post office.

THE SCHOOL WAS always so much calmer without the children in it. Calmer, quieter, but also emptier in a way that was more about spirit than actual space. It was always a little sad to see the place without kids, and it reminded Hope that the school might not be around forever. She needed to make sure Amy was on top of the petition.

She burst through the classroom door, an apology already on her lips. "Sorry, sorry, sorry, the post office was a nightmare."

Ava was sitting at her desk, glasses perched on the end of her nose. "Not a problem."

Hope looked around. "Where's Alice?"

Now Ava frowned. "I thought you knew."

"Knew what?" asked Hope, heart starting to pound hard in her chest.

"Knew that her father came for her."

Hope squashed down the panic and the fear and the anger and yanked her phone out of her bag, her hand shaking so much she had trouble pressing Noah's icon. She held her breath while the phone rang.

"Hello?"

"Noah? Where's Alice? Is she with you?"

There was the sound of a groan that made Hope's stomach clench. "Yes, yes," Noah said. "I meant to call you, I honestly did."

"You could have been anyone," said Hope, releasing some of the panic.

"But I'm not," Noah said. "I'm sorry. I came to pick her up at yours and Caz said that you were running late so I thought I'd catch you at the school and then you were out and Alice was there. But I should have called. I meant to, I just got so caught up in Alice telling me about her day. You know what a chatterbox she is when she gets off school."

Hope took a big breath. A big, calming breath. "You need to let me know if you pick Alice up."

"I will, I will, I swear," Noah said. "And I'm driving, I've got to go."

He hung up and Hope's legs started to feel shaky so she leaned against a tiny desk, almost toppling it over.

"Is everything alright?" Ava asked.

"He could have been anyone," said Hope.

"But he wasn't," shrugged Ava.

"Not the point. He could have been."

Ava pushed her glasses up on top of her hair and for once lust wasn't the first thought that Hope had.

"I hope you're not implying that I'd let a child go with a stranger," Ava said.

"Isn't that what you did?"

"He came to the classroom," said Ava. "The second Alice saw him, she shouted 'daddy' and flung herself at him. They're almost mirror images of each other. Obviously it was her father."

Hope closed her eyes, trying to center herself. Ava didn't understand, perhaps couldn't understand, that feeling of looking at the space your child was supposed to occupy only to find it empty. That echoing, gut-churning, scream of pure terror that wanted to rip itself from her mouth.

"You can't just let him take her."

Ava stood up now, seeing that Hope was not in good shape. "Alice is fine," she said. "But you're obviously not. Are you sure this has nothing to do with your feelings about your ex-husband, your protectiveness over Alice?"

"This has everything to do with the fact that you let someone take my daughter from your classroom," said Hope.

She could feel Ava take a breath, feel the oxygen soak out of the room.

And for the very first time she considered the fact that whilst she might be attracted to Ava, Ava might not be the right person for her. Not if she couldn't understand this, not if she couldn't fit into a life that had not just Hope but also Alice in it, even if it was for a short time.

"You're right."

Hope was adrenaline-pumped, ready to defend herself and her anger. So those two words rather took the wind out of her sails. "What?"

"You're right," Ava said. "It was irresponsible of me to let someone take a child out of this classroom when I didn't personally know him. I should have checked with someone, I should have called you. I'm sorry. It won't happen again. To Alice or to any other child."

Hope deflated a little. "I was worried."

"I could see that, and I understand why," Ava said. She was looking earnest. "I know I've got a lot to learn about being around small kids, and I know that's why you're here to help me. I'm used to kids that can take responsibility for themselves, hell, that can drive themselves. I screwed up and I understand why you got mad."

"Wow." Hope scratched her head. "Um, yeah, well, okay then. I'm not sure I was expecting such a complete apology."

"I did wrong," Ava shrugged. "The least I can do is apologize and make sure it doesn't happen again."

"I'm sorry I snapped," Hope said.

"You had every reason to," said Ava. She took a step closer. "I didn't mean to hurt you."

"I know." Hope could smell her, sense her, could fill herself up with the presence of Ava. And just as sometimes she swung from adoration to irritation, now she could feel herself swinging back again. "Um, I thought we decided this isn't an appropriate place," she said, voice sort of squeaky.

Ava stepped back. "You're right."

"Um, Alice is with her dad. I'm not sure where mum is, but I can check," Hope said. "By which I mean, you could come to my place. If you wanted."

The air crackled with energy. For a long moment Ava looked at her. Then she looked away, picking up her bag from her desk. "I've got a lot to do," she said. "You know, it's a school night." She was trying to make a joke out of the rejection, but Hope felt it anyhow.

She felt it and knew that Ava was afraid, fragile, just as Mila had said. And she knew that no matter how much she might want the woman, she'd have to be patient. She'd have to show Ava that she was trustworthy.

So she smiled and nodded. "Alright then, let's walk home, shall we?"

CHAPTER TWENTY THREE

Ava clapped her hands and twelve sets of eyes turned her way. She really was getting the hang of this. "Hand in hand please," she said. Immediately, the children all joined hands into a large, uneven circle. Ava sighed. On second thoughts, maybe she wasn't getting the hang of this.

"Pair up with your outside friend," Hope said. The kids separated, coupling up and then forming a neat crocodile line.

Ava blew out a breath and Hope grinned at her. "Alright, you know the rules," Ava said. "Stay with your outside friend. No running, no shouting, no leaving our sight. We're not going to the park to play, we're going…"

"To find insects," shouted the kids in glee.

"To look at insects," Ava corrected. "We look, we don't touch. When you see an insect then you can check it off on your checklist and draw a picture. Whichever pair has the most insects will win today's prize."

Little eyes turned big and round and there was a lot of whispering, debate, Ava suspected, about what the prize might be. She smiled to herself.

"Ready for this?" Hope whispered.

Ava felt the stir of her breath on her neck and nodded. This was her first field trip with the kids, but she was feeling confident. Which was more than she could say about whatever was happening with Hope.

Inside the school, apparently everything was going fine. As long as Hope was in a classroom, Ava couldn't get enough of her.

Commit to anything further than that though, and all bets were off. For God's sake, she'd spent nights dreaming about the woman, dreaming and touching and wanting. But the second Hope invited her over, she turned her down flat.

Because that made so much sense.

The children trooped out of the classroom led by Hope, and Ava followed on behind.

She wasn't exactly sure what the problem was. Okay, so she hadn't been with anyone since Serena. But her body was obviously ready and responsive. She could think of no logical reason why she shouldn't be an adult and spend some time with Hope doing adult things.

So why did her instincts kick in and make her say no all the time?

They came to a stop at the school gate and Ava almost tripped over Alice and Clara who were last in the line. Alice looked up at her.

"Yes?" Ava asked cautiously. She'd learned to be wary when Alice gave her the look that was currently being utilized.

"You're supposed to go out into the road and stand there so we can all cross," Alice said.

"So that the cars will squish you and not us," Clara added helpfully.

"No," said Alice. Then she looked doubtful. "Or maybe."

"I'm sure it's because I'm bigger and drivers see me better," said Ava. "I have no intention of getting run over."

She strode out into the street and let the children file past her, Hope bringing up the rear now. "So far, so good," Hope whispered with a smile.

Ava felt herself blush. Like she needed Hope's approbation. Except it did make her feel good. Everything about Hope made her feel good. So why was she being so stubborn about spending any alone time with her at all?

Along the sidewalk they all walked, slowly making their way to the small town park. The day was sunny and bright with only a hint of chill in the air, and the children were happy to be outside, chatting merrily as they walked.

Ava opened the park gate and let the kids go in. "Alright, what are the rules?" she asked. She'd learned to get anything important repeated back to her if she wanted to be sure that the kids really got it. "No…"

"Running!"

"Shouting!" shouted Daniel Monroe so loud that Ava almost laughed. She changed her laugh into a frown and Daniel grinned widely back at her.

"And no going out of my sight," Ava said. "You know what you're doing, so get started. If there are any problems, find me or Ms. Perkins."

And then there was the job.

The job that should be the solution to everything and yet was keeping Ava awake at night just as much as the thought of what might be lying beneath Hope's mostly-buttoned shirt.

This should have been easier. Running away is what it was, to be honest. Something that Quinn didn't hesitate to tell her.

But she'd thought that running away meant leaving everything behind her, when in fact it just meant taking everything with her to a new place.

And now she'd thrown Hope into the mix and things seemed even more complicated than before. Before she'd at least been able to focus on being heart-broken. Now she had to focus on being heart-broken and mostly turned on with periods of irritation which definitely did not make things easier by any stretch of the imagination at all.

So why was she doing this? Why didn't she just pack up and go back home, take the job Stan had offered her, crash on Quinn's couch until she found an apartment? Or hell, why didn't she pack up and go to Peru or Cambodia or somewhere else where her feelings might not find her?

There was a startled squeal and Ava spun around, locating the source of the sound immediately.

Nathan Jackson was holding his arm protectively against his side, cradling his hand, and a growing crowd of classmates was beginning to gather around him.

"Miss, miss!" shouted Clara. "Nathan got stinged by a bee."

"It was a wasp," Alice put in.

"But we wasn't supposed to touch nothing," added Daniel. "But then Nathan must've touched the bee."

"It was a wasp," Alice said again.

"And the wasp touched him, silly," said Sara Gonzalez.

Ava hurried in closer, squatting down so she could see Nathan's tear-stained face a little better. "Let me see."

He shook his head and pressed his lips together.

"He definitely got stinged," Clara said. "I saw it."

"Stung," Ava said, remembering that she was supposed to be the teacher here. "Show me, Nathan."

He shook his head more violently this time.

"What's going on over here," Hope said, joining the class. "Haven't you all got work to do?"

"Yes, miss, but Nathan got stinged," said Clara.

"Stung," said Ava and Hope in unison.

Hope squatted down beside Ava. "Show me," she said to Nathan. To Ava's surprise, Nathan shakily held out his hand. Hope tutted and then looked at him quite seriously. "I'm afraid we're going to have to cut this finger off."

Nathan snorted. "No, you're not. It's just a sting."

"It looks like a terribly horrible sting, we should definitely think about cutting it off," Hope said solemnly.

"It's only a sting," laughed Nathan.

Hope sighed. "Well, if you're sure," she said. "I do have a little package of vinegar in my bag that'll stop it hurting."

"Okay," said Nathan cheerfully.

Hope fumbled in her bag. "You're sure about not cutting it off?" she asked doubtfully as Nathan held out his hand to have a sachet of malt vinegar poured over his finger.

"Double sure," he laughed.

"Oh well then, off you go and get your work done," Hope said.

"Uh-oh."

Ava turned around again. "Uh-oh, what?" she asked, knowing full well that the sound couldn't bode well.

"Nothing," said Daniel Monroe edging off behind Hope. "Ms. Perkins, Ms. Perkins," he said in a whisper that was as loud as his regular speaking voice. "Ms. Perkins, I've had an accident again."

"It's fine," Hope said calmly. "I've got wet wipes and a spare pair of jogging pants in my bag."

This was some magic bag, Ava was starting to think. She watched as Hope lead Daniel off into the public bathroom to get cleaned up and shook her head.

That was the reason she was going nowhere. No Peru, no Cambodia, not even Quinn's couch. Because of Hope Perkins and her magic bag. Hope Perkins and her luscious curves, Hope Perkins and her ability to irritate and enchant with a smile.

She could go nowhere, Ava suddenly realized, without seeing where this went, without knowing just what it was about, without kissing Hope one more time or a dozen more times or a million more times.

Which meant she needed to get over this mental block of taking the next step.

Because, like it or not, Hope Perkins made Ava's life better by pretty much every single measure. Whilst before she'd been so busy being heart-broken that getting out of bed was a chore, now she found that she wanted to hurry to work, wanted to see Hope, if only to say good morning.

There was a reason Nathan Jackson hadn't shown her his hand. A reason that Daniel Monroe hadn't confessed his accident to her. Because they trusted Hope implicitly, trusted her to do what was right for them, to care for them.

And it was about time that Ava learned a little from her kids, rather than the other way around. It was about time she trusted Hope and maybe trusted herself a little too.

The rest of the morning managed to pass without incident,

and it was ten minutes before lunch as they ushered the children back into the school gates.

"Hope," Ava said, as she passed by.

"Mmm? Clara Buxton, don't you dare think about running in that corridor."

Ava swallowed. "Um, do you, er, that is, would you—"

"Nathan Jackson, walk smartly to the classroom and stop hitting people's coats."

Ava took a breath and tried again. "Er, I was thinking—"

"Alice Perkins, let go of Sara's hand, she doesn't want to be attached to you for life." Hope turned to her. "You'd better think quickly," she said, with a grin. "Because they'll set the place ablaze otherwise."

Ava cleared her throat. "It's just that, I thought maybe... Doyouwanttocometomyplaceafterwork?"

Hope frowned as she deciphered what Ava had said, then a smile began to spread across her face. "Yes," she said gently. "Yes, I think I'd quite like that."

Ava watched as Hope danced off down the corridor after the children. She didn't trust her legs to carry her that far they were shaking so badly.

She'd done it.

She was going to trust Hope Perkins.

And perhaps do a little more than just trusting...

CHAPTER TWENTY FOUR

Hope bounded down the stairs, practically bouncing into the kitchen. Her mother raised her eyebrows.

"So you're all primped and perfumed, are you?" Caz asked knowingly.

"What of it?" asked Hope, helping herself to an animal cracker off the plate Caz was preparing for Alice.

"Nothing of it," Caz said, moving the plate out of Hope's reach. "Just be careful, that's all."

"I always am." Hope leaned against the kitchen counter. "You don't mind, do you mum? I mean, I don't have to go, you don't need to stay in and look after Alice if you've got other things to do."

"Mind? I'm delighted," said Caz, pouring juice into a cup. "It's about time Alice and I had a little alone time." She looked her daughter up and down. "As for where you're going, well, I've got to say that I'm proud of you."

Hope bit her lip. "Mum, can I ask you something?"

"You just did."

"Yeah, something else." It had been preying on her mind. "Why now? I mean, you just start dating again out of nowhere. So why now?"

Caz moved Alice's plate and cup to the kitchen table and put her hand on her hip. "Maybe it occurs to me that I haven't always set the best example."

"In what way?"

Caz sighed. "In the way of making sure that you knew that I had my own life too, that the world didn't just revolve around you." She held up her hands as Hope opened her mouth. "I'm not saying you're spoiled or anything of the sort, I'm just saying that it might have been helpful to you as a woman if you'd had a mother that modeled healthy relationships."

"And you've decided to do that now?" asked Hope, raising an eyebrow.

"Better later than never," Caz said defensively. "Anyway, it's worked, hasn't it? You're off next door to see your fancy woman and I'm here babysitting."

Hope laughed. "I'm not sure how Ava will feel about being called a fancy woman."

"You need to do this," Caz said more seriously. "It's no life being alone. You and Noah have been done for a while now and it's important that you have something for yourself. It's important that Alice sees you have something for yourself. I'm proud of you for putting yourself out there, honestly, I am, Hope."

"If I'd have known that the only thing I needed to do to make you proud of me was kiss girls I might have come out a little sooner."

Caz snorted. "You're doing more than kissing if the amount of time you've just spent primping is any sign. And you'd better go, else you'll be too late to do anything."

"I'll be back—" Hope started.

"You'll be back when you're back," interrupted Caz. "You're only next door. Stay the night. Do whatever you need to do. We know where you are."

Hope paused. "When you say we…?"

"I mean I know where you are," Caz said firmly. "I haven't said a word to Alice except that you're going out."

Hope breathed more easily. She didn't want Alice getting all mixed up in this, not until she knew what was happening, what all this was. It had more than crossed her mind that this could just be a silly infatuation. One of those situations where sex happened and then the magic was gone. Not that she'd experienced that, but she'd heard that it happened.

Would that be a relief or just unimaginably painful? She wasn't sure. But she knew that she needed to figure it out sooner rather than later. And maybe finding out could be fun.

She was smirking to herself as she left the house. A smirk that rapidly disappeared as she walked up Ava's garden path and got an attack of the nerves.

She was shaking, her heart was in her mouth, and she was debating whether or not she really had the gall to ring the doorbell when she saw movement in the bushes by the door. She bent down and Rosie's beady yellow eyes looked back at her.

"Rosie, get out of here, go on, scat. Get home," she hissed.

Rosie narrowed her eyes, then turned and began to saunter back next door. Hope was watching her go when the front door opened.

"In my country we tend to ring the bell or at least knock on the door," Ava said. "It does rather take some of the mystery out of proceedings, but then, it prevents visitors from having to stand on the doorstep for hours at a time."

Hope turned with an acid comment already on her tongue and stalled when she saw Ava.

She'd showered, her hair was still slightly damp, pushed back off her face by her glasses. A long, white shirt billowed over leggings, a cloud of perfume enveloped her. Her eyes were delicately smudged with eyeliner and there was a hint of color on her lips, but other than that she was bare of makeup.

And she was about the most breathtaking woman that Hope had ever seen. Breathtaking enough that Hope found that she actually literally couldn't take a breath. Like there was a chance of her being able to touch this, kiss this, heaven forbid, bed this goddess.

"Jesus," said Ava. "I'd ask if the cat got your tongue, but I've just seen the cat and she looked empty-handed. And you look like you're about to choke. Maybe you should come in?"

Hope nodded and stepped over the threshold just as she managed to gulp a mouthful of oxygen into her lungs. Then she started coughing so hard that Ava had to pound her back. Not exactly the contact she was hoping for.

"And I thought I was nervous." Ava stood back as Hope finally straightened up.

"You're nervous?" Hope asked, grateful for every breath.

"Aren't you?"

Hope nodded.

"Living room?"

Hope nodded again.

They went into the sparsely decorated living room and it occurred to Hope that she'd never been in this house before, even if it was right next door. And then it occurred to her that maybe she shouldn't be here at all. Maybe Ava had asked her out of... what? Out of peer pressure? Like they were sixteen?

Or maybe because she thought she was expected to. Hope's stomach wavered a little and she sat on the very edge of the minimalist black couch.

Ava sat down at the opposite end of the couch. "I've got wine," she said.

"Um, I'm fine," said Hope, afraid now that if Ava got up she might not come back.

Ava sighed. "This is ridiculous, isn't it?"

Hope nodded for the third time. "A bit."

"We're both adults."

"And we don't have to do anything," Hope said hurriedly. "I mean, we can have a drink maybe, talk, I don't want you to think that there are any expectations here."

Ava bit her lip and Hope nearly passed out again. "But there are, aren't there? Expectations, I mean. Unless... unless you don't have any?"

"If you're asking whether I shaved my legs, then the answer is yes," Hope said rather more glibly than she'd intended.

"I did too," admitted Ava. She looked down at her hands. "But I find that now that I've got you here, I don't really know what to do with you. I mean how to start. It's been a very, very long time since I've been in this position."

"You're not the only one," Hope said. She crossed her legs. This was nothing, just a meeting with a friend, she told herself. Take the pressure off. "Maybe I should get us that wine," she said, standing up.

"I don't think I asked you here for wine," Ava said in a small voice.

Hope rolled her eyes. "Then why did you invite me here?"

There was a silence long enough that Hope thought Ava might not answer. But she did. "Because when I kiss you everything seems right."

"Right?" Hope said.

Ava shrugged. "My life has, not to put too fine a point on it, been a bit shit lately. And mostly it's still not great. Yet for some reason, the second I kiss you everything clicks into place, everything just seems right."

Hope took a breath to ask another question except she didn't have to. She knew exactly what Ava meant. There were a thousand reasons not to get involved with someone like Ava, not least that she wasn't around permanently. But when their lips meant every single one of those reasons went out of the window.

"Okay," she said slowly. "So why don't we start there?"

"Start where?" asked Ava.

"With a kiss," said Hope, holding out her hand. Ava laced her fingers into Hope's and warmth traveled up Hope's arm as she pulled Ava up off the couch, pulled her in closer, their heights almost matching, so they were almost nose to nose. "No expectations," Hope whispered.

But Ava was already reaching up, already cupping Hope's face in her hands, leaning her head until she could slide in to fit their lips perfectly together.

Hope's knees turned to jelly, her heart started to beat harder and there was a rush of warmth between her legs. She was struggling to breathe again, but this time she didn't care, she could suffocate as long as this kiss didn't stop.

She leaned into it, let herself disappear into Ava's lips, let her eyes close and her body feel and then Ava was pressing up against her, pushing her back, then she was leaning against a wall and Ava was melded to her, their bodies connecting with every atom, so close that Hope couldn't tell where she ended and where Ava began.

Ava pulled back, her green eyes heavy-lidded and her lips bruised, voice hoarse. "So much for no expectations," she said.

And Hope was going to ask her what she meant, but Ava's lips were already descending onto her neck and then her collarbone, and then the carefully buttoned shirt she'd put on was being torn from her and her hipbones were pressing up against Ava's and then this was happening whether they'd planned on it or not.

CHAPTER TWENTY FIVE

Ava could taste her, a salty, fruity taste like a margarita but better. She nuzzled her head into Hope's neck and closed her eyes, willing herself to make the right decision here.

What if this is all it was, argued one side of her. What if this was just pure physical lust? In that case, shouldn't she just jump in with both feet and get this, her first sexual encounter after her divorce, out of the way?

But what if this wasn't all it was, argued the other side of her. That was the side that terrified her, the one that made her freeze inside and wonder if she should be backing out, if she should stop leading Hope on.

Then Hope's hands went to her hips and pulled her in and Ava groaned softly into Hope's skin, and they were kissing again and Ava could feel every pulse of Hope's heart in her lips. Her breath was coming faster, there was heat between her legs, and all she wanted was more of this.

She pulled away, just enough so that she could look into Hope's dark eyes. "Care to move this to the bedroom?"

"If we stop, are you going to start again?" Hope asked. "Because if the only way this is going to work is to get screwed up against this wall right now then I'm not going to complain."

Ava laughed, then Hope's hands grasped her backside and the laugh turned into a moan. "We're not stopping," she said, suddenly knowing it was true, knowing that they wouldn't stop.

Hope raised an eyebrow. "We're not stopping. I've got your word on that?"

"Solemn promise," Ava said.

Then Hope was pushing her away and sliding out from between her and the wall. "In that case, race you."

She was gone, pounding up the stairs and with a gleeful laugh, Ava followed her, running up the stairs and practically crashing through the bedroom door until she stopped, paralyzed at the sight of Hope sitting there on the edge of her neatly made bed. The sight of Hope with her long, dark hair messed up in curls, her lips swollen, her eyes clouded and dark.

"You promised," said Hope, voice deep.

She stood up, quickly flicked open the button of her jeans and pulled them down, baring slim, smooth legs and leaving her only in a white shirt and underwear.

Ava's heart stopped. "I did promise, didn't I?" she said, voice cracking.

"I'm not a teasing kind of girl," Hope said, sitting back down on the bed.

"You're not a girl at all," said Ava, taking a step toward her.

"So, what happens now?"

Ava stopped. "What?"

"I've only been with Noah, remember?" Hope said with a half-smile. "Not that I'm not anxious to change that situation, I just don't quite know what I'm supposed to be doing."

A huge wave of wanting swept over Ava. "You're supposed to be doing nothing," she said, low and deep, as she took another step forward and then dropped to her knees. "Nothing at all."

"Nothing?" Hope asked, confused.

But Ava was already parting her thighs, was already insinuating herself between them, inhaling the scent of Hope, bitter and sweet at the same time, mouth salivating and stomach pulsing at the thought of tasting her.

"Ah," breathed Hope. "Nothing."

"Except perhaps stop talking?" suggested Ava, as she snuggled in closer, letting her hair brush against the soft skin of Hope's thigh. She leaned in, pressed her face against the lace of Hope's underwear and felt Hope's thighs tighten around her as she gasped.

"No teasing," Hope said. "And in exchange, no talking."

As if Ava could wait, as if she could stop herself now, with Hope right in front of her, with the smell and taste of her filling up all her senses. She'd been worried that visions of her wife would come to her, but they didn't. Her mind was so full of Hope that nothing else intruded.

With firm hands she pushed Hope's thighs further apart, hooking her arm around one and using her other hand to slide her fingers under the side of Hope's underwear and pull it to one side.

She heard another gasp, but true to her word, Hope didn't speak, she wriggled a little and pushed her hips up and Ava, who'd somehow forgotten that foreplay existed in the last few seconds, knew that even if she'd been inclined to toy with Hope, now really wasn't the time.

She pressed her face in, quested with her tongue, slipping deep into slick wetness. Jesus, Hope was turned on. Why that surprised her, she didn't know. It wasn't like the exact same thing wasn't happening between her own legs. It wasn't like she hadn't been ready the second that Hope's lips had touched hers.

Her tongue slid upwards, finding swollen hardness and Hope's hands tangled in her hair, pressing her face into her center. Obediently, Ava began to suck and then to circle her tongue and Hope shouted out something incomprehensible.

Ava tried to pull back, fearful that she'd done something wrong, but Hope's hands clutched her closer until she could feel Hope's heartbeat pulsing through her center and understood that even so fast, Hope was so close that every movement brought her exquisite agony.

She smiled, hummed lightly and pressed her mouth against

Hope who responded by pressing her fingers into Ava's head, lifting her hips, and then shuddering as her breath stopped.

Ava held her position until she heard Hope's first gasping, desperate breath, then pulled away.

"Jesus."

"No, just Ava."

"Jesus," Hope breathed again. She collapsed backward onto the bed. "Jesus."

"Wide vocabulary you've got," Ava observed, climbing onto the bed beside her.

"It's, um, it's been a while."

"No shit," Ava said, but she was grinning, her smile so wide it was in danger of splitting her face.

"And why are you looking so self-satisfied?" Hope asked, regaining herself now and propping her head up on one elbow.

"I don't think I've ever made a woman orgasm so fast in my life," Ava said. Her lips still tasted of Hope.

"That sounds like a challenge," said Hope. Her hand was on Ava's chest.

"Not at all, no challenge."

"Really?" Hope's hand pulled at Ava's shirt, lifting it until her fingers were touching the bare skin of Ava's stomach.

"Really."

"Really, really?" asked Hope, as her fingers slid underneath the waistband of Ava's leggings and then in the same movement beneath her underwear.

"I thought you didn't know what you were doing?" Ava said and she was proud of how controlled her voice sounded.

"I didn't say that, did I?" Hope said, as her fingers moved downward, stroking at wiry hair. "I said I wasn't sure what happened next, but I didn't explicitly say I didn't know what I was doing."

"Ah," was all Ava could manage.

"After all, I simply do to you what I'd do to myself, don't I?" Hope asked innocently, as one finger slid between Ava's lips into the slickness beneath.

Ava moaned because she couldn't form a word because the thought of Hope touching herself was too much to bear because Hope actually touching her was too much to bear.

"Having said that," Hope said, as the same finger slid back upwards and very gently circled around Ava's center without actually touching it at all in a way that made Ava want to slap Hope and kiss her all at the same time. "Having said I know what I'm doing, I mean. I'm not exactly sure whether or not the no talking rule still holds."

Ava bit her lip, feeling pulsing inside her already as Hope's slender fingers finally found their target and began to move rhythmically. "Mmm," she managed to groan.

"Mmm yes or mmm no?" asked Hope.

Ava's hips bucked up of their own accord and her eyes screwed shut.

"I guess you're not really in a position to answer," Hope said as her fingers moved faster and Ava's breath caught in her throat. "In which case, I'll tell you a secret." She leaned in close, whispering so that the hairs on Ava's neck stood up. "You're the sexiest woman I've ever met, Ava Stanford. I've dreamed about doing this, touched myself when I dreamed about doing this, touching you is almost enough to make me cum again."

Ava whimpered and Hope dropped a delicate kiss on her neck which was enough to push her over the edge.

Her hands grasped the bedsheets in fists as she disappeared off over the edge of the cliff into beautiful, starry nothingness, where the only thing that mattered was the touch of Hope's hand and the feel of her lips on her skin.

THEY WERE ENTANGLED together under the sheets, finally naked, their skin sweat-soaked and salty.

"We should eat something perhaps," Ava said lazily.

Hope put a hand on the curve of Ava's waist. "Perhaps," she said. "You know, I was worried. No, worried is the wrong word. I was... I was thinking, before this, thinking that maybe this was just physical, that maybe we just had to get it out of our systems."

"I had a similar thought," Ava said, stroking Hope's hair. She swallowed. "Um, I don't really think that was it, do you?"

Hope shook her head. "No. But then, I'm not sure what this is."

Ava felt Hope's weight on her chest. "We've both been married," she said. "We both know that there's more than this. That there's watching each other floss our teeth, arguing over directions, watching crappy documentaries on TV. A relationship is made up of a million moments that have nothing to do with love and yet are only held together by love."

"You said the L word, not me."

Ava smiled. "I didn't say it to you. And I don't expect you to say it to me. Not yet at any rate. I'm just saying that there's a lot to think about."

"And you'll leave one day and then who knows where we'll be."

"Exactly," Ava said. "But then, I'm not leaving today, am I?"

"You're not," agreed Hope. "And living for tomorrow sounds like a terrible plan."

"You might get hit by a bus tomorrow."

"You might get hit by a meteorite tomorrow."

"So I suppose what I'm saying is that I'd quite like to do this again," Ava said, her heart beating harder again as she admitted this.

Hope sighed and propped herself up on one elbow again. "So would I," she said. "But there's a condition here."

"I can't promise you to stay here, I can't promise long-term, I can't promise anything," Ava said.

"I'm not asking you to," said Hope. "We've both been through this before and we both know how life works."

"Then what's the condition?"

Hope took a breath. "Anyone that's part of my life has to be part of Alice's life too. We come as a package, Ava. I'm not dragging you into step-parenthood or anything, but Alice is important to me and I can't separate her out."

"I haven't asked you to," said Ava, relieved that that was all it was. "I like Alice."

Hope bit her lip, then nodded. "Alright then," she said. "So I'm inviting you to family dinner on Saturday. Me, you, Alice and mum."

"That's your condition? A home cooked meal?"

Hope laughed but Ava could see that she was wary, afraid that she was asking for something too big.

"I'd be honored," Ava said.

CHAPTER TWENTY SIX

Hope tramped across the grass to where she could see Noah waiting, wrapped in a scarf against the autumn chill. He waved when he saw her coming and in his smile she saw a glimmer of what she'd used to love about him.

She had loved him once. It would be ridiculous to assume that she hadn't. So now she couldn't help but compare the way she'd once felt about Noah to how she felt about Ava.

Feelings weren't absolutes, she couldn't measure them, couldn't make her feelings for Noah stand up against her feelings for Ava so she could judge which were taller or fatter or better. All she could do was go with her gut.

Her gut said that her feelings for Ava were bigger than her brain would care to admit and that she was better off not trying to calculate.

There were feelings there, she was sure of it. In that moment when Ava had talked about teeth flossing and TV watching there'd been an instant when all Hope could think was that yes, she wanted to be there for those things. That the sex was good, brilliant even, but that she knew there was more than that, more to uncover, to experience, more Ava to have.

And she wanted more Ava.

Which meant letting go of control to some extent. Okay, so

maybe she'd get hit by a bus on the way home, or a meteorite for that matter. But chances were that she wouldn't. Which would mean that at some point she and Ava would have to make decisions about the future.

Not until next summer, she told herself as she stumbled on the scrubby grass of the park. Who knows what will happen before then? Let the future belong to itself, don't screw this all up just because one day it might be over.

"You alright?" Noah asked, jogging a few steps to catch up with her.

"Fine," she said brusquely. Then couldn't help but ask: "Why?"

"Dunno," he said. "Funny look on your face, I suppose. Sure you're okay?"

She nodded and looked around for Alice, finally finding her tearing around on a red bike, pursued by Amelia on a far larger blue bike. She sniffed but clamped her mouth shut.

"Thanks for coming to pick her up like this," Noah said.

"Yeah, why was that again?" She hadn't asked. Alice had needed picking up and that was all that registered when Noah had called.

"Well, half because we've got a doctor's appointment on the other side of town," Noah said.

"And the other half?"

"I wanted you to see this," he said, nodding to where his daughter and girlfriend were racing down a straight section of path.

Hope sighed. "Alright, I've seen it now, so what?"

"Amelia's good with Alice," Noah said. "Alice likes her. Ask her yourself. They get on well together."

"I've never disputed that."

"Have you not?" Noah asked. "Cos I know it must be difficult. Believe it or not, I do get that. I can empathize, put myself in your place, imagine how I'm going to feel when you find someone else and some other man gets to tuck my daughter into bed at night. Really, I understand."

Hope had a sudden vision of Ava tucking Alice into bed and

looked away so that Noah wouldn't see the gleam in her eye. "That's not my problem."

"Then what is?" Noah said. "I'm a good dad, you can't deny that. Amelia's a decent person and Alice likes her. I've got a nice house, Alice has clothes and toys there. I get her to school on time and can have her picked up. I'm responsible. So why exactly is it that you don't want me to see more of Alice?"

Hope looked down at the grass. She'd had no intention of arguing with Noah today. No intention of even discussing this and now she felt like she'd been trapped into having a conversation she didn't want to have.

"Alice lives with me," she said. "We agreed on that."

"At the beginning," Noah said. "When I moved out and I was getting set up again. You were right, Alice needs stability. But I've got that stability now. Things have changed, and I think it's only fair that our arrangement changes."

Hope shook her head. "And what about later?" she asked.

"Later?"

"What about when you and Amelia have kids of your own? What then? You're going to keep seeing Alice every other week? You're going to treat her the same as your other kids? The ones that live with you full time?"

"I could ask the same of you," said Noah. The tip of his nose was white. "And of course I'd treat Alice the same. How could you ask that of me?"

"Because you're the one that left, Noah. You're the one that walked out, not me."

"So this is my punishment, is it?" Noah asked. "Not getting to see my daughter? That's the price I have to pay for being honest and speaking the truth that we both knew?"

Hope firmed her jaw and said nothing because there was nothing to say.

"Tell me you weren't feeling the same way, Hope. Tell me you weren't just going through the motions, waking up every morning and pretending everything was alright, when deep inside you knew that we weren't a good fit."

"I..." Hope started, but she couldn't finish it. She remembered sitting at the kitchen table in her old house, Alice opposite her, chatting as they ate. She remembered the faintly irritated feeling she had when she heard the front door open, when Noah interrupted their private time together.

But then, wasn't that what life was? What marriage was? A constant cycle of getting annoyed and then remembering why you loved someone?

Except maybe in the end there hadn't been much love. Maybe that love had turned into something else, into tolerance perhaps. And the sadness of that took her breath away.

"I was brave enough to say it, Hope. I took the blame. I knew that you never could, so I did it, I let myself be painted as the bad guy, the one leaving. I don't deserve to be punished for that."

"I'm not punishing you," Hope said.

"You are," said Noah. He pressed his lips together in a gesture so familiar that Hope could have drawn it. "You want to know about this doctor's appointment we've got?"

"Not really," said Hope. "That's your business."

"It's a fertility doctor," Noah went on, ignoring her answer. "Not that it's going to make much difference. It's a technicality really."

"Fertility?"

Noah nodded. "Amelia can't have children. She was told that a while ago. But we thought we'd check."

Hope looked over to where Amelia was bending down, helping Alice tie her shoelace. "She can't have children so she wants mine?" was the first thing she said.

Then she hated herself for it. Hated that she was so petty, so selfish, but she hadn't been able to help herself anyway.

Noah shook his head. "That's not what this is about," he started.

But then Alice was running towards them both, shouting 'mum' and 'dad' in a way that always made Hope's heart swell. This perfect little creation with her muddy knees and her tangled hair, it was unthinkable to her that she and Noah had made this.

"Mum," Alice said, breathless as she caught up with them. "Mum, 'Melia showed me a new way to tie my shoes. Shall I show you?"

"Show me when we get home," Hope said, because Amelia was walking toward them now and she didn't want to face her. Didn't want to face the woman that she'd just been so horrific to even though Amelia hadn't been around to hear it. She was embarrassed and felt a little sick at what had been a knee-jerk reaction.

"Bye, Al," Noah said, leaning down and kissing his daughter.

But Hope already had Alice by the hand. She flashed a brief, shameful wave at Amelia and then practically dragged Alice back off toward the car.

"Mum, why didn't you say goodbye to 'Melia," Alice said as they hurried toward the car park.

"I waved," Hope said defensively.

"Do you not like her?" asked Alice.

Hope exhaled but didn't say anything.

"She's really nice," Alice added helpfully. "I like her. She's quite funny, you know, even if she looks a bit serious. She likes eating only the jam part of the bread and she cuts all the crusts off. I told her she wouldn't have curly hair like mine if she didn't eat the crusts, so now she eats them though."

"Right," Hope said, unlocking the car and helping Alice in.

"And she doesn't mind if I cry in the night. It only happened once, but she wasn't cross or anything. She said it was alright to sleep in bed with daddy and then she went to sleep in my bed. So that was nice, wasn't it?"

"Mmm," said Hope, checking Alice's safety harness.

"I think that you would like her if you'd stayed at their house too," Alice went on. "You know that Nathan said that when he goes to his dad's he's allowed to eat all the sweets he wants and he doesn't have a bedtime. But my dad's not like that. There's no sweets except on Saturdays and my bedtime is the same like when I'm with you."

"I see," Hope said as she got into her own seat and closed the door.

Alice was quiet for a minute. "I like going to dad's and Amelia's," she said quietly. "I like going to yours and gran's though as well." She sniffed. "I don't have a favorite."

"You don't?" Hope couldn't help but ask as she looked into the rearview mirror at her serious daughter.

"Nope," Alice said firmly.

Hope sighed. She really didn't want to think about this now, didn't want to talk about it, especially with Alice, who was getting smarter and more observant by the day.

"Want to know a secret?" Hope said, anxious to deflect Alice's thoughts from her father.

"Yes!"

"Someone's coming to dinner tomorrow night, so you're going to have to be on your best behavior." She started the engine and put the car into gear.

"Who? Who? Who?" chirped Alice like a little owl.

Hope laughed. "Ms. Stanford is coming."

"Hurray!" Alice shouted and Hope laughed even louder. She'd been right to invite Ava. Whatever the future held, Alice deserved to know what was going on, at least to some extent.

CHAPTER TWENTY SEVEN

"Behave yourself," Hope said.

"Oh, come on," said Caz. "Alice is a big girl now, and her table manners are really coming along."

"I wasn't talking to Alice," said Hope, shooting her mother a look.

"And what's that supposed to mean?"

"It's supposed to mean that the first time Noah came over for dinner you grilled him on his career prospects and almost made him cry," said Hope.

"Well, I won't do that." Caz sniffed. "She's already got a job, I'm more than clear on Ava's career prospects."

Hope's lips tweaked into a smile. "Careful calling her Ava in front of Alice."

"Yes, yes, yes," said Caz. "I'm going to be a good girl, don't worry." She had been chopping tomatoes for salad, but she paused now and looked at her daughter. "You've got it bad, haven't you?"

"Got what bad?" asked Hope, tongue sticking out of the corner of her mouth as she arranged slices of garlic bread to go into the oven.

Caz snorted. "You know exactly what I mean, young lady. And don't think I didn't notice that you didn't come home until the wee hours of the morning the other night."

"I'm not the only one," Hope protested. "When are we going to get to see your fancy man?"

"Never, if you're going to call him my fancy man," said Caz. She sighed. "Let's get you dealt with first, shall we? Then we'll see about making things official."

"So there's something to make official, is there?" Hope slid the baking tray into the oven. "You know, I don't know anything about him, other than the fact he lives over by the church. That's all you've said."

Caz shuffled her feet uncomfortably.

"Mum?"

"Fine, fine. He lives up at the big place."

"Banks' House?" asked Caz. "But I thought that was some sort of corporate retreat or something?"

"No, not there." Caz's face flushed pinker. "The other one."

"What other one? Oh." Hope stopped. "Oh. He, er, he lives up at the old people's home, does he?"

"Don't call it that. It's a retirement home. For people who're retired. You don't have to be that old to be retired, you know."

"I know. I know. I just…" Hope looked at her mother, saw the traces of gray in her hair and the lines that had been laugh-lines for so long that she'd forgotten they were wrinkles too. "I just don't think of you as that old, that's all, mum."

Caz snorted. "I'm not moving in with him. Well, at least not yet. If I get rid of you fast enough then he might move in here."

"Mum!"

"You deserved that," said Caz. "Besides, have you seen that place? It's like a country club on Viagra."

"Mum!"

"Well, it is. It's dead fancy, and pricey too, so you'll be saying goodbye to your inheritance."

Hope rolled her eyes and shook her head. "I don't need an inheritance. And if moving in there will make you happy, well, we'll have to talk about it, I suppose."

Caz patted her arm. "There's nothing serious yet, don't you

worry. Anyway, I might like to keep my options open. I've not exactly done a lot of dating. There's a fair few eligible bachelors around town that I've got my eye on."

"Mum!"

The doorbell rang and before Hope could turn to answer it, Alice came thundering down the stairs. "I've got it, I've got it."

Hope followed her daughter into the hall and let her open the door to reveal Ava standing in a floaty dress, a cardigan over her shoulders to compensate for the autumn chill.

"Hello, Ms. Stanford," Alice chirped. "Please come in and can I take your coat?"

Hope laughed. "She's not wearing a coat, but nice try."

"I am carrying a gift though," Ava said, gently handing a bottle of wine to Alice.

"I'm not allowed to drink this," Alice said seriously.

"I know dear, but perhaps you could carry it very carefully into the kitchen?" said Ava, equally seriously.

Alice walked slowly into the kitchen and Hope turned to Ava with a smile. "Unnecessary, but thank you anyway."

Then Ava was stepping in closer and Hope could smell her scent and then her stomach was flipping and her pulse was racing again and Ava brushed her lips against Hope's and Hope about fainted from the pleasure of it.

"Hello," murmured Ava. "It feels like it's been a while."

"It has," said Hope, putting her hand on the curve of Ava's waist and pulling her in closer. "At least a day, maybe more. An eternity."

Ava's hand snuck into the small of her back until Hope could feel her heart beating in her throat. "We'll have to do something about that later."

All Hope could do was moan softly as Ava's thumb traced circles at the base of her spine.

"Mum, mum!"

Hope slowly stepped away. "Dinner first," she said, though her voice was still shaking.

Ava grinned and followed her into the kitchen.

"Mum, this is Ava Stanford from next door," said Hope.

"She's my teacher," added Alice from where she was arranging books on the kitchen table.

"Of course," Caz said with a wide smile. "We've met, but not formally. It's nice to have you. Can I get you something to drink? I could open that nice wine you brought?"

"Just a glass of water would be lovely," Ava said.

"Ms. Stanford, I brought my new library books to show you," Alice said.

"Al, not now, it's almost dinner time," said Hope.

Ava smiled. "There's always time for reading," she said. "Isn't that right, Alice? Why don't you come over here and we'll be out of the way and you can show me your books?"

Hope watched as Alice skipped over to the armchair in the corner of the kitchen and Ava sat down with Alice by her knee. Ava's red-gold head bent down next to Alice's dark curls as they both peered at the book that Alice was showing, Ava rapt with interest so that Hope bit her lip.

This is what it was supposed to be like, she thought. Comfortable. Home-y. Safe and warm.

The oven dinged and she rescued the garlic bread and Caz leaned in and gave her a nudge.

"What?"

"Nothing," Caz whispered. "Just well done, that's all."

"Well done?"

"A date that can connect with your child, well, a single parent can't ask for more than that, can they?"

"It is her teacher, mum."

"Yeah, but still," said Caz. "Look at the two of them."

But Hope didn't need to. The picture of Ava and Alice in the armchair was seared into her brain.

"WELL, THE PETITION is filed with the council," Hope said. "I don't know how much difference it's going to make, but I'm pretty sure every parent signed it."

They were sitting around the dinner table, empty plates in front of them. Alice had been dispatched off to take her bath and brush her teeth with promises that she could come down to say goodnight later.

"They'll take it into consideration, I'm sure," said Caz.

"Yeah, but do you think that the other two schools haven't done exactly the same thing?" Hope said. "I mean, none of us want to close."

"Is it common to close schools?" asked Ava, toying with her water glass.

Hope shrugged. "Getting more so, I'd say. The problem is that all of us little towns and villages have always had our own schools. Then a fair few years ago, the government decided that education needed to be standardized and equalized, so we all got the same basics wherever we went, state or public."

"State or public?" asked Ava.

Caz laughed. "Over here, state means public and public means private."

"Obviously," Ava said.

"Anyway, that meant that the smaller schools couldn't very well teach older kids, since they needed science labs and the likes. So secondary education moved more toward larger schools, having our kids bussed into towns for school. The primary kids stayed though."

"Until recently," cut in Caz. "Now it's all about cost-cutting. People are having fewer kids, school sizes are shrinking, and it's not economical to keep the small schools open, so they merge them."

"It seems a pity," said Ava. "I've got to say, I've vastly enjoyed teaching twelve children as opposed to the thirty that I've normally got. It's easier to give everyone attention, the kids obviously profit from it."

"It's all about money though, nowadays," said Caz.

Hope nodded in agreement. "And unfortunately, there's not much we can do. If we were a richer town we could perhaps get sponsors and become a kind of charter school, but that won't work here. We'll just have to wait and see, I suppose."

"What do you think our chances are?" asked Ava.

Hope smiled as she noticed how Ava used the word 'our'. She was shrugging as Ava's phone started to ring.

Ava dug into her pocket, apologizing, looked at the screen and pulled a face. "I'm really sorry," she began.

"Oh, take it, take it," said Hope, standing up. "I'll get started on the cleaning up. Go out into the living room if you like."

Ava went, phone already at her ear, and Caz and Hope began scraping plates.

"I like her," said Caz.

"You do?" Hope asked. "You haven't grilled her or anything. I'd have thought you'd have given her the third degree by now. Maybe the fourth and fifth as well."

"Don't be cheeky. No, I do like her. She's honest and genuine, you can't ask for much more in a person than that. She's clever too, and Alice likes her. I'd say you're onto a winner."

Hope's heart grew another size. She was an adult and definitely didn't need her mother's approval. But she was glad to have it anyway.

Ava came back into the kitchen and Hope turned to see that she was pale. "What?" she asked.

"That was Stan Gardener," Ava said.

"Who?"

"From the school that wants to hire me," explained Ava. "Um, there's a problem."

"What kind of problem?"

"The job's been moved up. They need me starting from January."

"But you're supposed to be working here in January," Hope said, stating the obvious but unable to think any further ahead than that.

"If the school doesn't close down for good," said Ava.

"Then... then you want to leave?" Hope asked, stuttering over the question.

But Ava didn't answer.

In the doorway, Alice, dressed in her pink and yellow pajamas, began to cry.

CHAPTER TWENTY EIGHT

It had hardly been ideal. And in her defense, Ava truly hadn't meant to blurt out what she'd said in front of Alice. Even she wasn't that heartless.

But Hope had looked askance and Ava had been in shock, and the words had just come tumbling out.

She hadn't even answered Hope's question.

Maybe because she didn't know the answer yet.

Hope had asked if she wanted to leave and Ava had stood there with her mouth open long enough that Hope was the first to break eye contact. Long enough that she saw the shadow of disappointment, of hurt, pass across Hope's face and her first instinct had been to yell that she'd stay, of course she'd stay.

Because hurting Hope was the last thing she wanted to do.

Except she hadn't said anything because Alice had been crying and Hope's attention had turned to her daughter and in that quick second Ava had had a chance to gather herself just enough to stop herself relying on her instincts.

Trusting was one thing. She'd decided to trust Hope and taken the risk and she was glad that she had. But the whole rest of her life?

How was she supposed to decide the course of her life on a dime like that?

So Hope had gone to Alice and picked her up and Caz had stared from one to the other and Ava had swallowed and straightened her spine and said "it's late, I should be leaving."

And no one had stopped her.

So she'd walked out of the little cottage, away from the cozy dinner table, down the little garden path and into her own, cold, practically empty house.

At which point she'd panicked and tried to call Quinn about three hundred times and then taken herself to bed. Which didn't help because the dark just gave her more time to think. More time to worry, to weigh options, to try to solve the impossible.

So the lights had gone on again and in between randomly dialing Quinn's number and attempting to read a book and remembering the smell of Hope's body and the touch of her skin, Ava came to absolutely no decision at all.

THE SUN ROSE later than she'd thought, the sky orange and red, the air cold and misty for the first time since she'd arrived. She shuddered under her comforter and then figured she might as well get out of bed since she had nothing else to look forward to except going back to bed.

She made herself tea in the freezing cold kitchen and watched as Rosie the cat balanced expertly on the back fence, strolling without looking, walking the tightrope and making it look easy.

She made it until half past nine, at which point she'd done the dishes, vacuumed, dusted, and marked what little homework there was to mark. Without a hundred essays to grade a week she found that she had more free time on her hands, one of the downsides or benefits to teaching younger kids, depending which way you felt about it.

So she put on her coat, wrapped a scarf around her neck, and let herself out of the front door, praying that she wasn't about to run into Hope.

Walking into town, leaves crunched under her feet and she could smell burning. She didn't know where she was headed until she was already pushing open the door to the bookstore.

"Oh, thank God it's you."

If she'd have been in her right mind, and a little faster on her feet, Ava would have registered the screaming child and run before opening the door. But it was too late now. Mila was standing in the middle of the floor, a yelling child on her hip and a harried look on her face.

"Here," said Mila before Ava could do a thing, and shoved the child into Ava's arms. "Hold her for a second, I'll be right back."

Then Ava was standing alone holding a crying infant and panicking more than just a little. The cries were piercing and loud and Ava had a headache after not sleeping all night and her patience were thinner than a Kleenex.

She looked at the child's red, sweating face.

"Stop!"

In an instant there was silence.

The child stared up at her with watery blue eyes and Ava stared right on back.

"That's better," she said, more quietly. "Honestly, if you think you have something to cry about, you really should stop this process of growing up right now. It doesn't exactly get easier, you know? I wish being hungry was the extent of my issues."

The child's mouth smacked and a bubble of snot appeared in its nose.

"Oh, really," said Ava, using one hand to pull a tissue out of her pocket and swiping it around the child's face. "You can't go around in public looking like that."

The child chortled as Ava screwed the tissue up and then, failing to find a waste paper basket, laid it gently on the counter.

"I suppose things do get better in some ways," she went on, not wanting to discourage the child from growing entirely. "I mean, language proves an effective tool once you can use it properly. Then there's wine, that's quite nice too."

"Oh, dear Jesus," Mila said, bustling back in with a baby bottle in her hand. "For a minute there I thought you'd suffocated her she was so quiet."

"And yet you didn't hurry back," said Ava, arching an eyebrow.

"I was busting for a pee and I needed to get the bottle out of the warmer," Mila said, retrieving her daughter and taking her to an armchair next to the counter. "Now, what can I do you for?"

Ava shrugged. "I... I have no idea."

Mila put the bottle into her daughter's mouth. "Well, as long as Ag's got a bottle she'll be quiet and I'll have time to talk." She sniffed. "Assuming you wanted to talk, that is?"

Ava shrugged again. "I mean..." She let out a long, shuddering breath. Mila was, strangely, as close as she got to a friend on this side of the Atlantic. Or at least someone who wasn't Hope.

"Jesus, you sound dead miserable," Mila said. "Come on now, tell your Auntie Mila all about it."

So, out of other options, Ava did. "I've been offered a new job. In the States."

"Sounds good."

"Except I'll be starting in January."

"Ah."

"But then Whitebridge Primary might be closing anyway."

Mila's mouth dropped open. "The school might be closing?"

Ava blushed. "Oh God, was that supposed to be a secret, I had no idea."

Mila laughed. "Nah, just messing with you. The whole town knows, we're all up in arms about it, don't you worry. But I see your problem. Well, actually, maybe I don't. I mean, you take the new job, don't you? You don't turn down a sure thing for another six months in a school that you planned to leave at the end of June anyway. So in the long run, I guess it doesn't matter that you leave early, or if the school closes or not. At least not to you."

Ava bit her lip.

"Unless," Mila said. "Unless there were some other reason to stay. Or to go, I suppose."

Ava sighed and closed her eyes and Mila laughed again. "So, things went further than you'd thought with Hope Perkins, did they? She's a persuasive girl, that one. Got her head screwed on straight too. Couldn't think of a better catch."

"What about if you're not sure whether you're fishing or not?" asked Ava.

Mila pursed her lips. "That puts a different light on things then, doesn't it?"

Ava leaned against the counter. She'd already started, so she might as well be honest. "I like her, I truly do. But there's more to consider than that, isn't there?"

"Not least that Hope has a family," Mila said. "A child."

"Which means committing to not just Hope but Alice as well."

Mila cuddled her daughter closer to her. "Can't say that I've been in your position," she said. "But I do know that I'd forgive my husband most things, but I'd never forgive him hurting Ag. Not that he would, but do you see where I'm going with this?"

"Hurting Alice would be unforgivable," Ava said. "The problem is, I think maybe I already have. I spilled the news about the job in front of her, I didn't know she was there. Now she knows her teacher's leaving and she seemed destroyed by the news. Imagine how she'd feel if she thought her mother's, um, whatever-I'm-supposed to be was leaving. She's as defensive of Hope as Hope is of her."

Ag gurgled and Mila tipped the bottle a little more. "It all comes back to what you want," she said. "It doesn't get much simpler than that. You, Ava Stanford, need to decide just what you want and go for it."

"But what if what I want and what's sensible aren't the same thing?" argued Ava. "What if I derail my whole life for the wrong reason?"

"Then you'll have made a mistake. Life's full of them, unfortunately."

Ava closed her eyes again. "I can't base my whole future on one night."

"Why not?" Mila asked. She looked down at her daughter. "We're all based on one night in the end, aren't we?" She smirked. "Well, in Ag's case it was one rainy afternoon, but my point stands."

"Why not?" Ava said. She looked out of the shop window at

the cool morning outside.

Whitebridge was a nice place, a place she'd almost belonged for a little while. But she had to try to build her life again, she had to make something to replace what she'd lost. Expecting Hope to help her do that was unfair. Expecting Hope to risk herself and her daughter on someone who, in the end, would probably have to leave anyway, was unfair.

"Why not?" she said again. "Because we don't always make decisions for ourselves, do we?"

"Don't we?" Mila asked. "You could've fooled me. We're not all as self-sacrificing as you might think, you know."

But Ava already knew what she needed to do. Calling a halt to whatever this was between her and Hope was best for everyone. Stop things before they got too serious, before anyone, including Alice, could get more hurt.

She needed to take the job and prepare to leave. It was the best thing for everyone.

CHAPTER TWENTY NINE

Alice tucked her hair behind her ear and concentrated on coloring in her book. Hope kept half an eye on her as she washed up the breakfast things.

"Alright," Caz said. "I'm off to get in the shower and then it's a busy day for me up at the hospital. You two have a good day at school."

She stood up and Hope smiled at her, but Alice just frowned over her coloring book. "What do you say to gran, Al?" Hope prompted.

"Bye, gran," Alice said dully.

Caz moved to sit down again and hash this out, but Hope shook her head. Caz shrugged and went off up the stairs to get ready for her day. Hope dried her hands on a tea towel and then pulled out a chair to sit opposite her daughter.

"Everything okay, Al?"

"Mmm." Alice colored in the wing of a dragon bright purple.

"You know, you can tell me if something's not okay," Hope said. "Like, if something's making you sad, or angry, or whatever."

"Mmm-hmm." A collection of scales became red.

"You were a bit rude to gran a minute ago," Hope tried. "We don't do that, do we? Taking out our feelings on someone else, that's not really fair."

"'kay."

Hope sighed. Okay, Alice had had a melt-down after Ava had left. Not that that was unexpected. She was all of six years old and had already dealt with her father leaving and a move of house. She didn't do well with upheaval, with things changing. It was, Hope supposed, a natural reaction in a kid with divorced parents. One that unfortunately, she couldn't do much about.

But they'd talked things through and Hope had done her best to explain to Alice that Ava had a life and a home of her own to go back to. That the plan had never been that Ava should stay. And in the end, she'd thought that Alice had gotten the picture.

She'd been quiet, but that was okay. She might be only six, but she had the right to her own feelings. She had the right to be sad.

Hope had spent most of Sunday trying to cheer her up, putting on DVDs and getting ice cream. And Alice had laughed and talked, but still hadn't quite been herself. It had been a shock, Hope had told herself. A shock that it would take her a little while to get over.

"Are you almost ready for school?"

Alice said nothing, scrubbing a blue pencil into the page so hard that the paper ripped slightly.

A shock. It shouldn't have been. After all, Hope had known going into this that Ava would leave eventually. Maybe that had even been a part of the attraction, knowing that things couldn't get too serious.

So why was she shocked? Why did she feel like something was crumbling away beneath her, like a wave was sweeping her feet out from under her?

That wasn't how things were supposed to be.

She was angry, she reminded herself. Angry that Ava had just spilled the news like that in front of Alice, angry that Ava could be so careless of a child, so clueless that she'd just up-end Alice's world without thought.

"I said, are you ready for school?"

Alice grunted and changed her pencil for a new, sharper one.

"Alice Perkins, I asked you a question and I expect an answer," Hope said sharply.

"Not going."

Hope was already in strict mode, already getting herself riled up for a fight with her daughter, but Alice's words took the wind out of her sails. "What?"

"I'm not going," Alice said, looking up now defiant and angry.

"Why on earth not?" was all Hope could think to ask. No mention of the fact that there was no choice, that they both had to go. No mention of the fact that actually, come to think of it, Hope would also quite like to curl back up in bed and not have to go, not have to face Ava.

Alice sniffed. "You could tell her to stay."

"What?"

Alice took a deep breath and said louder: "You could ask her to stay. Tell her to stay."

"Who?" asked Hope, knowing full well who Alice was talking about.

"Ms. Stanford. You could tell her to stay here."

Hope let out a breath. "Love, I can't do that."

"But you like her," said Alice. "I know you do. And she likes you too. I thought you were friends. Best friends. Even maybe special friends. You know, like daddy and 'Melia."

"Special friends?" Hope spluttered. "Why would you say that?"

Alice looked at her with shrewd brown eyes. "Because you smile at her the same as 'Melia smiles at daddy and 'Melia said to me that she loves daddy. She said she loves me too if I want. But if I don't want then it's okay."

Hope took this in, sitting back in her kitchen chair like she'd been gut-punched. "Alice," she said eventually. "Al. We can't, I can't... Things are complicated."

"Grown ups always say that when they don't want to explain."

"Because some things are difficult to explain," said Hope as patiently as she could. Time was ticking. They needed to leave.

Alice bent over her coloring again, tongue sticking out of the corner of her mouth in concentration.

"Al, we need to get ready to go."

Alice sighed heavily and Hope dearly wished that she could give in. She wished they both could give in and go back to bed.

One of the advantages of having a child though was that there was no time to wallow, no time to be self-indulgent, no time to think of what could have been. Not that it didn't hurt. It hurt so bad that Hope was still reeling from it. Reeling because she hadn't expected it to hurt so badly, hadn't planned on falling so far so fast.

"You could ask Ms. Stanford to stay if you wanted to," Alice said stubbornly.

She couldn't though, could she? How do you ask someone to give up everything for you?

More than that though, how do you recover from asking someone to give up everything for you only to have them refuse?

When Noah had walked out, Hope had been so numb that nothing had hurt for days. She'd assumed that because the love was gone, the pain was less. Then one morning, she'd dropped Alice off at her mother's, gone home, sat at the kitchen table and started to cry.

Started to cry and hadn't stopped until the sky was already dark.

Cried with the sheer weight of it, the crushing failure of it all, cried for the dreams that were ending and the ones that would never get a start. Cried because the pain caught up with her.

And if that happened after Noah, who she knew she had fallen out of love with, how much would it hurt after someone she was falling *in* love with?

She couldn't take that chance. Couldn't risk losing herself to that sadness. Couldn't risk her daughter's feelings as well as her own. No, she needed to take a page out of Ava's book. She needed to build a wall, defend herself, protect herself and her daughter.

"If we don't leave right now, we're going to be late," she said.

Alice bit her lip. She hated being late.

"And who knows what you might miss?" Hope said. "This is

the last week of insects. You might miss a quiz or some painting. You might miss the next part of James and the Giant Peach."

Alice put down her pencil. "Do you think?"

Hope nodded.

With a sigh, Alice got down off her chair and went to get her school bag. "I like insects," she said.

"I know," said Hope, relieved more than anything that she didn't need to fight with Alice.

"I don't understand though," Alice said as she struggled into her coat. "Insects have hard outsides."

"Called?" prompted Hope, getting her own jacket.

"Carapaces," Alice said dutifully. "They're all hard so that their squishy insides are safe. But then, insects get squished anyway, don't they?"

Hope picked up her handbag. "I suppose."

"So why do they have hard outsides then?" pressed Alice.

"I really don't know," said Hope, catching a glance of the time again. "You can ask Ms. Stanford, maybe she'll know."

"I think it's just to make them feel better. So they don't think so much about being squished," Alice said as Hope ushered her toward the door. "Like when I fall over and you kiss me better."

"What?" Hope asked, distracted now at the thought of not only being late but also having to see Ava again.

"It doesn't work," Alice clarified. "I know that your kisses aren't magic. I'm six now. I'm not a baby. But they make me feel better anyway. Just in my head."

"Right." She found her house keys.

"So the insects have hard outsides, carapaces, to make them feel better even if they don't work in the end." Alice sighed. "It's still silly though, isn't it? I'm glad people don't have shells."

"You are?" Hope asked, practically pushing her out of the front door.

"Yes," said Alice. "They'd be difficult to cuddle, wouldn't they?"

Hope took a deep breath of cool morning air and wondered if it was too early for a drink. "I suppose," she said. "Are we ready to go?"

Alice nodded.

Hope narrowed her eyes, then turned to open the front door again, grabbing Alice's backpack from inside, closing the door, and handing the bag to her child. "Now you're ready."

Alice danced off, pulling her bag on as she went and Hope followed.

A hard shell like an insect. Well, at least it would stop Ava cuddling her, she supposed. Though, if what Alice said was true, she'd end up getting squished anyway. So maybe, in the end, it was better that Ava was going away. That way she wouldn't have to worry about being squished. That way she could keep her hard shell intact.

CHAPTER THIRTY

It helped, Ava found, if she didn't look at Hope. Which was easier than one might imagine, given that twelve six-year-olds demanded pretty much constant supervision.

That didn't mean that she never looked at Hope. Of course she did. During the course of the day she hadn't been able to help it. Like picking at a scab or pushing at a wobbly tooth. It was a bitter-sweet pain that she was in danger of becoming addicted to.

The sight of Hope bent over a child's desk, the sight of her cross-legged on the reading carpet, the sight of her smiling at her daughter.

Looking wasn't the problem. Looking hurt, but she could deal with that.

More of a problem was the fact that she couldn't touch Hope. Couldn't brush a hand against her leg, couldn't pat her arm. It was more of a problem that she had to be there, act normal. The kids were like sharks, they'd scent something wrong a mile away.

At least Alice had kept things quiet. Or Ava assumed she had, since there hadn't been a classroom revolution yet.

"Take the football back to the football area," she barked as she rounded the corner of the playground and almost tripped over the ball.

"Yes miss, sorry miss," said an older boy, laughing as she

picked the ball up.

She was on playground duty, something she'd never have done in the States, but that she strangely enjoyed here. A little time to herself, as long as she kept her eyes wide open, but there was rarely any trouble. Whitebridge Primary was small enough that everyone knew each other and for the most part, the older kids kept an eye on the younger ones.

She was approaching the school gate, where she'd left a mug of coffee balanced on the wall, when Jake Lowell strode through it.

"Afternoon, Ms. Stanford," he said.

"Afternoon. Been taking a sneaky long lunch?"

He smiled at her and Ava thought that he looked tired. "I wish. Been at the council meeting."

"Ah."

"Ah, yes," said Lowell. "They got the parent's petition."

"And?"

He shrugged. "And now we wait and see. There's nothing that can be done."

"Fingers crossed then."

"Fingers crossed," agreed Jake.

"Ms. Stanford, what's a petition?"

Hope looked down to see Alice Perkins looking up at her with big dark eyes, Clara Buxton right next to her.

"I think I'll leave that one to you," Lowell said to Ava as he walked off toward his office.

"Well," Ava said, considering this carefully. "Let's say that you want to stay in the classroom but everyone else wants to go out and play."

"Okay," said Alice.

"I wouldn't want to stay inside," Clara put in.

"Hush," Alice said. She was much better at dealing with hypotheticals than the very concrete Clara.

"It wouldn't be very fair if you made everyone stay inside with you," Ava went on, talking directly to Alice. "But how do you know what other people want?"

"You ask them," Alice said immediately.

"Well, a petition is a way of showing that other people support your idea," Ava said. "So if you want to stay inside you write on a piece of paper that staying inside is a good idea. Then you ask people to sign their names on your paper. When you've asked as many people as you can, you take your petition to someone in charge, like a president or a prime minister or a teacher, and show them that you're not the only person that wants to stay inside. Lots of other people want to stay inside too."

Alice looked thoughtful.

"It's like if I want pizza for dinner," Clara said. "It's better if I get my brothers to ask for pizza too, that way my mum gives us pizza. If it's just me and they want hamburgers then I don't get pizza."

"Power in numbers," Ava agreed. "The more agreement you have, the more likely you are to get what you want."

Alice nodded in understanding.

"Off you go," said Ava. "Break time's nearly over."

Alice and Clara walked away, heads bent together in earnest discussion and Ava smiled as she watched them.

She liked Alice, she truly did. She liked her and she didn't want to hurt her.

A few months ago she'd never have considered having a child in her life. Now she was putting a child's needs and wants above her own.

She supposed that she had changed, which meant that she'd accomplished what she'd come over here for. At least partly.

The big school bell rang and the children began to run toward the school doors.

"Walk, don't run," Ava said, and hurried after them to ensure that no one got hurt in the crush to get back to class.

THE CHILDREN FILTERED out of the classroom and Ava and Hope were alone.

She'd been dreading this moment, truthfully. Dreading it but knowing that it had to happen.

"We need to make a decision about the nativity play," Hope said, putting chairs on desks.

"Right," said Ava, who'd forgotten all about it. "Er, do you think it's a good idea?"

Hope shrugged. "Traditionally it's our class that does the nativity in the evening before the older children do their carol concert. The younger infants do one in the early afternoon. But there's no reason we have to if you're uncomfortable with it."

"It's not that I'm uncomfortable, I just don't know if it's appropriate."

Hope perched on the edge of a desk and Ava tried very hard not to look at her and failed miserably. "We have a diverse school. But we celebrate as many holidays as we can. Diwali, Hannukah, you name it, we'll include it and teach our kids as much as possible about as many people as possible. I'm not sure I see why Christmas should be any different."

"Fair point," Ava said. She nodded. "Alright then, we'll do a nativity. Are there costumes? Sets?"

"Even a script," said Hope. "I'll get everything together and you can look things over and then we'll tell the kids about it at the end of the week."

"Sure."

Hope hesitated. "Assuming that you'll still be here for the end of term, that is?"

Outside there was the noise of children running and playing, the sound of crisp leaves crunching underfoot. But inside, the classroom was quiet.

"I'm sorry," Ava said.

"For what?" asked Hope. "You never promised me anything. We knew what we were doing. We decided not to think about the future, and so we pay the price for that. You have nothing to be sorry for."

"And yet I feel like I do," Ava confessed. She came around the table so that she was opposite Hope, so that she had to put her hands behind her back to stop herself reaching out to touch her.

So that she had to admit to herself that she very much wanted to touch her.

"It's... fine." Hope bit her lip. "Well, it's not fine. But you know what I mean. We're adults. We know how these things go."

"We do," Ava allowed. "I'm sorry it had to end sooner than we imagined." Because after all, they'd barely had anything at all.

"I'm sorry that you had to tell Alice like that. She was devastated."

Which reinforced what Mila had said. Ava nodded. "I'm sorry too. I shouldn't have blurted it out, I should have been more careful."

Hope looked down at the ground and Ava wasn't sure she'd ever seen her look so beautiful.

"Thank you."

"For what?" Hope asked.

Ava laughed a little. "I would say for giving me hope, but that doesn't sound quite right. I do mean it though."

"Do you?"

"I do. I came here thinking... I don't know what. Thinking I was broken, knowing I was, but thinking that maybe I was unfixable. Maybe that I wouldn't have anything again. You... you showed me that I'm not quite unfixable. That maybe I can build something new one day."

"You're welcome," Hope said. She smiled a little too. "And thank you."

"For?"

Hope sighed. "For teaching me that maybe it's important that I have something of my own, that I don't turn into my mother, that Alice learns from me what a sensible relationship should be like. I don't... I don't want her thinking that I sacrificed everything for her."

"Even if you did?" Ava asked.

"I don't want her to carry that guilt. So thank you."

Ava blinked, her eyes feeling gritty and tired, her body feeling heavy. "I will be here."

"What?"

"For the end of term, of course I'll be here," Ava said. "I've got no intention of running out and leaving the school in the lurch. I'll stay until the end of term and then leave straight after."

"Right."

"Which means…" Ava swallowed. "I mean, that means you and I have a few weeks together. Not together-together, but—"

"I know what you mean," Hope interrupted. "And it won't be a problem."

"Friends?" asked Ava, not at all sure that this wasn't going to be a problem. Not at all sure that she could stop herself kissing Hope in the next five minutes, let alone the next five weeks.

"Friends," Hope said. "And co-directors."

"Ah, I see you have your heart set on next year's Oscars," Ava said. "Well, I'd better see that nativity script before we make any decisions."

"I'll dig it out for you," Hope promised.

"You know, I was thinking about Alice for the role of Mary."

"Were you?"

"Mmm," Ava said. "But actually, I think she's more suited to being a Wise Man. Well, Wise Woman, I suppose."

Hope laughed. "I see your point." She stood up, went to the cupboard to get her coat and bag. "We can talk about casting tomorrow, I'll find the script and you can read it at lunch."

"Sounds like a plan," said Ava.

Hope pulled on her coat. "Alright then. Well, good night, I suppose. I'll see you tomorrow."

"Bye."

Ava watched her leave, heart aching, thinking that one day the leaving would be for real. One day she wouldn't have the promise of seeing Hope in the morning. One day that she needed to prepare herself for, because leaving Hope was going to be a lot more difficult than she'd planned.

CHAPTER THIRTY ONE

Hope looked out of the kitchen window, hands soapy with dishwater. She was tired. Bone-achingly, terribly tired. She was also no fool and knew damn well that she was depressed and miserable.

Like it or not, her feelings for Ava were stronger than she'd realized, and now, well, now things were broken.

As she watched, she saw Rosie jump up over the fence and stride confidently across the garden. She was about to grab some cat food when she saw something else. Another cat hopped up onto the fence then gingerly dropped down onto the lawn, following Rosie at a distance.

Rosie paused, the other cat caught up, rubbed its face against Rosie's, then the two continued onward toward the back door. The cat flap opened, Rosie slipped through, followed closely by the other cat.

Hope just stood and watched, she had no clue what she was supposed to do about this interloper. Rosie yawled impatiently, looking up at Hope, and the male cat, because it was very clearly a male cat, stood behind her.

With a sigh, Hope got two bowls from the cupboard and filled both of them.

"What's this?" Caz asked, coming into the kitchen.

"Looks like Rosie's got a boyfriend."

"We have two cats?"

"What am I supposed to do? I'm not going to throw him out into the garden, am I?"

Caz sniffed. "Suppose not." She eyed her daughter. "And now you're getting all upset because the cat has a love interest and you don't, I suppose?"

Hope rolled her eyes even though deep in her mind that was exactly what she'd been thinking. "Of course not."

Caz sat down at the kitchen table. "You are moping though."

Hope took a seat opposite her. There was no point lying. Caz knew her better than anyone in the world, and she'd ferret out the truth eventually. "Yes, fine, I'm moping."

"Sometimes things don't work out," said Caz.

"I know that, I'm not a child. I'm a divorced woman, for God's sake." Hope rubbed at her tired eyes. "It's just... I don't know. I feel like there's more to this, that this isn't the way it's supposed to go."

"Let me ask you this," Caz said, leaning forward. "What would make you happy?"

"Honestly?"

"If you lie to me, Hope Perkins, I'll have your guts for garters. Of course honestly."

"More time to figure this out. More time to consider the possibilities." Hope bit her lip. No, more honest than that. "If Ava stayed." Once the words were out there, they seemed like the only possible truth. She wanted Ava to stay, no matter how selfish that might be.

"And can't she?"

"How?" Hope asked. "And how could I ask her to? You don't just ask someone to up-end their life for you, just on a whim."

"Is this a whim?"

"No," Hope said immediately.

"Well then," said Caz. "Besides, we ask people to up-end their lives for us all the time. We ask people to marry us, to have children with us, we ask people if we can move in with them and bring our child and live all together."

"Okay, okay, I get your point. But that's different."

"Is it?" asked Caz. "Is it really? Because I feel like you might be cutting off your nose to spite your face here. Have you asked her to stay? Or even floated the possibility that you'd like her to stay?"

"No, of course not," Hope said. "I don't want to put this on her, that's unfair."

"Why do you want her to stay?"

Hope looked into her mother's kind, brown eyes and shrugged. "No reason," she said, still determined to be honest. "Just… My life is better with her in it, that's all. As irritating and annoying as she can be, I look forward to seeing her in the morning. Which is why I can't ask her to stay, because what kind of reason is that?"

"The best one," Caz said quietly. "What more can you ask of life than that? To be with someone that you look forward to waking up next to? Someone whose very face makes you want to be alive? You know what we call that? A reason for living, Hope. And if Ava gives you a reason for living, well, you've got it worse than even I suspected."

Rosie jumped up onto the kitchen table, her meal finished. She purred and rubbed her face against Hope's hand. Her boyfriend jumped up too, sitting quietly on the corner of the table, watching.

"It's no good, mum. I like her. I like her a lot, more even than I'd realized. But I can't ask her to stay here. Stay here for what? With the school maybe closing it's not as though she'll have a hope of finding a job. She's better off going back to America."

Caz shook her head. "You're a fool to turn down a chance of happiness, Hope."

"I'm not turning it down. I just… I don't know how to get it. I don't know a fair and equal way of making everyone happy."

"Then find a way," said Caz, pushing her chair back. "Otherwise, you're going to be miserable." She stood up and went to the sink, picking up a tea towel to dry the dishes Hope had washed. "You coming to help here?"

Hope stood up and went back to the sink.

It was all very well her mother doling out advice. It was all very well being able to admit to herself that she liked Ava a lot. It was all very well saying she wanted Ava to stay. But she wasn't a child. She knew that life didn't always work out.

"If you want something, then you need to reach out and take it," Caz said softly. "She wouldn't be staying for nothing. She'd be staying for you. And you're worth it."

"You have to say that, you're my mum."

"I mean it," said Caz. "The other stuff, it's just... details. There are other jobs in the world, other places than Whitebridge, you know?"

And a glimmer of light appeared in Hope's mind.

There were other places, weren't there? And other jobs too.

* * *

"You fell in love."

The way Quinn said it made it sound like an accusation.

"I did not," Ava said to the screen.

"Bullshit," said Quinn. "Ava Stanford, you actually did it. You learned how to love again. I'll be damned. You know, I was doubtful about this whole disappearing off to England to change yourself thing, but I think it's worked."

"I'm not in love," Ava tried again.

"Are you not?" Quinn asked. "Because it sounds a lot like you are."

"No, I'm not. I just... It's just..."

"Just what?"

Ava sighed. "Just... Leaving is harder than I expected, that's all."

Quinn mimicked her sigh. "Because you're in love."

"I am not."

Quinn rolled her eyes. "Alright then, little miss 'I'm not in love,' why are you so miserable about leaving a woman you've barely even kissed then?"

"We've done more than that," Ava said, slightly smugly. Then she remembered the smell of Hope's body and her cheeks flushed.

"You what? You've… you two have… Ava!" Quinn looked gratifyingly shocked.

"I'm an adult."

"You left here a heartbroken adult. Apparently, we're feeling better."

"Maybe," said Ava. She thought about the way Hope made her feel, about the way she looked forward to seeing her, the way she made her smile. "But that doesn't change how things are."

"Does it not?" asked Quinn. "Because from where I'm sitting, this Hope has changed your life for the better and you're about to walk away from that. Not that I don't want you home, but, well, I can see how there might be other priorities here."

Ava shook her head. "It's unrealistic."

Quinn snorted. "Fuck realism."

"Quinn!"

"What? Can I remind you what your life was like before? You slept on my couch. You barely moved to go to work. You walked around in a haze of pain and heart-break all day and cried yourself to sleep at night. Are you going to argue that there hasn't been an improvement?"

"No."

"You found the balm, the magic potion that makes things better, that helps you heal. But you're willing to walk away from it?"

Ava closed her eyes. "Isn't it easier that way?" she said. "I know what life was like before, Q. I was living it." She opened her eyes. "And what if it happens again? What if this doesn't work out and I end up back where I started and…" She couldn't finish the sentence.

Quinn was quiet for a moment, letting her gather herself. "That's life," she said finally.

"That's life? That's your come-back to that?"

Quinn shrugged. "I wish it was better, but that's what I've got. That's life, Ave. It beats you down, leaves you bruised and bleeding on the sidewalk, and you pick yourself up, dust off the dirt, and keep on walking. That's what we do, all of us, every day, and you're no different. Because if you're so afraid of falling, you'll never walk. And if you don't walk, well, you'll never get anywhere, will you?"

Ava bit her lip and said nothing. There was nothing to say.

"Ava, my love, she's fixed you somehow. She's bandaged your wounds and got you back on your feet. And if you're not willing to take risks to be with her then you don't deserve her, it's that simple."

"Take risks to stay with a woman that I barely know, a woman I've barely kissed in your words?"

"When you know, you know," Quinn said. "And you know. I've known you long enough to know that you're no fool, Ava Stanford. If you know one thing, it's your own mind. You might be doubting your judgment a little, and that's understandable after everything you've been through, but I, for one, don't doubt you in the slightest."

"Q, I can't... How? What am I supposed to do? I can't just sit around here pining after a woman. I'll have no job soon enough and then I'll run out of money, and..." She trailed off.

"So? You'd better get things figured out before you end up living under a bridge," Quinn said sweetly. "But I do know that if you don't take this risk, Ava, you're going to regret it. What does coming back here give you? What are you trying to re-claim? You can't get your old life back and I don't think you really want it."

Ava swallowed. It was true. She hadn't thought of Serena's face in days, maybe longer.

"Think about it," Quinn said. "And lunch break's over and I've got to go. Call me later if you need me?"

Ava nodded and Quinn's face disappeared from the screen.

Maybe she was right. Maybe she did need to take some risks. The problem was she was absolutely terrified.

CHAPTER THIRTY TWO

"Mu-um, Robbie looks sad."

Hope pushed her computer away. "You'd look sad too if you were being castrated."

"What's castrated?" Alice asked, coming into the kitchen.

Hope couldn't help herself. "I think that's a Ms. Stanford question," she said. "And I need to get going to the vet. You're staying here with gran, alright?"

Alice nodded, her attention on Hope's computer.

"Nope, no computer games. Gran's going to take you to the park."

"O-kay," Alice said. She sniffed. "You should close your web browser if you're not using it."

"Where—" started Hope, but then she gave up. Alice was picking things up at a rate of knots, and she had no idea where she was getting computer lessons from. Maybe her father.

"And anyway, you're not a teacher, silly mummy. You're looking at the wrong page."

Hope glanced over then quickly pulled her laptop over and minimized the page. Teaching jobs. There were more of them than you'd think. And all over the place too. Not that she was planning on getting Ava another job or anything. She was just looking at possibilities. Looking and hoping as time was slowly running out.

Two weeks until the Christmas concert. Two weeks until the nativity play and the end of term and then...

There was the sound of yowling from the hallway. "I'd better go," said Hope.

She pulled on her coat and picked up the cat carrier. Alice had insisted on the name Robbie, saying it went well with Rosie. Hope had insisted that the animal be fixed. The last thing she needed was even more cats. Despite the signs they'd posted around town, it looked like Robbie was here to stay.

"I'm off," she shouted to her mother and Alice. And she went out to the car with a very irate cat in tow.

IT WASN'T THAT she didn't want to ask Ava to stay, it was that she couldn't. And with all the good will and advice in the world, she really couldn't come up with a workable plan that was a compromise, that didn't involve somebody giving up too much.

Then there was the fact that in the last three weeks Ava had barely looked at her, let alone touched her or kissed her or anything else.

Not that she wanted that.

No, strike that. She very much wanted that. But she understood that Ava was trying to create a distance, trying to make things easier in the long run. She should be grateful that Ava was strong enough to do that, because there were at least fifty times when Hope would happily have thrown herself into Ava's arms.

It turned out that planning someone else's life for them was more difficult than she'd thought. She'd had the idea that perhaps she could find other possibilities, other reasons for Ava to stay. In the end, all she'd done was confuse herself and chase down empty leads.

"Come back at around half four," the friendly vet receptionist said. "He'll be done by then and you can take him home. We'll ring if there's any change, but you shouldn't worry, we do this all the time and it's a perfectly safe operation."

"Thanks," said Hope, who hadn't considered that the operation would be anything but safe until the receptionist mentioned it.

"No problem," grinned the receptionist cheerfully.

Hope pushed out of the glass doors and out into the cold autumn air. Autumn. Practically winter really. It was cold enough to snow now and the air had a crisp, clean scent to it that made Hope think of Christmas and home.

Whitebridge had always been home, something she was starting to consider as she walked toward the car.

The little town had been her whole life and she'd been perfectly content to stay there, perfectly content to have her little place in the patchwork of Whitebridge, to bring up her family here, to live out her days here.

But if she couldn't find reasons for Ava to stay, maybe she needed to find reasons for herself to leave.

"Hope!"

She sighed. Okay, yes, she did love living in town. But it was impossible to get any privacy, impossible to have a moment to herself. Knowing everyone meant everyone knew her, and, to be truthful, she wasn't entirely sure how much gossip there'd been about her and Ava.

"Hope!"

She turned around just as she reached the car, trying to figure out who was calling her, only to see Noah's familiar figure jogging down the street toward her. She groaned. She really wasn't in the mood for an argument today and that's what any discussion with her ex-husband was bound to lead to.

"Hope," he said, as he got closer. He was slightly out of breath, his cheeks pink with running and the cold.

"Noah."

"Got a minute?"

"Not really," said Hope. "I just dropped the cat off at the vet and I really need to get home."

"Oh no," he said, eyes widening. "There's nothing wrong with

Rosie, is there?"

"All is well with Rosie, more than well, which is sort of the problem. Robbie's the one in, he's getting fixed."

"Robbie? You got another cat?"

"Another cat got us," Hope said. She tucked her hands into her armpits to keep them warm. "What do you want?"

"Five minutes," said Noah.

"It was a minute before."

His chocolate brown eyes pleaded with her. "Come on, please Hope. I just want to talk. No arguments, I swear. I just saw you here and took my chance. There's always someone else around when I want to talk to you. Your mum, Amelia, Alice. I really do want to speak with you. Just you."

Hope sighed. "Fine," she said. "But get in the car, it's freezing and catching a cold is the last thing I need."

Noah smiled gratefully and opened the passenger side door as Hope went around to the driver's side.

"So?" said Hope, once the doors were closed and she was starting to warm up.

Noah sat back in his seat. "It's about Alice."

"Of course it is."

He looked at her. "It's just... Alice isn't a thing, she's not a possession, she's a person."

Hope stared at him incredulously. "Are you being serious? Do you really think—"

"Wait, wait." Noah took a deep breath. "I'm not explaining this properly."

"Well you'd better start doing a better job or I'm throwing you out and getting on with my day."

"Okay, okay. Alice... She's amazing. Truly amazing. She's funny and kind and smart." He looked at her again. "I'm not kidding myself that I had much to do with that. I know it was you. You're the one that spends the most time with her, you're the one she takes after."

"Flattery will get you nowhere," Hope said, thawing a little bit, both figuratively and literally.

Noah sighed. "It's just... It's like you've painted this beautiful picture but you won't let anyone look at it. I know you want to protect Alice, but you can't. She's a person. She deserves to be out in the world. The world deserves to have her. God knows there aren't enough kind and beautiful people in the world."

"Noah—"

"No, let me finish. I know that she's just a child. But I also know that she has to grow up and she can't be wrapped in cotton wool. I know that there's only so much we can do. Having said that, I do see your point." He cleared his throat.

"What point would that be?" Hope asked carefully.

"That perhaps she needs her mum a bit more than her dad right now."

"Meaning?"

"Meaning... I don't want to take this to court. I'm not going to get lawyers involved. If you say that Alice shouldn't spend half her time with me, then I'll accept that. For now. Not that I'll stop asking. I'll wait until she's seven and then ask again, and again when she's eight, and I'll keep on asking. But I'll also respect your judgment."

Hope felt stress leave her body, literally felt herself getting lighter. She hadn't realized just how much it had affected her that Noah wanted to create problems over custody. "Respect my judgment," she said, shaking her head. "I'm not sure that's always the best idea."

"Are you kidding?" asked Noah, looking surprised. "Hope, you're the best judge of character that I know, not to mention the most sensible person."

Hope raised an eyebrow at him. "And yet I chose a philandering husband."

"Philandering?"

"Sorry, do you not know what the word means?" Hope asked a little acidly.

"Of course I do," Noah said. "But I'm no philanderer. I never cheated on you Hope, not once. I'll admit that I knew Amelia before we split, I even knew that I was developing feelings for her. But I didn't speak to her about them, ask her out, or even have a full conversation with her until after you and I had split and gone through mediation. I swear to you."

Hope could tell from the look on his face that he was serious. "Really?" she asked, not wanting to believe him. She'd comforted herself for a long time with the idea that Noah was the bad guy, that he'd cheated and wronged her.

"Really," he said. "Amelia is a lovely person. I adore her and I won't hide her away. I think you might even like her if you gave her a chance. Alice adores her. But I absolutely had nothing to do with her until we were split up."

Hope breathed slowly and evenly.

"You can trust your judgment, Hope. Whatever it is that you're worried about, whatever decision it is that you're trying to make, you can trust yourself."

"Who says I'm trying to make a decision?" Hope asked, thinking again about the gossip potential of small towns.

Noah grinned at her. "I've known you a long time, Hope Perkins. I know when you're in the middle of a crisis. Whatever it is, whoever it is, that has you like this, well, if you like them then they must be worth it."

"They must be, mustn't they?" Hope said, smiling back at him. "After all, you were worth it."

And she meant it. Whatever had happened between them, Noah was still her first love, still the father of her child, and she wouldn't change that.

"Listen," she said. "I'm not promising anything and nothing's decided yet, but how would you feel about a change of circumstances. You might not love the idea of what I'm about to say, but it could mean that you have Alice for every school holiday..."

CHAPTER THIRTY THREE

Two sheep were fighting over a red lego brick, one wise man was crying whilst another was standing on top of a desk with a He-Man sword in hand, the virgin Mary had cut her own bangs the night before and Joseph had wet himself. Again.

Ava clapped her hands. "Enough!"

Twelve pairs of eyes swiveled to her.

"Everybody to the reading carpet," she said. "Now." Obediently the children trotted toward the carpet until Ava spotted the flaw in her instructions. "Not you, Daniel," she added to Joseph, whose white robe sported a yellow stain. "Go to the office."

"Yes, miss," Daniel said.

It was her own fault. As long as she stayed observant and watched out for wiggling she could catch Daniel before he had to go. Rehearsals for the nativity were driving her insane though. Put a kid in a costume and suddenly said kid thought he or she was invincible, invisible, and, in Ava's opinion, infuriating.

"Sit down, hands in laps, please," Ava said.

"Are we going to have story time?" asked Clara, her bangs slanted across her face in a way that made her look slightly cross-eyed.

"Because it's not really story time," added Alice, who had a package of frankincense tucked under one arm, a bag of gold coins circling her wrist, and a bottle of myrrh tucked in the cord of her robe.

"Why do you have all three gifts of the Magi?" Ava asked.

"What's a Magi?" piped up Nathan.

"It's a wise man, stupid," said Carter Edwards.

"Well why didn't she just say so?" asked Nathan with a sigh.

"Because Adesh and Sara can't be trusted with their presents," Alice explained.

Which was probably true, given that Sara was mopping her eyes and Adesh was currently ferreting a finger inside his nose, but that wasn't Alice's decision to make. As mature as Alice was, Ava sometimes worried that she was too mature. "Let's return the gifts to the appropriate Magi, shall we?"

Alice huffed but tossed the frankincense to Sara and then threw the myrrh at Adesh, neatly hitting him on the head, his finger so far up his nose that he didn't have time to extricate it to catch.

"Story time," Ava said firmly.

For the last thirty minutes of the school day, the children managed to sit quietly and listen to a chapter of Stig of the Dump. When the bell finally rang, Ava let out a sigh of relief. Not that the day was over yet, far from it.

"Remember, everybody needs to be back here at six o'clock sharp," she said. "That gives us plenty of time to get back in costume and get ready for the play. Understand?"

Twelve heads bobbed up and down, but Ava knew better than to trust a six-year-old's word. She'd had Hope send letters home to parents and knew that everyone would be more or less on time.

The children scattered and Ava was left alone. Hope had taken the last hour or two to stay in the school hall and set up chairs and decorations for the Christmas Concert.

Ava stayed on her chair and closed her eyes, letting the empty classroom echo around her.

It was almost her last day, almost the last time that she'd sit here. And despite what Quinn had said, despite agreeing with her, she still hadn't taken any risks. Maybe because she thought she didn't deserve Hope.

Maybe because she was afraid.

Maybe because even though she'd looked she couldn't bring herself to commit to moving to the UK. Not right now. Not to a whole new place, not again.

Which was stupid and ridiculous and foolish and all she wanted was an excuse to stay here.

Her heart told her she didn't need an excuse, her brain told her she might not need an excuse, but she definitely needed a job and a place to stay wouldn't go amiss either.

But she was going to take a risk. She'd promised herself that. She'd promised herself that come what may she wasn't going to let Hope walk out of her life forever. Alright, so they might not have the kind of relationship that she wanted, but they could be friends, couldn't they? They could write emails and have phone calls and maybe, one day, the world would align and they'd come together.

Or, said the little voice in the back of her head, you might never see each other again and you'll lose this forever.

Not helpful.

What she wanted, truly wanted, was for Hope to walk through the door and beg her to stay.

Just as she was thinking that, there was a knock on the classroom door and Jake Lowell poked his head into the room. "Got a minute?" he asked, looking flushed and red and about as un-put-together as Ava had ever seen him.

"Sure," she said. "Come on in. I've got two and a half hours until all hell breaks loose, so make yourself at home."

Jake laughed. "It's not that bad."

"The Virgin Mary hit an Ox over the head with a book this morning and the Innkeeper drew glasses on the baby Jesus."

"Ah," said Jake, still laughing. "Don't say that they don't entertain you."

"Oh, they very much do," Ava said. She smiled. "I've got to say that even though this wasn't the original plan, well, I've come to be glad that I stayed. It's been quite the experience. I'm not sure that I can go back to teenagers swearing at me again."

Jake lifted an eyebrow. "And is that still the plan?"

"Ah."

"Ah indeed," Jake said. He pulled out a small bookshelf and perched himself on top of it. "Something you want to talk about?"

Ava exhaled. Not really. What was there to talk about? She'd turned the job down in the end, she'd told Stan Gardener she couldn't do it, that she wasn't planning on teaching high school again, and that was it.

She might not be able to ask for the life she thought she wanted, but she wasn't going to go back to trying to make things the way they were before.

"Not really."

Jake held up his hands. "It's completely your business, of course. But I did have a phone call from a... Stan Gardener? He asked me if there was anything I thought I could do to persuade you and I told him... Well, I told him I don't know you that well, but that if you've got your mind set on something you don't strike me as the kind of person to make a u-turn."

Ava smiled a little at this.

"So you're not going back but you're still leaving us after tomorrow?" Jake said.

Ava nodded because she was. Because the hard part was already done and what difference did it make if she left now or months from now, she'd still have to leave. She couldn't draw out the agony of walking away from Hope any longer.

She'd fly home, talk to Quinn, start investigating how she could move to elementary school teaching, find a new school district, start all over again.

"Are you sure?" Jake asked.

"I'm only temporary," said Ava. "Besides, the school might not exist for much longer. I'm sorry, truly I am, but I do have to think about my future."

"I completely agree," said Jake. He folded his hands in his lap and looked at her thoughtfully.

"What?" asked Ava.

"It's just that... something's come up," said Jake.

Ava frowned and crossed her legs. "What kind of something?"

THERE WAS MUCH hushing and shushing which made the Upper Infants procession toward the stage not quite as quiet as the children might have believed they were being. Ava led them, Hope brought up the rear, and when they reached the front of the hall, they stopped. Ava gave a gesture and all twelve children sank silently to the floor, crossing their legs and arms.

She gave them a small smile of approval and got a toothy grin from Alice in return. Her heart burst with pride at the sight of them, all dressed in their costumes, ready to go, excited and tamping down nerves.

Keeping a strict eye on them, she took her seat in the front row, Hope sitting beside her, parents and friends chattering quietly in the seats behind them.

Ava was just starting to worry that the kids wouldn't be able to sit still for much longer when the heavy spotlight shone on the stage and Jake Lowell strode out to the podium.

"Good evening, good evening," he said, with a broad smile.

Ava's heart started throbbing hard in her chest because she knew what was about to happen.

"We're delighted to welcome you all to this year's Christmas festivities," Lowell said. "And we've got plenty of treats lined up for you. The children have been working fantastically hard."

Ava eyed Daniel and he caught her gaze, grinning and shaking his head vigorously. He didn't have to pee. That was one less thing to worry about.

"But before we get to the main events of the evening," Jake said. "I do need to make a small announcement."

There was some mumbling at this from parents who already had phone cameras ready to record. Jake held up his hands.

"As you have all heard, Whitebridge Primary has been under threat of closure for the last few months."

Hope sat up straighter and Ava could feel her almost shaking. Without thinking, she took Hope's hand, squeezed it tight in her own.

"I had a phone call from the council yesterday," said Lowell, the bright light shining on him and beading sweat on his forehead. "But I thought it only fitting to save this announcement for tonight, when we're all together as a community."

Hope's fingers interlaced with Ava's and Ava's mouth went dry, her pulse pounding through her veins until all she could think about was the touch of Hope's skin on her own.

"I'm happy, no, ecstatic, to tell you," Jake said. "That Whitebridge Primary will be remaining open."

There was a loud cheer from parents and children alike, but Ava didn't hear it. The only thing she heard was Hope's erratic breathing as she yanked Ava into a hug that pushed all the air out of her lungs and left her breathless and dizzy.

CHAPTER THIRTY FOUR

Hope ushered the children off the stage, grinning widely at each of them and praising them to the heavens.
"You were wonderful, perfect, excellent work."

Alice had forgotten two of her lines, the innkeeper had offered Mary two rooms for the price of one, a sheep had tripped over, and after his afternoon accident Joseph was wearing a long white dress shirt rather than a robe, but on the whole, things had been very good.

Of course, Hope would have told them they were amazing anyway, but just at the moment she had little time for anything other than frantic mental gymnastics revolving around the school staying open.

The older children trooped onto the stage to begin their singing and Hope corralled her kids into the classroom next to the stage, where Ava was waiting for them.

"You were all excellent," Ava pronounced as they walked in. "I'm so proud of you."

Hope turned away because she could see that Ava was getting choked up and if she saw a tear then she was likely to start as well.

"Gather in," Ava said. "We've got time for the very last chapter of our story before the juniors are finished and you can go and find your parents."

The children gabbled away happily as Ava gathered them onto the carpet to sit quietly.

And Hope couldn't watch.

She couldn't watch as Ava read the last chapter of the last book of the last day. She couldn't listen to Ava say 'the end.' So she slunk away toward the hall.

The juniors were giving an off-key rendition of Away in a Manger as she walked quietly down the halls of the school.

They'd stay open. Whitebridge Primary was safe. She should be happy. She was happy. She was filled with joy at the idea of keeping the school. Keeping her school. But with every second that went by she was closer and closer to losing Ava.

It wasn't that she didn't have ideas. She had those. One that might even be somewhat workable.

It was more that she lacked the... the courage perhaps, to bring it up.

There was something here, she knew that. She and Ava shared something, a connection, a biological imperative, something that made her know that together they could be something amazing. She knew in the same way that she knew the first moment that she held Alice that nothing would ever be the same again.

It was the same kind of deep-seated sense that she had found someone, her someone, someone that made her better and bigger and stronger than she really was.

Now all she needed was someone to push her into asking that other someone if perhaps, maybe, there could be a future that didn't involve them living the rest of their lives apart. Or maybe she needed a stiff drink. Neither of which she was likely to find in a primary school.

"What are you doing out here?"

Hope looked up to see Jake Lowell walking toward her. "I might ask you the same thing."

"Can I tell you a secret?"

Hope nodded.

"I've been a teacher for thirty years," Jake said seriously. "And if I have to listen to one more version of Away in a Manger, I think I might take to drink."

"Funny," Hope said. "I was just thinking about drinking myself."

"Well, we did get some excellent news," said Jake. "I can't quite believe it yet, but we live to fight another day and I can't say that I wasn't a little teary-eyed when I got the phone call. Of course, a few things are going to have to change around here."

"Like what?" asked Hope, leaning against the wall with one shoulder.

Jake shrugged. "There's going to be more kids, for a start. Not a horrific amount, but class sizes are going to go up. On the same note, our budget increases as well. So we're going to be looking for at least one new teacher, and we'll be turning the music room back into a classroom, which was what it was originally intended to be, of course. And then—"

Hope's brain finally caught up with what he was saying. "A new teacher?"

Jake nodded. "I'll start the interview process next term, try and get someone on board before the summer so that everyone's around to vet them. I'll take the rest of the staff's thoughts into account, don't worry about that."

Hope swallowed. "Um, that's not really what I was worried about. I was just wondering…"

It was the perfect solution, of course it was. It was like an answer was being handed to her on a plate.

"Ah," said Jake.

"Ah what?"

"I sense that you're having the same thought as I did."

"Which is?" Hope asked carefully.

"That Ava Stanford would be perfect for the job."

"Well, she would be," Hope said, heart beating hard in her chest. "She's already a part of the school community, the kids already know her, as do the parents." She blew out a breath, trying to be fair and just. "She is an American, of course."

"Psh, that's nothing nowadays," Jake said. "With the new QTS rules she wouldn't even have to re-train. She could work here and just apply for UK qualifications, it's quite simple really given her vast experience."

"Well, there really shouldn't be a problem then," said Hope, insides on fire now, heart beating hard enough to hear. This could work. Really work.

"Unfortunately," Jake said. "There is a problem."

"Which is?"

"I asked her," Jake said. "And she turned me down."

It was like the world came crashing down around Hope's ears. She'd dared to have hope and then it was taken away from her. Ava didn't want to stay. She could, but she chose not to.

"Which is a shame," Jake continued. "Since we all wanted her to, not least the kids." He pulled a wrinkled piece of paper out of his pocket and handed it to Hope. "Young Alice gave me this right before the concert started."

Hope looked down at the crumpled sheet of paper. At the top in shaky hand-writing was 'We want Ms. Stanford to Stay as our teacher.' The F in Stanford was back to front and capitals were used haphazardly and Hope recognized her daughter's writing.

Underneath were twelve names, written in crayon and pencil, spelled correctly or crossed out and written again.

"It's a petition," Jake said helpfully.

"I can see that," said Hope. And it broke her heart just a little bit more.

Jake ran his fingers through his hair and shrugged again. "There's not much I can do if she doesn't want the job," he said. "But, well, I was thinking that maybe you could ask her to stay?"

"Why me?" Hope asked, looking up quickly. Did he know something?

Jake smiled at her. "Because you're persuasive."

"Ah." So no, he knew nothing.

"And because I get the feeling that Ava Stanford might do more for you than she would for me," he added.

Okay, so maybe he'd guessed. Hope swallowed. She

desperately wanted to ask, but she shook her head. "I can't ask her to stay. If she says she doesn't want to, then she doesn't want to. I won't emotionally blackmail her."

"Good heavens, Hope. I wasn't implying that. Simply that the two of you have spent a lot of time together over the last term and maybe you have better insight into her than I do."

"Oh," Hope said. But she still shook her head. "If she turned you down then she doesn't want to stay."

There was the sound of applause coming from the hall and Hope stood up straighter.

"They're almost done," said Jake. "I'd better re-claim my seat. We'll talk about the coming changes later, don't worry about them though, you'll all have input."

He hurried off and Hope took one second to close her eyes and breath before she too turned around and headed back to the classroom.

IT WAS OVER. The children had been sent home with their parents, over-excited and over-stimulated. Hope didn't look forward to trying to put Alice to bed tonight. She'd run off quite happily with Caz though, so maybe her grandmother could calm her down.

The classroom was quiet and empty, the chairs had been stacked in the hall, and all Hope needed to do now was pull on her coat and go home.

Except Ava was there, wiping off the white-board, collecting things together on her desk.

"It went well," Hope said, the lingering thought that Ava didn't want to stay still at the back of her mind.

"It did," said Ava, not looking at her.

Hope took a breath. "So, um, I suppose, well, I should say goodbye."

Ava still didn't look up. "I'll be in tomorrow. There's class in the morning and then cleaning up to do in the afternoon."

"Right," said Hope. "Yes. Well, goodnight then."

"Goodnight," Ava said, still not looking up.

Hope put her coat on, put her bag over her shoulder, closed the cupboard door and walked toward the exit.

She was two steps from the door when she heard a small sniff.

She might not even had heard it. It might have been nothing.

She took the last two steps, put her hand on the door and then...

And then she thought about all the sleepless nights she'd had, all the sleepless nights she would have. She thought about regretting this moment for the whole rest of her life, about thinking this could be the moment she could have changed everything.

And she thought about Ava crying, stifling her sobs so they couldn't be heard, building her wall higher and hiding herself behind it.

She didn't turn around.

But she did speak.

"Don't leave me."

CHAPTER THIRTY FIVE

There was a long silence as Ava tried to understand the words that she thought she'd heard.

Then Hope turned around. "What?" she said. "I didn't say 'don't leave.' I said 'don't leave me.'"

"Entirely different," Ava said, mouth dry.

"Oh, but it is." Hope came closer, dropping her bag on a desk. "Entirely different. I would never ask you to stay here for me. That would be wrong and cruel. But I can ask you not to leave me behind."

"You mean…" Ava swallowed, not quite able to believe it. "You mean you want to come to the States with me?"

"I want to be with you."

"What about Alice?" It was Ava's first real thought.

Hope smiled. "Well I'll be damned, Noah was right."

"Noah? Your ex? What was he right about?" asked Ava, thoroughly confused.

"He said I should trust my instincts. I did, and you just put my daughter ahead of your own wants and needs. So he was right. I should trust you. I do trust you."

"Thanks," Ava said, no less confused. "But can we go back to the part where you flee your country for me?"

Hope sighed. "It's not ideal. I get that. Noah doesn't love the idea, but he's prepared to compromise and give it a try as long as he gets Alice for all the holidays. It might not be forever."

"What would you do?"

Hope blushed in a way that was quite charming. "I haven't thought quite that far ahead yet, but I'm sure something will turn up."

Ava had to sit down, her legs were shaking. She managed to seat herself on the edge of her desk. "Hope, I'd never ask for you to come with me."

"I know you wouldn't, that's why I'm offering."

Ava didn't really know what to say to that.

Hope watched her.

"This is crazy. We barely know each other. We've spent one night together, that's all."

"So?"

"What do you mean, so?" Ava said. "It's insane. We're talking about up-ending our lives and changing everything to take a chance on... on something."

"On us," said Hope.

"But why?"

Hope's eyes cleared and she smiled. "Because I love you."

Ava was very, very glad that she was sitting down. "You..."

"I love you," Hope said again perfectly calmly and naturally. She laughed. "Look, Ava, I get it. It's soon, it's way too early to say something like that, but we are kind of under time pressure right now. It's not like this is something that's going to change. I'm not sure when I realized. Maybe I've always known. But that's the truth and I can't un-say it now."

"Don't un-say it," Ava said, voice a little shaky because she still wasn't sure what was happening.

Hope smiled wider. "I won't."

"But it's still crazy."

"Why?" Hope asked. "I knew the moment I saw my daughter that I loved her, you can know the second you sit down at the piano that you want to play, you can see a dress in a shop window and decide you want it in milliseconds, life is full of infinite decisions made in the smallest amounts of time."

"But this isn't a dress in a shop window," said Ava.

"All the more reason for this to be a snap decision," Hope said. "Think about how many millions of decisions you make like that every day, from what to have for breakfast to which foot steps out of the door first. We have a lot more practice making snap decisions than we do considered ones."

Ava couldn't help but laugh a little at this. "Alright, alright."

"We haven't known each other long," Hope said. "But that doesn't change how I feel about you. And I'm not wearing rose-colored glasses here. You do my head in, Ava Stanford."

"That hardly seems like a good thing."

"You irritate me beyond measure, you're stubborn and annoying. But I can't help wanting to wake up next to you every morning."

Ava looked down at her feet. She'd been waiting for this. She'd been waiting for permission to love again and now that it was being handed to her she didn't quite know how to handle things.

"My life is in ruins," she said quietly. "I have nothing, Hope. I don't want to ask you to stand by while I build something again."

"Why can't we build something?"

Hope came closer, her warmth bathing Ava until Ava looked up and saw complete honesty in Hope's eyes. "You have something. You have your daughter, your home, your mother and friends and job. Why would you want to build something with me?"

"Because you make me want to tear my hair out at the very same instant as you make me want to pull the stars from the sky for you."

The wind blew outside, making the windows rattle. Inside, in here, Ava felt safe and warm. She felt, she realized, as though she belonged, as though she was part of something.

Hope took Ava's hands in her own. "Trust me, Ava. I know it's hard for you, I know I'm asking the impossible, but just trust me. I'd do the impossible for you, can you not say the same for me?"

Ava closed her eyes and slowly, very slowly, Hope let go of her hands and her warmth began to fade away.

Ava's eyes shot open. "Where are you going?"

Hope flushed. "Home."

"Are we not in the middle of something here?"

Hope raised one eyebrow. "Well, I was. But I rather think I might have got the wrong end of the stick, I mean, you don't seem to want me to be here, to want—"

"Jesus fucking Christ." Ava leaped from her desk and pulled Hope into her arms, crushing her with a kiss that left them both breathless.

"Jesus," Hope echoed, when she finally pulled away.

"Right, let's start from the beginning," said Ava, finding herself again, finding her feet, as though kissing Hope had finally knocked some sense into her stupid brain. "I love you too."

"You do?" Hope asked, lips twitching.

"It's far too soon to say so, but as you say, we're under time pressure here. You're absolutely right, of course, we all make decisions every day and there's no reason that this one should be any different. For whatever reason, you also drive me insane but make me want to hang the moon for you. Clear?"

"Clear," Hope said. "Um, would you like me to sit down for this, or are you going to kiss me again."

"No kissing."

"Right," Hope said, sitting on a child's desk.

"To be clear, not because I don't want to, but because if I do then we might not stop and I think we've got some sorting out to do first."

"We do."

"You would really leave everything for me?"

Hope nodded. "I would."

"And what if I stayed?"

The wind blew again outside and Hope rolled her eyes. "Why didn't you just accept the job when Jake offered it to you?"

"Because we'd already said goodbye, because it already hurt enough, and because I don't want to up-end your life with all my baggage and bullshit," said Ava.

Hope snorted. "As though we don't all go around up-ending people's lives all the time. You do know that only important people can do that, right? You don't get your life up-ended by the cashier at the supermarket."

"I may be starting to realize that," Ava said. "And let's stay on topic for a second."

"Yes, miss."

Ava pushed her glasses up on top of her head. "So, I stay."

"Obviously."

"No, not obviously. And not permanently," Ava said gently. "We can't put that much pressure on us, not yet. I'll sign a contract for a school year and we see where we go after that, is that fair?"

"Eminently reasonable," agreed Hope.

"I'll see if I can continue renting the cottage."

"Fine," Hope said.

"And then, er, I suppose we just get on with things."

Hope smiled. "Is that a euphemism?"

"Would you like it to be one?"

"I think I would." Hope shifted on the desk. "Have we reached the kissing part yet?"

"Not quite yet," Ava said. "There's the question of Alice. You should tell her, I wouldn't want to confuse her or upset her. She might not want me around, you know."

"She very much will," Hope said. "And even if she didn't, we'd find a way to work with it. I can't protect her from the world forever. She's growing up and she needs to see reality, she needs to see what love looks like, she needs to learn that she's not always the center of the universe."

Ava bit back a smile and nodded. "Alright then, I suppose that about covers everything."

Hope stood up again. "That was very logical and considered, well done."

Ava shook her head. "There's nothing logical and considered about the way I feel about you, Hope Perkins."

Hope grinned up at her. "Good. Logical and considered is boring. And are we at the kissing part now?"

Ava pulled her in closer. "We're getting close."

Hope cupped Ava's face with her hands, looking straight into her eyes. "Ava Stanford, I have no idea what's going to happen in the future. I can't tell you that this will all work out. I can tell you that I'll try my best."

"Now who's being logical and considered?" Ava asked, drawing closer, watching Hope's lips as she spoke.

"Me," Hope said. "I will make you one promise, and I ask that you make one in return. I promise that I will never deliberately hurt you, Ava Stanford, and you—"

"I promise that I will never deliberately hurt Alice," Ava said, knowing exactly what Hope was worried about, knowing that she'd put her daughter before herself every time. She leaned in even closer. "But I'm good for two promises. And I'll never hurt you either, Hope Perkins."

The wind blew outside, the glass rattled in the windows, the old school creaked in the coming winter storm as the first flakes of snow began to twirl to the ground. And inside the little classroom it was very, very quiet as the kissing part finally began. It didn't end for a very long time, until snow was dusting the playground and the little town of Whitebridge was settling into winter.

EPILOGUE

The kitchen table was cluttered with just about every dish in the house.

"How are we supposed to eat?" Hope asked.

"Just push things aside," said Caz. "Trust me, I know what I'm doing. If you leave all those glasses and plates in the wall cabinets, the building work is going to end up shattering them to pieces."

"Since when do you know so much about building work?" Hope said, lifting an eyebrow.

"Since Joe told me to make sure I empty the kitchen cabinets."

"Ah," said Hope, still kind of getting used to the idea of her mother having a partner. "I forgot he was a builder."

"Speaking of," Caz said. "I've been meaning to talk to you about him, I mean—"

"Why is everything we own on the kitchen table?" Ava said, coming into the kitchen and kicking off her running shoes by the back door.

"Are we having a party?" Alice said, coming downstairs at pretty much the same time.

"No, love," said Caz. "It's just to protect the dishes from the builders, that's all."

"Are they going to steal them?" asked Alice.

Hope rolled her eyes and decided to put a stop to things. "All of you sit down and make a space on the table to eat breakfast," she said. "Nice run?" she asked Ava.

"Excellent, thanks," Ava said as she sat down. "Better since it's the holidays and I don't have to go into school after it."

"Agreed," piped up Alice.

Ava grinned. "I'll have breakfast, jump in the shower, and then go and do the shopping in town if you want?"

"I can do it," both Hope and Caz said.

"Eh, I need to pick up something from the bookstore anyway," said Ava.

Before they could argue further about it, the sound of drilling began in the next cottage. Alice clamped her hands over her ears. "Why is it so loud?"

Hope put a dish of cereal in front of her, pulled one hand away from one ear, and leaned in. "You'll be happy when it's finished," she said. "Twice the space, a spare bedroom for sleepovers, brand new wallpaper in a brand new bedroom."

Hope caught Ava's eye and smiled. It had taken some planning, not to mention far more appointments with the local council and inspectors than either one of them had anticipated, but their big project was finally underway. Ava had snapped up her rental cottage eight months ago when it had finally gone on the market, using the money she got from the sale of her house in the States. Now, with Caz's enthusiastic permission, they were knocking the two cottages together.

"Here," said Hope, handing Ava a cup of coffee.

Ava stared down into it. "It's full of dust."

"Get used to it," said Caz, settling down with some crackers and cottage cheese. "Those builders'll be months in there, take my word for it."

"We planned on six weeks," said Ava.

"And it'll take double that. Something always comes up in projects like this," said Caz.

Ava looked at Hope and Hope mouthed the word 'Joe' at her and Ava smiled. "We'll see."

"I've been thinking," Alice said loudly over the noise of the drilling.

"Mmm?" said Hope, taking a plate of toast and moving a fruit bowl, a blender, and a set of decorative wine glasses out of the way so she could sit.

The drilling next door stopped as Alice started speaking again, meaning her words rang out far louder than she'd intended.

"I thought I might go and live with daddy."

Hope's heart exploded into a million pieces.

* * *

Ava strolled her way into town, letting the early summer sun stroke her skin. She was glad to be out of the house. The building noise was definitely getting on her nerves. More than that though, she was glad she didn't need to be around for the conversation that Hope and Alice were about to have.

She had seen the destruction on Hope's face, seen just how much it had hurt her to hear Alice's words. And she'd offered to stay, but both she and Hope knew that this was a conversation that needed to be between just her and Alice.

So she'd gone out to get the shopping done and was glad of it.

Whitebridge was so pretty in the spring and early summer, people smiling more as the sun came out. Besides, with all the noise of the building work, it was good to get out.

"Morning, Ms. Stanford," piped up a young boy, holding his mother's hand.

"Morning, Davie," she said. "Mrs. Flitt."

One of the eighteen children in the class that she'd just finished teaching. Next term there'd be twenty, but she felt confident that she could handle that now.

She was just about to step into the bookstore, planning to treat herself to the final Detective Dennis book, when a harried looking man ran out of the store, practically barreling her over as he did so.

"Morning Max," she said, then spotting Ag clinging like a

limpet to her dad's side she grinned and winked. "Morning, Ag."

"Ava, Ava, thank God," Max panted.

Ava took a step back. "What's wrong?"

"Mila, it's Mila, she went, and now she's gone and then I came here and then they're gone and now—"

"Calm down!"

Max took a big breath.

"Mummy has a baby," Ag said seriously.

Ava laughed. "Is that all this is?"

Max nodded. "I was out on a walk with Ag and my phone was out of battery. Ant and Ad have taken her to the hospital."

"So they're not here to take care of Ag," Ava said, finally understanding what was happening.

"But now you're here…" Max began.

Ava sighed, eyeing Ag. She wasn't a baby anymore, but three years old was young. Younger than Ava was really used to. Max's eyes were pleading and she could see the sweat on his brow and the fear and excitement in his eyes.

"Okay, okay," she said.

"Thanks, Ava, you're the best." He unslung a huge bag from his shoulder and passed it over to Ava, before kissing his daughter soundly on the head and handing her over too. "I'll be back as soon as I can," he said, already jogging toward his car. "Bye, Ag!"

"Bye bye, bye bye," Ag chanted, bouncing up and down on Ava's hip.

Both Ag and Ava watched as Max drove away, Ava with the huge bag weighing down her shoulder. When Max was out of sight, Ava looked down at Ag. "We have to do some shopping."

"Shop?" Ag asked.

"Yes."

"Sweets?" asked Ag hopefully.

Ava frowned. She had no idea whether or not Ag should have candy. "We'll see," she said provisionally.

Ag seemed happy at this and Ava grinned. This child-rearing stuff was a piece of cake.

Ten minutes later, Ava was standing in the middle of a puddle of juice in the far aisle of the town general store.

"I'll get a mop," Sylv, the rotund shopkeeper, said, bustling off.

"Ag," Ava said, preparing herself to reprimand the toddler. But the child was nowhere to be seen. "Ag?" Ava said again. Then she started to panic. "Ag?"

"Oh, leave off," Sylv said, reappearing with a mop. "She'll be over there under the cheese display. She likes to hide under there now that her mum's too pregnant to get down and pull her out."

Ava gritted her teeth, went over to the display, and tugged at a small foot sticking out.

"No, no!" Ag giggled.

"Yes, yes," Ava said firmly.

The child slid out from under the display, jumped to her feet and toddled off, leaving Ava to follow her thinking that shopping had been a bad idea.

"This one," said Ag, pulling a chocolate bar off the shelf.

"No."

Ag's face started to crumple. Jesus. Ava looked around, thinking hard and fast. "Wait. Shopping first."

"Shop?" Ag said.

"Shop first," Ava said firmly. "We do the shopping and then sweets."

"Sweets?" Ag said.

"Yes," said Ava, losing patience very, very quickly.

Ag grinned and picked up the dropped chocolate bar, putting it into the basket Ava was carrying.

With a sigh, Ava took the child's hand and pulled her the rest of the way around the small shop, chattering constantly to keep Ag's attention. When they finally arrived at the check out, she was exhausted.

"That's not the kind you like, love, is it?" Sylv said to Ag, holding up the chocolate bar.

"It's not?" asked Ava. "She insisted."

"It's not like she can read the label," pointed out Sylv. She reached over and picked a small bag from the front of the counter display. "These are the ones Mila lets her have."

"Thank you," said Ava in relief. "She's a bit of a handful."

Sylv laughed. "That'll be because it's her nap time, I expect."

"She naps?" Ava asked, surprised because frankly, Ag was walking and talking and as far as Ava was concerned was plenty old enough to make it through the day.

"She does indeed," Sylv said. "And I'll give you a piece of advice. You'll probably find pull-ups in that bag on your shoulder. Mila buys them here. Make sure you put a pair on her before nap time or else you'll likely wake up to a wet bed."

"Pull-ups," Ava said as though the word was foreign to her. Yet another thing she hadn't thought of. "Right."

"More?" Ag said, tugging at Ava's sleeve.

Ava looked down to see Ag's face covered in melted chocolate and the empty bag of chocolate buttons screwed up in her hand. With a sigh she picked up another bag and put it on the counter. It was beginning to dawn on her that she was very, very unqualified for her current position as baby-sitter.

She needed Hope.

※ ※ ※

Hope was flicking through a magazine at the kitchen table when Ava came in, dragging what seemed like far too much stuff behind her.

"Did you shop for the army?" Hope asked her.

Before Ava could answer, Ag came flying into the kitchen with a bellow of delight, chasing after a fleeing Rosie who disappeared through the cat door.

"And you brought reinforcements, I see," Hope said, with a questioning look.

"Um, I ran into Max on the way to the shops and he was panicking, Mila's gone into labor."

"That explains that then," said Hope, watching as Ag tried to stick her head out of the cat flap.

"Did you talk to Alice yet?"

Hope sighed. "Not really. She didn't seem inclined to talk about it, and I don't want to forbid her to go or anything. So I just told her that she was free to go to her dad's if she wanted to, that we both loved her and she was welcome anywhere.

Ava pulled a face. "Alright then, how about this? After two bags of chocolate buttons and having garnered information about the possibility of pull-ups being involved with nap time, how about we swap?"

"Swap?" Hope asked. Ava looked harried and it almost made her want to smile. The thought of logical, authoritative Ava chasing around after a wild, three year old was kind of funny.

"You put Ag down for a nap and I'll go and have a word with Alice."

Hope cocked her head to one side, trying to get a better view of where Ag was trying hard to get her head stuck in the cat door. She nodded. "Deal."

Far better that Ava handle things with Alice. Hope had a feeling that her emotions would just get too much in the way for that conversation.

* * *

"I got you some of that juice that you like," Ava said, putting a glass of fruit juice on the patio next to where Alice was sitting in the sun playing on her Switch.

"Wow, cool, thanks," Alice said, beaming.

"Want to put your game away for a minute? I think we need to talk."

Alice put the console down and nodded seriously. "I've been meaning to discuss something with you," she said.

Ava bit back a smile. Alice had been a precocious six year old. She was now a very precocious almost nine year old.

"Do you really want to go and live with your dad?" Ava asked.

Alice shrugged. "Maybe. I was just thinking about it."

"You know that no one would stop you," Ava said. "But on the other hand, if there's a problem, some reason that you'd rather not live here or rather live there, we should talk about it."

Alice shrugged again. "I guess."

Ava sat down on the patio next to her. Something was bugging Alice, she could see that. She could also see that demanding answers was going to get her nowhere. So she tried another method. "What did you want to talk to me about?"

"Well, I was just wondering what I should call you," said Alice.

"After more than two years?" Ava laughed.

"I know, I call you Ms. Stanford at school and Ava at home. But then I was thinking. I mean, Amelia lets me call her Mel now. And I call mum mum, so I thought maybe there was something I could call you like that."

"Ah," Ava said, starting to feel out of her depth. "I see. Did you have any ideas on that front?"

Alice sniffed and looked away as though it was nothing important. "I thought maybe I could call you Mom Ava, you know, like the American kind of mum."

Ava's heart swelled about five times in size. She couldn't speak over the lump in her throat.

"Unless you don't want me to," Alice added hurriedly. "I don't have to."

"No," Ava said, voice tight. "No, I think I'd like that. As long as you wanted to. And we should probably ask mum too."

Alice nodded. "Yeah, we should. So…" She trailed off and scratched her nose.

"I thought you might be happier than that," observed Ava.

"I am," said Alice. "It's just… well, I wondered if that meant that you're staying here."

Ava frowned. "Staying? Alice, I've bought a house. We all live together. What did you think was going to happen? Did you think I was going to leave?"

"Dunno," Alice said, looking at the grass. "Maybe. You were going to before and then you didn't. But then Dad and Amelia are married and you and mum aren't. And then I was thinking that maybe it might be easier if you didn't have to think about me as well. After all, you have children at school all day. And I know Amelia wants to have a baby and she can't and that they're going to maybe adopt one but it's hard and there's no guarantees and —"

"Stop," Ava said sharply.

Alice took a deep shuddering breath and stopped speaking.

"Alice Perkins, that's about the silliest thing I've ever heard. How could you think that it would be easier without you? We're..." Ava almost stuttered, not quite believing that she was saying the words, but knowing they were the truth and she had to say them. "We're family. It's that simple. I'm going nowhere."

"You're not?" Alice asked, finally looking at her.

"I'll stay here as long as you and mum want me," Ava said, stomach tightening into a knot as she said it, aware that she'd been putting all of this off for far too long. "You're free to go and live with your dad if you want to, but don't do it on my account. My life would be smaller and sadder without you in it every day."

Alice was smiling now. "You mean it?"

"I mean it," Ava said, putting an arm around Alice's shoulder. "And how about this afternoon you and I take a bike ride over to your dad's? I think we can find a route that's safe enough that you can go by yourself if you want to. That way you could bike to your dad's over the holidays whenever you fancied it."

Alice's smile widened. "Yes!"

✽ ✽ ✽

The pounding next door was vibrating through Hope's bones. She had no idea how Ag was sleeping through it, but the toddler was safely wrapped up in a blanket on the couch, pull-ups on and thumb in mouth.

"Coffee?" Caz said poking her head around the door.

Hope got up and followed her mother into the kitchen. "It'll have dust in it," she said.

"Beggars can't be choosers," said Caz turning the kettle on.

"And you and I have unfinished business."

"Do we?" Hope pulled two mugs from the collection on the kitchen table.

"I told you this morning that I wanted to talk to you, and I do. So sit down and let's have this out."

Hope's hands trembled a little. Her mother sounded serious. Too serious. She forgot sometimes that Caz was over sixty now, that she wasn't as young as she used to be. "What is it?" she asked, wanting to get this over with.

"It's about Joe," said Caz, sitting down as she waited for the kettle to boil.

"Joe?" asked Hope, confused and relieved that it wasn't something more serious.

"I'd like him to move in." Caz was looking at her hands, cheeks flushed pink.

"You want your boyfriend to move in?" Hope said and then realized that she wasn't talking to Alice, she was talking to her mother and that Caz had every right to have someone move into her own home. "I mean, I'm happy for you."

"It's a complication," Caz said. "I understand. But we're getting more space now, and it seems practical and… Well, to be truthful, I want it. I want to live with someone again, I'd like to have a life of my own. You've got Ava and, well, I think it's time, don't you?"

"I think it's past time," Hope said, the idea growing on her.

"You don't mind then?"

Hope took a breath. "I think it's wonderful, mum. He's a nice man, I like him. We'll have to run it past Ava, but she adores Joe. I hope you're going to be really happy."

"Thanks, love," Caz said. She stood up, dropped a kiss on Hope's head and went back to making coffee.

Hope was happy for her mother. Happy and a little anxious and, now that she was thinking about it, a little sad as well. It had been her and Caz for so long. She wasn't stupid enough to think that Joe would replace her. But she knew that now Caz would have a confidante, someone else to turn to.

Which was a good thing, of course, but a little sad at the same time.

A little sad and... And perhaps exactly what Alice might be feeling. Maybe this was why Alice wanted to move in with Noah.

Hope groaned. She was an idiot.

* * *

Ava looked around the broken living room. "It's a start, I suppose," she said.

Hope laughed. "It's the first day of construction. I wouldn't expect more than this."

"You'll sound like Caz if you're not careful," Ava said. "Her and Joe are convinced that this project is going to take months."

Hope shrugged. "So? We have months, don't we?"

Ava's heart beat in her throat. She'd thought about this long and hard. She'd consulted with Quinn, who had told her to stop being an idiot and to just do it. She'd semi-consulted with Alice during their talk in the garden. The only thing she hadn't done was mention the idea to Hope. Which, since it involved Hope rather integrally, was a bit of a problem.

"About that," she began.

But Hope's phone rang before she could get any further.

Ava wandered over to the fireplace while Hope talked, checking the brickwork, wondering if they should take the fireplace out altogether, maybe put a nice stove in.

"That was Max," Hope said, coming to join her. "Mila had a baby boy about an hour ago. Dashiell."

Ava grinned. "After Dashiell Hammet, I'm assuming?"

"Got it in one," said Hope. "Mother and baby are doing fine and Max is on his way to pick up Ag to take her to meet her baby brother."

Ava paused for a second, a thought striking her. "Um, babies. Kids."

"Ye-es," said Hope. "What about them?"

"We've never discussed them," said Ava. "Do you want more of them?"

Hope blew out a breath. "I never thought about it, to be honest. I always wanted one, and Alice is the light of my life. I suppose I could be persuaded if you wanted…" She looked up at Ava. "Do you want?"

"Um…" Ava rubbed her face. "Well, I sort of feel like I've got eighteen of them at school every day. And then, well, I don't know if Alice has mentioned anything?"

"About what?"

Ava swallowed. "Um, she did ask if it was alright to call me Mom Ava." She felt herself blush. "I told her it was fine by me but that she needed to run it by you."

But Hope was already throwing her arms around Ava. "That's brilliant," she said. "Thank you."

Ava pushed her away a little. "I'm not quite done here," she said. "So, I talked to Alice and I think she's fine now. She was just feeling a bit… insecure, I think, about all of this. Us and Amelia and Noah and everything."

"I'd kind of figured that out," Hope said. "I'll talk to her about it."

"That's just it, I think maybe there's something we can do to make her feel better. And, well…" Ava's heart beat harder and faster, her mouth started to dry up and her palms got clammy. "Well, it's just that I thought we could…"

"We could what?" asked Hope, frowning up at her.

"How long are we going to pretend this is temporary?" Ava said, changing course. "We've been going along not making any commitment and I just thought. Jesus." She rubbed her face again. "I just thought that we could get married if you want," she added in a rush.

Hope stepped back. "We could get married if I want?"

"Well, we're quite literally building something together," said Ava, feeling on firmer ground now that the words were out of her mouth. "And I figured since you were the one that asked me to stay here then I should be the one to ask you to marry me."

"I didn't ask you to stay," said Hope.

"Fine," Ava said, gritting her teeth. "I take the proposal back then."

Hope smiled and came a little closer again. "I'm not sure you're allowed to do that."

"Of course I am. It was my proposal, if you don't want to get married then we don't have to."

"Did I say that I didn't?"

"You really are the most infuriating person," Ava groaned. The movement by the open front door caught her attention. She groaned again. "Oh no."

"What?" asked Hope.

Rosie strode through the door like she owned the place, closely followed by Robbie, closely followed by… a small cat that Ava had never seen before.

"They adopted a baby!" Hope said.

"I'm going to nail the cat door closed. You're some kind of cat magnet," said Ava.

"I'll put up signs, I'll get the kitten adopted," Hope said hurriedly.

But Ava sighed and shook her head. "No. Rosie brings home strays because she trusts you. Because you looked after her and took her in and I guess I of all people can't complain about that. It's just the price I have to pay for having a girlfriend that's so trustworthy."

"A wife that's so trustworthy," Hope said.

Ava's head spun around to look at her. "What?"

"Did you or did you not just ask me to marry you?"

"I did," said Ava. "But you didn't say yes."

"You didn't give me a chance to."

"Oh."

Hope stepped in and wrapped her arms around Ava's waist. "So, yes."

Ava's eyes felt heavy, she could feel her throat tightening. "I love you," she said quietly. "I can't promise we'll always be perfect, I can't promise that nothing bad will happen. But I do love you. I came here broken and you've fixed me."

"No," Hope said, equally quietly. "I didn't fix you. You fixed yourself. And that's okay. Because that's what life is. It's not perfection. It's just being constantly broken and constantly repaired, and that's a good thing. The repaired places are better and stronger, even though they might be uglier."

Ava bit her lip and nodded. "So, we're going to do this?"

"You can't take it back now," Hope joked.

"We'd better go and tell Alice," said Ava.

Hope leaned in closer. "Oh, I think that can probably wait a few minutes, don't you?"

"Can it?" Ava said, but Hope's hands were already traveling down over her waist, grasping at her hips. "Hmm, I suppose it can. Hold on." Ava darted away, quickly shutting the front door of what had been her house and was now about to be their house. "Can't have any more cats getting in."

"Oh, there's going to be cats. Lots of cats. And children and family and arguments and making up and meals and holidays and laughter and tears and all kinds of everything else."

"Sounds fantastic," said Ava, taking Hope back into her arms.

And then there was silence other than the soft sounds of breathing and moaning for a long, long time. Until the sun was setting and the light was orange and Ava couldn't imagine being anywhere else in the world.

THANKS FOR READING!

If you liked this book, why not leave a review? Reviews are so important to independent authors, they help new readers discover us, and give us valuable feedback. Every review is very much appreciated.

And if you want to stay up to date with the latest Sienna Waters news and new releases, then check me out at:

www.siennawaters.com

Keep reading for a sneak peek of my next book!

BOOKS FROM SIENNA WATERS

The Oakview Series:

    Coffee For Two
    Saving the World
    Rescue My Heart
    Dance With Me
    Learn to Love
    Away from Home
    Picture Me Perfect

The Monday's Child Series:

    Fair of Face
    Full of Grace
    Full of Woe

The Hawkin Island Series:

    More than Me

Standalone Books:

    The Opposite of You
    French Press
    The Wrong Date
    Everything We Never Wanted
    Fair Trade
    One For The Road
    The Real Story
    A Big Straight Wedding
    A Perfect Mess
    Love By Numbers
    Ready, Set, Bake
    Tea Leaves & Tourniquets
    The Best Time
    A Quiet Life
    Watching Henry
    Count On You
    The Life Coach
    Crossing the Pond
    Not Only One Bed

The Revenge Plot
The Queens of Crime
The Hotel Inspector
Teaching Hope
That French Summer

Or turn the page to get a sneak preview of That French Summer

THAT FRENCH SUMMER

Chapter One

The eight o'clock Eurostar left St. Pancras precisely on time and Delia Holland caught it by the skin of her teeth. The man behind her didn't catch it, which was just as well because the last thing she needed was to spend the trip to Paris in the same carriage as a paparazzo. The door slid shut just in time, the photographer yanking his lens out of the way, and Delia slid her comically huge sunglasses further up her nose.

On reflection, she might have gotten away with it better without the sunglasses, she thought as she dragged her case to her seat. The hat was definitely going too far. She pulled it off with one hand. Large and floppy it did rather scream 'I'm famous and don't want to be noticed.'

Not that she was famous.

"Are you somebody terribly famous dear?"

Delia stopped struggling to lift her suitcase onto the luggage rack and looked down at the little old lady looking up at her.

"No," she said carefully.

The case wasn't as heavy as it looked, just awkward, so she gave it a hefty push.

She wasn't lying. Lying to sweet little old ladies wasn't the sort of thing that Delia Holland did. Mind you, of late, her life had changed so much that she wasn't entirely sure what was the sort of thing she did anymore.

She definitely wasn't lying though. Famous was the wrong word. Infamous, alright, but not famous. Famous implied she'd done something and since she'd spent the last few weeks staunchly denying that she'd done anything at all, she could hardly claim to be famous now, could she?

She could certainly lay claim to infamy though.

Infamy was like fame's annoying baby brother, constantly hanging around as a reminder that whilst she couldn't reap the benefits of fame, she could expect the consequences of infamy. No window seats in posh restaurants or VIP lines at clubs for her. Yet there were paparazzi outside the house, and eventually inside the hotel foyer once the house was gone, every second of the day.

Not that she went to clubs. Or wanted to. Still, the option would be nice.

She settled herself down into her seat and the old lady rustled a sweet bag in her general direction. "Sweetie, dear?"

"No, thank you," said Delia because she was well brought up and had excellent manners.

In France this would all go away. Or so she hoped. The French didn't care who you were if you weren't wearing Chanel or Dior, or if you weren't at least topless or preferably fully naked and caught in flagrante.

Particularly, the French didn't care who you were if you weren't actually French, and Delia definitely wasn't that. A year at finishing school and a solid education had given her a decent grasp of the language, but she was very definitely English.

No, she was pretty certain that the French press would not be waiting at the station when she arrived. Nobody else would be waiting either, which was more depressing than she'd thought it would be, but there'd be no clicking cameras and barked questions.

It might be nice to walk to the shops again. Or to draw the

curtains in the morning without worrying about whether too much cleavage was showing.

Christ.

She closed her eyes and lay back in her seat.

Forty one years old. Forty one. And sometime in the last twelve weeks she'd been picked up and planted into the life of a cheap reality TV star or one-hit-wonder plastic singer or... or... she couldn't come up with any other examples.

The ones she had were unfair as well. She enjoyed the odd evening in in front of some soppy reality TV, and she'd definitely downloaded more than her fair share of one-hit-wonders.

The point was though, that she was a grown adult and until twelve weeks ago had been living a grown adult life. The kind where you buy opera tickets and worry about the dry cleaner's ruining your silk blouse, rather than the kind where you buy comically large sunglasses and worry about the paparazzi getting too close to the wrinkles around your eyes.

There was the sound of someone clearing their throat. Delia opened one eye. The old lady was staring at her and smiling politely.

"Is everything alright?" Delia asked. The last thing she needed was some sort of disaster now. She did know CPR, but the fuss that would come from Delia Holland performing CPR on an elderly lady on the Eurostar was not the sort of fuss that she needed.

God, the woman might even die.

She'd be well and truly fucked then, wouldn't she?

"Yes, dear," said the woman, still smiling. "It's just... are you sure you're not someone terribly famous?"

Delia nodded. "Quite sure," she said firmly.

"Only..." said the woman, nodding in the direction of a gaggle of schoolgirls who were peering over the tops of their seats and pointing.

Delia gritted her teeth and took a deep breath before smiling wide and whipping off her sunglasses. "Selfies, anyone?" she caroled.

The girls took her up on her offer and Delia spent the next few minutes beaming because, after all, none of this was their fault. They had no conception of what happened, they couldn't, they were kids, even Delia herself barely understood what was going on.

All they knew was that they'd seen her face on TV and in the papers and online.

"Are you a singer?" the old lady asked as Delia settled back down in her seat.

"Can't hold a tune in a bucket," she answered, smiling sweetly.

"An actress then?" pressed the woman.

"Well, I was a very convincing Viola in my school production of *Twelfth Night*, but on the whole, no, I don't think I've missed my calling there."

The woman sighed in frustration. "Well, who are you then? Now you've taken those glasses off I do recognize you, I'm sure I do."

Delia's mother had always told her that the best way to eat a frog was in one gulp. In other words, if you had to do something terrible, you might as well go all in and do it fast and furiously. The woman would remember at some point anyway.

"Delia Holland," said Delia, smiling and holding out her hand.

The woman took her hand, more out of habit than anything else, Delia thought, then dropped it like it was hot.

"Oh," she said. "Oh, I see."

She shuffled her things closer to her side of the table they shared, as though being Delia Holland might be somehow contagious, and Delia sighed and closed her eyes again.

At least she could expect the rest of the journey to be quiet, she supposed.

THE TRAIN ROLLED into Gare du Nord as precisely on time as it had rolled out of St. Pancras, but this time Delia wore her sunglasses out of necessity rather than privacy. The sun was beaming down through the glass panes of the station ceiling, and despite the fact that it was only half past ten in the morning, it was boiling.

Boiling, busy, and yet after the kerfuffle of the last few weeks, strangely peaceful. She stood for a moment in the middle of the platform, hand on her case handle, and soaked in the feeling of being finally anonymous again.

Anonymity was much under-rated, she only now realized as she wheeled her case down the platform and toward the street where she hoped to find a taxi.

Being able to scratch your nose in public without the newspapers commenting on it, being able to break a heel on your shoe, wriggle your underwear out of the crack of your bottom, make a dentist appointment without comment on your name, all of those things were vastly under-rated.

She would, she swore to herself, never, ever complain about being ordinary again. Not if she got the chance to be ordinary.

She dragged her case out into the hot sun, smelling the Paris summer smell of dust, perfume, dog mess and uncollected trash, and reveled in the fact that not one person looked at her.

She got into the first taxi in the line outside and requested a trip to Gare de Lyon.

"Of course, madame," said the driver, with a grin. He pulled out of his space and budged his way into the morning traffic. "So, madame is heading south?"

"Absolutely," Delia replied. He wasn't psychic, Gare de Lyon was the station for French trains heading south.

"And what, if I may ask, is a beautiful woman doing heading south by herself at the beginning of the summer?"

Delia smiled. Things were going to change.

The truth was, she was depressed. The last few weeks had taken their toll and changed her into someone that she hadn't recognized in the mirror anymore. Someone she didn't especially like. Someone without her smile, without her lightness, without her happiness.

A part of the reason she'd come to France was to get that person back again.

Obviously, another part of the reason was to avoid the publicity in England.

The third part of the plan, well, that was the reason she was going to Gare de Lyon.

"I'm going to Marincourt," she said.

The driver raised a bushy eyebrow in the rear view mirror. "I'm not familiar with it."

She smiled. "It's a small town."

"And what is in this small town that it attracts the attention of such a fine English lady?" he asked.

"A chateau," she answered quite honestly.

He snorted. "There are many chateaux, too many, the whole countryside is littered with them. I could take you to more chateaux than you could visit in a week just in an hour drive from Paris. Ruinous places, all of them, money pits, sucking the money of the rich, the money that should go to better things, to health care, to education…"

She let him continue to rant for a good five minutes. "They are beautiful though," she said, when he was done.

He grunted. He was a Frenchman, he couldn't deny beauty, no matter how much he hated chateaux.

At least, she hoped this one was beautiful.

After all this fuss with Rupert, she could use a little beauty in her life.

Besides, this place was her last shot, the only property left, the only asset, in fact, that she had at all. Because she did have it. After weeks of searching and praying and hoping, there was this one last place that was in her name and not in her husband's.

The Chateau de Marincourt was hers.

CHAPTER TWO

Paris handed Clare the folder.

"What's this?" Clare asked, brow furrowing. She scooched forward in line a little and Paris took a step to keep up with her.

"Everything you need," Paris said. "Your passport, the landing card I filled in for you on the plane, directions to our hotel and the address and a little cash, just in case we get separated."

Clare looked anxiously at the guard in his little booth ahead of them. "We're not going to get separated though, right?"

"Absolutely not," Paris said firmly. She'd checked and double checked everything. Both their passports were valid, Americans didn't need a visa to enter France, and there was nothing in their luggage that could in any way be construed as contraband.

Clare grinned. "Exciting, right?"

Paris grinned back because it was exciting.

"I can't believe you've never been here before," Clare said. "I mean, with your name and all."

"Yeah, the irony of Paris never having been to Paris is not lost on me," Paris said. "But I've been waiting to do this properly, and now we can, so here we are."

Thirty two years she'd been waiting. Well, maybe not exactly that long, but for as long as she could remember. Longing to visit a place she'd been named after by a mother with a romantic soul and not enough cash to follow her dreams.

Paris looked up at the grubby airport ceiling. "This one's for you, mom," she whispered.

Clare took another step closer to the front of the line.

She'd waited until she was financially secure, and then she'd waited until she had the perfect opportunity, and then she'd waited until she had the perfect partner. And now, maybe, that waiting was over.

She was by no means rich, but she was doing okay. She'd just finished a job and was waiting to start another, so the timing was right, she had weeks to explore. And then there was Clare. Clare who was beautiful and thoughtful and not at all the kind of person that Paris had ever imagined for herself.

And, alright, they'd only been together a year, and they'd been arguing a fair amount recently, but this trip was going to change that. This was the trip where they'd really find out if they fit together as well as it had seemed at first.

Then, well, then Paris assumed everything would go according to plan. They'd get married, they'd have kids, they'd buy a house. Maybe not in that order. Definitely not in that order. House first, Paris did things properly.

"All okay?" Clare said, flashing her bright smile.

"Perfect," Paris said, clutching her green folder tight to her stomach. "Just perfect."

THE TRAIN RIDE to the hotel was longer than Paris had thought. The walk from the station to the hotel was even longer. By the time they reached the foyer, Clare was muttering about showers and naps and snatched the room key as soon as the concierge handed it over.

Paris carefully filled out the guest forms and slid them back to the concierge.

"Merci," he said, scanning the forms. Then: "Oh, madame, I'm afraid there is a misunderstanding." He laid the paper back on the desk. "Here we need your name, not the address."

Paris looked down then looked up at the concierge. "That is

my name."

"Paris?" He pronounced it the French way, Par-ee.

"Paris," said Paris, enunciating the S.

He raised an eyebrow at her. "Parissss."

"Right."

He blew out a breath. "Perhaps I shall name my first child Chicago and then there will be some balance in the world."

Paris laughed. "There are worse names."

He nodded seriously. "Moscow," he said. "Or perhaps Brussels." He grinned at her. "And will madame be requiring any services? I have maps, I can arrange tour guides, whatever you like."

"Oh no," Paris said, patting the green folder that was lying on the reception desk. "I'm prepared, thank you."

"Very well," he said. "You'll find your room upstairs on the second floor on your right."

She tromped up the stairs, pulling her case behind her and did not fall for the obvious mistake. The second floor in France was third floor American, she'd done her research. But when she got into the room, she saw Clare face first on the bed.

"No, no," she said, standing her suitcase by the door. "Up you get. It's not nap time yet."

Clare groaned.

"It's not," Paris said. "We agreed that we had to stay awake to beat the jet lag. We'll go to bed in the evening. Come on, up you get."

Clare groaned again but began to shift. Paris blew her dark bangs out of her eyes and tightened her ponytail. "Up, up, up," she said. "We've places to be." She took her green folder and patted Clare's behind with it.

"I'm starting to hate that folder already," Clare said.

"You've got time for a shower," said Paris temptingly.

With another grunt, Clare finally sat up. "Fine, a shower," she said, stomping off to the bathroom.

Paris sat on the edge of the bed to wait, opening up the green folder, looking at the carefully planned pages within. Every day was accounted for. Every hour was accounted for. France was a big country and who knew when they'd get a chance like this again? Certainly not for a long time, not if there were going to be children.

So they had to make the most of it, had to see as much as possible. Paris looked at her spreadsheets, her carefully planned schedule, then she looked at her watch. They were already running late.

"Come on," she shouted through the bathroom door.

"I've barely got in," Clare shouted back.

Paris opened the door and stuck her head around it. "Aren't you dying to see Paris?"

For a second, a look of irritation crossed Clare's face, then she sighed and smiled. "I can already see you."

"That joke is going to get old, fast," Paris said.

Clare stuck her tongue out. "How about you hop in the shower with me? That way we'll be more efficient, right?"

It wasn't that she didn't consider it, she did. She thought about running soapy hands over Clare's curves, she thought about the taste of her, the feel of her. Then she thought about the green folder. There'd be time for the grown up stuff later, she promised herself.

"Please?" she said. "Let's not destroy the schedule on the very first day?"

Clare closed her eyes for a moment, then nodded and disappeared back behind the shower curtain. "Give me two minutes," she said.

"Perfect," said Paris and went back to the bedroom to change into her walking shoes, bought new for the trip. She'd spent three weeks back home carefully breaking them in. No blisters were going to ruin this trip.

"PARIS, COME ON, please?"

Paris stopped, the late afternoon crowds streaming around her on the sidewalk. "We'll take a break in a few minutes," she said. "I promise."

"My feet hurt and I'm exhausted," Clare moaned.

"I told you not to wear those shoes."

Clare rolled her eyes. "We're in Paris and you want me to wear hiking boots?"

"You wouldn't have blisters if you'd worn hiking boots."

"Listen, we're supposed to be on vacation. Can't we just sit down for half an hour? There's, like, a million cafes around here."

Paris looked around the small square they were standing in. All around them, people were walking and talking, chatting at small round tables, busy living their lives. There were indeed plenty of cafes right here.

But she shook her head anyway.

They had a schedule to keep. And it wasn't her fault that Clare had insisted on wearing heels. She had told her, warned her, that there'd be plenty of walking. But Clare had put on the silly shoes anyway, even though half the streets were cobbled and she'd break a damn ankle at this point.

"Not yet," she said.

Clare sighed and Paris took pity on her. She was looking pale and tired, and, to be honest, Paris was starting to flag a little herself.

"Half an hour?" she said.

"I don't see the point of being on vacation if you act like it's a fucking boot camp," Clare said, but she started walking again anyway. Limping actually.

"I'm not acting like it's a boot camp. But we want to make the most of this opportunity. We want experiences, we want to do things and see things."

Paris looped her arm through Clare's, but Clare pulled her arm away, though she did still keep walking. "Is the whole trip going to be like this?"

"We have three beach days planned when we get down south," Paris said. "We can relax then. Although, there are probably some things we should discuss while we're lying around and doing nothing."

"Like what?" Clare pouted as they crossed out of the small square and back onto a wider street.

Paris took a breath. It was in the schedule. Maybe she should just spit it out, give Clare a chance to get her own thoughts in order. "Like the future," she said.

"The future?"

"Yes," said Paris, stepping to one side, slightly behind Clare, as a large group of tourists appeared coming in the opposite direction. "You, me, us, the future." She cleared her throat. "Um, kids, that kind of thing."

"Kids?" screeched Clare, making the oncoming tour group swivel all eyes in her direction.

"Or... or not?" asked Paris. "Or maybe. That's kind of why we need to discuss things."

It was a group of fellow Americans, not used to the narrower sidewalks of a smaller city. They plunged on and Paris carefully walked closer to the curb. She looked up at just the right moment, seeing the Eiffel Tower peeking around the side of a building, poking up over a rooftop. Her heart fluttered.

"Hey," she said, poking Clare's back. "Look at that."

It all happened at once.

Clare looked up, the tour group finally reached them, a man in a cowboy hat dodged to one side to avoid someone's elbow, Clare took a side step then began to slip, Paris reached out to grab her arm and haul her up away from the road.

But it was all a little too late.

Even over the traffic and the buzz of American voices, Paris could hear the snap as Clare's ankle turned over the curb.

Get Your Copy of That French Summer Now, Only from Amazon!

Printed in Great Britain
by Amazon